P9-DMU-361

31241010235979

NOWHERE BOY

ALSO BY KATHERINE MARSH

The Door by the Staircase

Jepp, Who Defied the Stars

The Twilight Prisoner

The Night Tourist

NOWHERE BOY

KATHERINE MARSH

ROARING BROOK PRESS
NEW YORK

Published by Roaring Brook Press
Roaring Brook Press is a division of Holtzbrinck Publishing
Holdings Limited Partnership
175 Fifth Avenue, New York, NY 10010

mackids.com

Library of Congress Control Number: 2018935592

ISBN: 978-1-250-30757-6

Our books may be purchased in bulk for promotional, educational, or business use. Please contact your local bookseller or the Macmillan Corporate and Premium Sales Department at (800) 221-7945 ext. 5442 or by e-mail at MacmillanSpecialMarkets@macmillan.com.

First edition, 2018
Interior design credit: Jaclyn Reyes
Printed in the United States of America by LSC Communications,
Harrisonburg, Virginia

7 9 10 8 6

To Sasha, Natalia and the world’s children

À Sasha, à Natalia et aux enfants du monde

إلى ساشا وناتاليا وأطفال العالم

CHAPTER ONE

They had purposely waited for a cloudy, moonless July night. It was less likely, the smugglers had said, that the Greek Coast Guard would spot them.

But now their invisibility was a problem. The top of the inflatable rubber dinghy bobbed barely ten centimeters above the Aegean, several centimeters lower than when they had started. There was no land in sight. The captain struggled to restart the motor while the silhouettes of eighteen men, three women and four children huddled together. Some had ill-fitting life jackets; only a few knew how to swim.

"If the motor doesn't start, we will drown," one of the women said, her thin voice rising in panic.

No one disagreed.

Ahmed Nasser hugged his life jacket against himself. It was too small for a boy of fourteen, especially one nearly as tall as his father. He remembered the stories he had heard in Turkey of smugglers selling defective life jackets that made people sink instead of float.

A hand touched his shoulder. "Ahmed, my soul, don't be afraid."

Ahmed looked at his father, his large frame crammed against the side of the boat. A black inner tube was slung over his shoulder and he smiled calmly, as if he knew they'd be okay. But the smell of bodies, unwashed and sweating, the terrified gazes, the sickly toss of the sea, told Ahmed otherwise.

"The lady is right," Ahmed whispered. "The boat's deflating. If the motor won't start—"

"Hush," his father said.

His voice was commanding yet gentle, as if he were soothing a child. But Ahmed was old enough to know the powerlessness that lay behind it. He thought about his mother, his sisters, his grandfather—would his death be worse than theirs had been? His father had assured him theirs had been painless. Surely theirs had been quicker than this. There had been no time for false words of comfort.

Less than ten kilometers separated the coast of Turkey from the Greek island of Lesbos. Ahmed tried to make out lights from land or even from another boat, but he could spot nothing. Where was Europe? Where was the rest of the world? There wasn't even a star to promise a better elsewhere existed. The sky was as dark as the water below it. He could barely see the face of the stainless-steel watch his father had worn until earlier tonight, when he'd fastened it around Ahmed's wrist. It had been

Ahmed's great-grandfather's Omega Seamaster, a name that seemed ironic now.

"Baba, you know I can't swim," Ahmed whispered.

"You won't have to," his father said.

But water was soaking Ahmed's sneakers. He could feel it rolling back and forth across the bottom of the boat. People tossed bags into the sea, trying to lighten the load. Ahmed watched the bags bob, then float away or sink. A few people tried to bail the water out with plastic bottles, but it hardly seemed to make a difference. The woman in front of them started crying. For the first time, Ahmed noticed she was holding a baby in a sling.

"Don't cry," Ahmed's father said to her, his tone light. "There is already enough water in this boat."

But this only seemed to make the woman cry harder.

"*Allahu Akbar*," several people prayed.

"Baba—"

"The woman is right," his father interrupted. "We must keep this boat moving. But you will not sink. Nor will the others."

Ahmed noticed him glance at the woman and her baby, then at the rest of the desperate, frightened strangers in the overcrowded boat. Baba pulled the inner tube off his shoulder and slipped it over Ahmed's head and around his torso. Then he leaned over and whispered in his ear.

"Forgive me, my soul. For a moment, I must leave you."

"Leave me? Where?"

But his father had already turned away.

"Baba!"

Ahmed tried to reach for him, only to realize that his arms were pinned to his sides by the inner tube. By the time he'd freed them, his father's leg was already over the side of the boat.

Ahmed lurched forward to grab him, but it was too late. His father slid into the dark water like an eel. A moment later he reappeared, treading water.

"What are you doing?" Ahmed shouted after him.

"We need to pull the boat." His father's eyes searched the passengers. "Can anyone else swim?"

They were from a medley of places—Syria, Afghanistan, Iraq—but Ahmed realized from the helpless way they looked at one another that they had one thing in common: none of them could swim.

But then a voice behind him said in Iraqi-accented Arabic, "I can."

Ahmed turned around. A slight, wiry man took off his jacket, then his shirt. He handed them to the woman beside him, who folded them neatly, as if to make a point that she expected him back. A little girl sat between them, half swallowed by her life jacket.

"I can, too," said the captain. He looked ashamed about the motor, but Ahmed felt it wasn't his fault. He wasn't even really a captain. He was just an engineering student from Homs whom the smugglers had chosen from among the refugees to pilot the boat. This thankless duty had earned him an oblong orange buoy. He tossed it into the sea, then dove after it.

Ahmed tried to give his father back the inner tube, but

he refused to take it, claiming it would slow him down. The men swam to the front of the boat and, as a passenger shined a flashlight across the dark water, they looped the boat's towrope around the buoy, conferring in tones too hushed for Ahmed to hear. Then each grabbed onto the rope with one hand, kicking with their feet and paddling with their free arm. Ahmed's father swam in front, the two men behind him.

The boat jerked forward, as if a giant hand had given it a shove.

Cheers and shouts of "Praise be to God!" rose up from the passengers. Those in the center of the boat scooped water from the bottom into bottles and passed them to those on the edge to pour out. As he emptied bottles, Ahmed felt his fear ebb, replaced by pride that it was his father leading the swimmers. It reminded him of long-ago weekends before the war, when his family had barbecued and picnicked with friends outside of Aleppo. Late at night, his father would lead the *dabke,* whirling the line of dancers as they held hands and stamped their feet to drum and tambourine. Ahmed would stare up at the star-filled sky and let himself be dragged along wildly, knowing Baba was in charge.

But a half hour later, he was jolted from his memories as the wind picked up and choppy waves rocked the dinghy. Occasionally they spilled over the sagging sides, and Ahmed could hear the water slosh in the bottom. He looked anxiously out into the beam of light that illuminated his father and the other swimmers. Whitecaps broke over their heads, slowing their pace, but their free arms continued to pinwheel around.

A hard summer rain began to fall. Within minutes, Ahmed was drenched. He told himself that rain this heavy never lasted long, but it stirred up the sea even more. The swimmers pulled the dinghy straight into the waves. It pitched and bucked, pulling the swimmers' rope taut, but it stayed afloat.

Then came the sideways wave.

Ahmed didn't see it, but he felt it. It tipped the dinghy to one side and seemed to hold it there, as if considering the worth of those inside. Ahmed sucked in air, expecting to be flipped. But the wave let the dinghy slide down its side and instead swept over the swimmers so that they vanished completely. Then it ripped the buoy off the rope and tossed it into the darkness.

There was a second of silent shock before everyone started shouting, shining their phones' flashlights across the water.

"Where are they? Can anyone see them?"

The captain sputtered to the surface. The Iraqi popped up next with a gasp, his hand still clutching the rope.

But where was Baba?

Far in the distance, through the driving rain, Ahmed thought he saw his father's head bob to the surface.

"Baba!" he shouted.

But there was no response, and when he looked again, all he could see were the endless whitecap waves.

CHAPTER TWO

Max Howard nearly choked on his waffle.

"You're what?!"

He knew he should have been suspicious when his parents had suggested a second waffle of the day. They had just left the Grand Place, the enormous square in the center of Brussels where tourists gawked at the ornate gold-adorned buildings. It was their third day in Belgium, and his mother had wanted to take a family photo there. Max had figured she would post it on Facebook with some goofy comment like "Beginning our exciting year in Europe!"

This was Max's first time in Europe, and, like most of what he'd seen so far, the Grand Place didn't seem real. The narrow cobblestone streets around it were filled with chocolate shops, waffle stands and souvenir stores selling beer steins and key chains of the *Manneken Pis*, the statue of the little peeing boy that was Brussels's mascot. Tourists speaking in a babble of languages passed by their table outside the waffle shop, and although it felt like morning, waiters were beginning to change the café chalkboards for dinner. But even in his jet-lagged fog, Max knew there was something very wrong with what his parents had just told him.

"I thought I was going to the American school. Like Claire."

He stared across the metal café table at his older sister. Had she known about this? But she just tossed her long blond hair and continued texting one of her millions of friends back home. Max felt like ripping the phone out of her hands and shouting, "Traitor!" In Washington, she'd always told him everything their parents were up to; she'd even given him strategies on how to keep them from freaking out about his grades. But she had been even angrier than Max when their parents had announced that they were moving to Brussels for a year so their father could be a defense consultant to NATO, a military alliance founded to protect Europe from Russia. And now, she was making it clear that he was on his own.

His mom leaned in from the chair beside his. She was small, not much bigger than him, but she somehow still managed to make Max feel trapped.

"Claire's in high school. She can't have an adventure like you."

But the word "adventure" didn't fool Max. He knew what she was really saying: *Claire is an A student on track to go to Harvard or Yale. You barely passed sixth grade, and we're afraid you're going to end up living in our basement.*

Max turned to his father. He was sipping a tiny European coffee, but with his sunburned face, cargo shorts and Marine

Corps Marathon T-shirt, he was clearly American. Max hadn't seen a single man in shorts outside the Grand Place.

"Dad?"

Max knew his parents rarely agreed. But his father just smiled, as if he knew what Max was up to, and shook his head.

"It's a good idea, Max."

Max stared at his parents in disgust. He would have included Claire too, if she'd bothered to look up from her phone.

"Um, you know I don't speak French?"

"You'll learn," his father said.

"Ms. Krantz said you have a good ear," his mother added.

Max had a feeling the lawyer part of her had been waiting to break out this crushing evidence. *What did you say?* he almost said. But it was a dumb joke, and he felt too depressed to make it.

Ms. Krantz was the learning specialist his parents had hired in Washington, D.C., after he'd nearly failed every subject but history. She'd told his parents he needed to work on study skills and focus, including on being less impulsive. But that was probably just because of the incident with the bike—after this crazy eighth grader took his friend Kevin's bike, Max had chased after him. It wouldn't have been a big deal except that when Max grabbed him, the crazy eighth grader had lost control of the bike and fractured his arm. The kid's parents had blamed Max, and even Kevin had been mad at him because his bike was twisted out of shape.

But the incident with the bike was nothing compared to this. Here, he was stranded in a weird foreign country where people ate horsemeat (his mother had pointed it out at the store, so he knew it was true) and spoke a language that sounded like someone hacking up phlegm, and he was being denied his basic right to drift off in class to a language he understood. Middle school had been bad enough in English. And forget about friends. At least he'd had a few in Washington, like Kevin and Malik, who liked role-playing games and comic books. But how was he supposed to make friends when he couldn't even speak to them?

Even the weather seemed to be messing with him. A few minutes before, it had been sunny, but now gray clouds covered the sky.

He could feel his mom pressing in on him, a storm front of forced enthusiasm.

"You can sleep in! The school is just around the corner. Claire has to get up early to take the bus—"

"He's not a *complete* idiot," Claire interrupted.

Max might have thought she was defending him, except for the way she emphasized the word "complete."

His mother shot her a look. "Excuse me?"

"He knows this isn't just some fun adventure. We all do."

"Claire," his father warned.

Max got it. She'd been happy in Washington with her million friends. She loved Walls, the super-selective high school where she had just finished ninth grade. But she acted like the move was somehow Max's fault when he'd had nothing to do with it. And he certainly didn't feel sorry for her now. At least she would be going to school in English.

Max pushed away his waffle. "I won't go."

His mother's voice was gentle but firm.

"It's not a choice, Max."

"How am I supposed to pass seventh grade in French?"

A group of tourists glanced over. He realized he was shouting. He hated the way everyone in Brussels walked around grim and silent, like they'd just been yelled at. Even the little kids were quieter than American little kids.

"Here we go," Claire murmured.

"Oh, shut up," Max said to her.

She looked up from her phone and fixed him with a stare. "You're not going to seventh."

From the nervous glance his parents exchanged, Max instantly knew that Claire was telling the truth.

"What?!"

"We thought it would be easier for you to learn French if you repeated sixth," his father said.

This wasn't a waffle-and-coffee stop—it was an ambush! Max jumped to his feet. "You're holding me back?"

"Just think how great your French will be when we get back to America," his mom said. "You'll be the best in your class!"

The best. Always the best. That was all his parents seemed to care about. Max picked up the soggy remains of his waffle and pushed past his mom to the trash. Then he chucked it in.

"Max!" she called after him.

Max ignored her, his arms crossed over his chest. A drop of water smacked against his face, and he wiped it away with the back of his hand. Perfect. It was beginning to rain. He'd been in Brussels all of seventy-two hours and he was already sick of it—the little cars; the clouds of cigarette smoke; the scrawny, overtrimmed trees that looked like amputees; the greasy snack shops selling fries and kebabs; the surly waiters who refused to do anything in a rush. In a single afternoon, he'd nearly been run over by a tram and stepped in dog poop (the entire city was like some poop obstacle course since no one in Brussels seemed to clean up after their dogs). Parts of the city looked the storybook way he'd imagined, with large windows and flower boxes and steep roofs; others seemed different (Max had never seen so many women wearing headscarves). But none of it felt like home.

A wave of homesickness washed over him. He just wanted a hamburger—not the weird raw beef the Belgians inexplicably called "filet Américain." He pictured Kevin and Malik munching on the greasy ones at the diner on Connecticut Avenue. What he wouldn't give to be sitting in the booth with them, discussing the new Avengers movie and making plans for a sleepover. He thought about texting them, but he was too embarrassed to admit that his parents were making him repeat sixth. Would they even be his friends next year if they were in different grades?

He'd never felt so completely alone.

He heard footsteps behind him and a hand squeezed his shoulder. His father wasn't a big man, but he had a strong, reassuring grip from years of golf and Washington handshakes.

"I know we kind of sprang this on you."

"Which part? Moving to Belgium? French school? Repeating sixth grade?"

"All of it," he admitted. "But like Mom was getting at, it's an opportunity. And it takes the pressure off. All you have to do is learn French—"

"All I have to do is learn French? An entire language. Wow, thanks. I'm glad that's all."

His father laughed and Max couldn't help feeling a little of his anger drain away.

His father's eyes crinkled as he leaned in closer.

"Anyway, there are only four French words you really need to know."

But Max wasn't going to let his father kid his way out of this. He stared silently across the cobblestone street. A woman in a headscarf stood on the corner, holding out a coffee cup. Max couldn't understand the handwritten sign in her other hand—only the words *faim*, hungry, and *réfugié*, refugee. Max wished he hadn't ordered the waffle, that he'd given her the five euros instead.

"Max, come on," his father said gently. "Just give it a try."

"I don't really have much of a choice, do I?" Max muttered.

"That's the spirit! Now, those words . . ." His father looked from side to side, as if checking to make sure no one was eavesdropping on them.

"*Où est la toilette*?" he whispered.

Max groaned. "Where's the toilet? Are you serious?"

His father playfully ruffled Max's curly brown hair. "Look at that. You understand already!"

CHAPTER THREE

Ahmed listened to Ibrahim Malaki without looking at him. It was easier that way to conceal how he felt about the latest bad news.

He had long since stopped thinking of Ibrahim as the Iraqi. He was his father's friend, even though the friendship had been forged in less than a minute as the men treaded water and traded vows: "If something happens to me, look after my family."

But now, after nearly a month of sleeping in a tent in Parc Maximilien in downtown Brussels, Ibrahim explained that the Belgian Office of Foreigners had refused to grant him and his family refugee status. "They are pressing us to return to Iraq," he said.

Ahmed looked out at the sea of camping tents that stretched past the one he'd been sharing with Ibrahim and his family. Refugees weren't eligible for housing until they had registered across the street at the Office of Foreigners. But all summer, the lines had been so long that people had to wait days, even weeks, leaving them no choice but to sleep in the Red Cross camp in the park. Ahmed liked the volunteers who ran it and brought everything from clothes and blankets to hot meals and diapers for the babies. They had even set up a little school. Ahmed had attended it once with Ibrahim's four-year-old daughter, Bana, and learned a few French phrases.

But the interior ministry had recently announced it would be closing the camp. Summer was ending, but Ahmed knew they were reacting to more than just the weather. The wooden crates repurposed as chairs and tables, the laundry drying on ropes strung between trees, the first-aid tent with its giant red cross, the piles of donated clothes—it all made for an unsettling contrast with the reflective glass office towers that surrounded the park. The authorities could no longer justify a tent city in the center of the European Union's capital.

Now, Ibrahim's wife, Zainab, explained that they hoped to stay with relatives living in the nearby neighborhood of Molenbeek while Ibrahim appealed the decision.

"As an unaccompanied minor, you must go into state custody while they process your case," she said gently.

Ahmed's stomach tightened. Since the Greek coast guard boat had rescued them and brought them ashore in Lesbos, he hadn't spoken more than a few necessary words. But now he found the ones that terrified him most of all.

"By myself?"

There were thousands of child refugees traveling in Europe alone. He'd met a few along the way, listened to the rumors and information they traded about which smugglers to trust or which routes were safest. Some, like him, were orphans; others had been sent ahead in the hope they could bring their families along later; a few had been separated from their families on the way. Ahmed had assumed he would stay with Ibrahim in Belgium, at least till he could finish high school. He had never considered the possibility that Ibrahim and his family wouldn't be allowed to stay themselves.

"You will have a better outcome without us," Ibrahim said. "You are Syrian, not Iraqi. They are taking Syrians—"

Ahmed hadn't even wanted to live in Belgium. He barely knew anything about this little country wedged in between France and the Netherlands like a pebble in a shoe. His father had planned to go to England or Canada, where at least they could speak the language. Ahmed had only gone to Belgium because Ibrahim was headed there.

"But where will I go?"

"There is a reception center just for unaccompanied minors. You will have a roof over your head—"

Ahmed winced. He had stayed in other reception centers in Greece and Hungary; they were little more than human pens where refugees were crowded together, given expired food and hollered at by impatient guards. He had sworn he would never end up in one again. He had heard enough about what the centers held for boys like him: the fights and nightmares and overwhelmed adults, the strange food and medical exams and language classes. It would take months for them to figure out what to do with him, months when people he didn't know or trust would be in charge of him. And what were the chances he would find another family? True, there were plenty of kind Belgians who had brought food and clothing to Parc Maximilien. But it was one thing to volunteer a few hours and another to adopt a teenager. He would end up in state custody until he came of age.

"Tomorrow, we will go together to the office of unaccompanied minors and get you registered," Ibrahim said.

"Don't worry, Ahmed," said Zainab. "We will keep in touch every day. If you have any trouble, we will help."

But Ahmed knew there wasn't much help they could give him from Iraq. And once he registered in Belgium, he would become ineligible to apply for asylum in England or anywhere else. That was the way the asylum rules worked. He would be trapped in Belgium forever.

An even worse fear gripped him. The only proof he had that he was even Syrian was a forged passport. His father had bought it on the black market in Turkey after they'd fled Syria. Their real passports had been destroyed on that terrible day. What if the authorities didn't believe he was Syrian? He had been traveling with an Iraqi family, after all. He would have been better off arriving alone.

And then there was his age. He'd only just turned fourteen, but everyone always thought he was older. The police might see not the face of a boy, but of a sullen young man, a possible terrorist. Wasn't that the fear he'd seen lurking in so many European eyes? He pictured them sending him back to Turkey—all those hard-earned kilometers in reverse, his father's death in vain.

Ahmed remembered the life he had imagined with Baba in England: going to school in a language he could at least partially understand, playing on a football club team, eating fish and chips while watching David De Gea's brilliant goalkeeping for Manchester United. Maybe, even though Baba was gone, fate was telling him not to give up on England. From gossip at the camp, he knew that the best chance of getting there was through the city of Calais on the northern coast of France. There was another large camp there called the Jungle, where refugees waited for the chance to travel through a train-and-car tunnel under the sea to England. There were always a few smugglers who hung out around Parc Maximilien, offering to arrange rides down to France.

Should he go to Calais and take his chances there, or stay in Belgium and try to enter the system alone? He had less than forty-eight hours to make a choice that would shape the rest of his life. He stroked the face of his watch, wondered what his father would tell him to do. But the Seamaster offered no answers. Then he tickled Bana so her giggles would distract him.

CHAPTER FOUR

On the morning of September 1, 2015, Max muttered a tense goodbye to his parents, then plunged into the crush of kids in navy-blue uniforms streaming into the courtyard of Ecole du Bonheur. He still couldn't believe the name of his new school was the School of Happiness. It was like some cosmic joke.

Max breathed deep and rubbed his clammy palms. In just seven hours, he told himself, his first day would be over. It was going to be fine. Like his parents had reminded him, he'd already done sixth grade once, and in Belgium it was still elementary school. He'd omitted this embarrassing detail when he'd Skyped with Kevin and Malik, but they had been too busy telling him about coding camp and the epic water-gun battle they'd had at Malik's house to ask him much anyway.

Max let himself be funneled past an enormous sliding door and into a brick passageway. The chatter and shouts blended together in a way that was at once familiar—the typical noise of a schoolyard—and strange. Here and there, a word registered in Max's head: *coucou*, the funny word for "hi," or *l'été*, summer, which already seemed a distant memory under the cool, cloudy sky. But mostly the words were incomprehensible, giving Max the same detached, dreamlike feeling he'd often had since arriving in Brussels, like he might still blink and wake up and find himself home in his bed in Washington.

As the crowd spilled into the asphalt courtyard, Max looked for the line for 6B. But if there was an order to the chaos of kids running around and giving one another adultlike cheek kisses and throwing their wide backpacks into piles on the ground and kicking around a soccer ball, Max couldn't see it. He finally spotted a paper sign for 6B, which had been unhelpfully hidden by the head of Madame Legrand, a tall, unsmiling blond woman.

"*Mex How-Weird*," she said, turning to him as he trotted over.

For a split second Max thought she'd called him weird, but then he realized that she was just pronouncing his name in her thick French accent. This made him grin until he realized she was staring at him without a smile, waiting for the answer.

"Yes," he said, then, feeling stupid, "*oui*."

A girl with thick glasses and long, dark hair who was standing in front of the teacher bit her lip and looked down. Max knew he'd done something not quite right.

"*Oui, Madame*," Madame Legrand said with an emphasis on the *Madame*.

"*Oui, Madame,*" Max repeated.

Madame Legrand pressed her lips together like she was considering whether this "*Oui, Madame*" was acceptable. Max wondered if maybe they would just keep saying this to each other like some sort of funny skit, but to his relief, a bell rang and she waved him into the line and led everyone inside.

The first hour of class passed quickly, as all everyone basically did was take out new school supplies and organize them in their desks. Max didn't know the names for most of the school supplies, nor did he understand Madame Legrand's instructions about where to put them, but he was sitting behind the girl with the glasses and long hair, whose name was Farah, and he just copied her. The classroom was small and old-fashioned, with rows of desks that opened for storage instead of lockers, blackboards and chalk instead of smart boards, and not a single computer. He even had to load a cartridge of ink into the fountain pen they were required to use, a task that made Max feel like he'd traveled not just to a different country, but to a different century.

When everything was in its place, Madame Legrand wrote some lines on the board. Twenty-nine fountain pens leaped upright as everyone started copying the phrases into their notebooks. Max started to write too, but the nib of his fountain pen only scratched dryly against the paper. He gave it a shake and tried again. He could see the impression of the letter in the paper, but there was still no ink. Max looked around—everyone else was busy writing. He unscrewed his pen and took out the cartridge. Had he loaded it wrong?

Max sensed movement behind him and turned around. A big, sandy-haired kid was staring at Max, his eyes on the pen. He unscrewed his own pen, then took the nib and mimed the action of poking the top of the cartridge with it.

Max instantly understood. *Merci,* he mouthed. The big kid grinned.

Then Max turned back around and did the same. The second he put the nib of the pen on the paper, he saw a comforting blot of blue ink. But the next thing he knew, the ink was pouring out over his paper and all over his fingers.

The big kid behind him made a sound halfway between a chuckle and a snort, but Max had no time even to shoot him a dirty look. The ink was everywhere. Max tried to blot his fingers on his blue Oxford shirt, soaking it with big blotches. He pressed his fingers against the paper, leaving fingerprints, but the ink was everywhere now—staining his nails, between his fingers.

Max raised his hand. But Madame Legrand, who was still writing on the board, didn't see him. He felt a trickle of sweat down the side of his face and rubbed it before he realized that he probably now had ink on his face too. Luckily, he knew what to say.

"*Excusez-moi.*"

Madame Legrand turned around with a look that seemed to say *How dare you interrupt me!*

"Où est la toilette?" Then he remembered and added, "*Madame.*"

Madame Legrand had a lot to say on this subject. Max was

pretty sure her passionate answer was not a simple "Take a left and then turn right." But he couldn't understand a word of it, so when she was done, he repeated the question.

"Où est la toilette, Madame?"

The big kid behind him was laughing even harder. Max felt the urge to turn around and kick him.

Madame Legrand sighed deeply. "*Où sont les toilettes?*" she corrected. Then she added, "At the end of the hall." Just like that. In heavily accented but perfect English. Instead of making Max feel better, hearing her speak English made him feel like even more of a moron.

Lunchtime wasn't much better. Max took the mystery soup and the plate of sausage, potatoes and something purple the lunch attendant handed him. It tasted better than it looked, but before he could really dig in, a bell rang and everyone rushed to clear the table. Then, in the same disorderly way as in the morning, kids mobbed the door for recess.

One of his favorite parts of middle school had been that he no longer had recess, only free periods, where he could hang out and play Talisman with Kevin and Malik. But now he was back to having recess, a full hour of it. As the hoard pushed Max out the door and into the rain, he realized something else. Unlike in America, where even the threat of rain had turned outdoor recess into indoor recess, which was basically computer games or a movie, the School of Happiness didn't cancel for bad weather.

From the spongy-topped athletic court where the kids

congregated, Max could see through a fence and over the wall to the backyard of the town house his family had rented. His bedroom on the third floor was probably less than fifty yards away, and yet it felt as far away and unreachable as his life back home. A group of boys began to play soccer, organizing themselves into teams, while several others surrounded Max with expressions of friendly curiosity.

"Do you speak English?" asked a boy with curly red hair from his class.

It was such a relief to hear English that Max didn't really think about the slight oddness of the question.

"Yeah," he said, returning the kid's smile. "You do too?"

The boy's face lit up. "Do you speak English?" he repeated.

Max nodded. "Yes, I said—"

But before he could finish, the red-haired kid burst out laughing.

"Coca-Cola!" said the boy next to him.

"Shut up and dance with me! This woman is my destiny!" the red-haired kid shouted back, swiveling his hips.

Max recognized the chorus from the Walk the Moon song that had been playing all summer on the radio. With a sinking feeling, he realized that they didn't know any English other than "Do you speak English?," "Coca-Cola" and some song lyrics.

"Yeah, guys, good," he said. *"Bonne anglais."*

A cheer went up from the boys as they high-fived one another. Max took the opportunity to slide away and insert himself into the soccer game, mainly by running up and down the sidelines. Some of the kids were pretty good and Max hoped they wouldn't pass to him, but they seemed to hog the ball less than the kids back home did, and inevitably someone kicked it toward him. He tried to stop it, but his foot slipped on the wet foam and it rolled out of bounds. Max gave an irritated look, like this wasn't the sort of thing that normally happened to him. He noticed the big, sandy-haired kid who'd given him the bad tip about the pen staring at him in disbelief.

"Oscar!" someone shouted, and the big kid started to run toward the ball, which was back in play, knocking over a smaller defender in his way. His huge foot reared back and hit the ball so hard that it shot across the court, bounced off the goal post and before Max had time to react, hit him in the face with such force that he was knocked backward.

For a few seconds, all Max saw was the gray Belgian sky, raindrops smacking against him. Then his field of vision filled with faces.

"*Ça va? Ça va?*" they said.

He was helped upright. He could feel the pain now, throbbing around his eye. More babble around him. Then an adult shouting, scattering the kids until only Farah remained. She took his arm carefully, like he was an old woman, and with the aide led him to the principal's office. Even though he was clearly a victim, Max wondered if he was in trouble. But instead of the principal, he was delivered to the secretary, who led him to a nook outside her office where she motioned him to lie down on a bench and covered him with a blanket. She made a lot of clucking noises, then fetched a cold pack. *Do they not even have a nurse's office?* Max thought. He could feel the skin around his eye bruise and tighten—he'd definitely have a black eye. *But at least,* he thought sourly, *I'm out of the rain.*

It was at this moment that Max came up with a new name for his new school: the School of Misery.

CHAPTER FIVE

The night of September 1, the temperature dropped and Ahmed could tell that summer was coming to an end. It had been a cool summer anyway, with nights that were only cozy in the tent because of the heat of the bodies beside him. Now the rain fell in sheets, and despite the blue plastic tarps that volunteers had pitched over their tent, the water seeped in, making the ground damp.

The silver hands of Baba's watch stretched up to midnight. Ahmed listened to Ibrahim snoring and Bana whining in her sleep till Zainab pulled her closer. Then he wedged on his shoes, checked to make sure he had the three hundred euros his father had tucked into his passport, and kissed Bana gently on the cheek, the way he had once kissed his littlest sister, Nouri. A smile flickered on Bana's face, but she did not wake. He scrawled a note to Ibrahim, thanking him for honoring his promise and promising in turn to get in touch when he reached Calais. By the time he'd swallowed the lump in his throat and crawled out the tent flap, a chilly wind was driving the rain sideways.

The ground was muddy, and he could feel water soaking into his sock where the sole of his sneaker was peeling off. But at least no one was out to see him leave the park and knock on the window of an idling van. An unshaven man with a prominent Adam's apple turned around in the driver's seat and waved him inside. Ahmed slid open the door, releasing a cloud of smoke and thumping Albanian techno music.

"Ahmed!" the man said, as if they'd known each other a long time.

The smuggler's first name was Ermir; Ahmed didn't know his last name, only that he spoke English and had agreed to drive him to Calais.

"You have the money?"

Ahmed handed him the three hundred euros.

Ermir counted it, then shoved it in his jeans' pocket.

"Great, great. Take a seat in the back."

Ahmed shut the door behind him. The van smelled horrible—like cigarette smoke and old cabbage. But it was a ride. The doors locked with a click, and Ermir pulled the van onto the road. Ahmed took a deep breath as the park disappeared behind him. Ermir smiled at him in the rearview mirror.

"I forgot . . . Hand me your phone."

Ahmed looked at the reflection of the smuggler uncertainly. His phone was the only way he could contact anyone. It was the only way he could get online, check in with friends back home. It was where he kept the only photos he had of his family.

"Don't worry, Ahmed. I'll give it back to you in Calais. I just can't have you using it in the van."

Ahmed hesitated, trying to remember if he'd heard other stories about smugglers collecting phones. The van jerked to a stop, and Ermir turned to face him.

"Look, Ahmed. We've got to trust each other. I'm taking a big risk here—"

Ermir glanced at the door as if he was starting to think Ahmed wasn't worth the effort. Ahmed shoved the phone toward him. "Okay."

Ermir pocketed it, then silently shifted back into drive. Ahmed pressed his face against the window. Since arriving by train from Germany, he'd seen little of Brussels beyond the park and the dirty, crowded Gare du Nord station a few blocks away. The skyscrapers that seemed half empty even during the day were dark and deserted. The broader avenues near the station gave way to narrow, curving streets lined with shabby row houses. Some had shops on the ground floor, but at this hour their entrances were shuttered behind metal grates. Tram lines crisscrossed above the streets like spiders' webs. The only hints of life were a few lone men smoking beneath overhangs and the neon signs of night shops. Ahmed knew they were convenience stores that sold mostly alcohol and cigarettes, but the English words seemed to hint at something darker.

Ten minutes later, Ermir bumped his fist against the radio power button, cutting off the wailing woman singer. Ahmed hadn't particularly liked the music, but now he wished it was back on. The only sounds were the mechanical swish of the windshield wipers and Ermir tapping his cigarette into the ashtray. Suddenly he caught Ahmed's eye in the mirror. He was no longer smiling.

"I'm feeling like three hundred is not enough here."

Ahmed stiffened. "But you say it is—"

"It barely covers the gas—"

Ahmed peered out the window. He had no idea where they were. *Be calm,* he told himself. Smugglers always pushed for more. But he couldn't help remembering a tale he'd heard about a smuggler who'd threatened to harvest a refugee's organs if he couldn't pay more. A healthy kidney was worth more than three hundred euros on the black market. Ahmed tried to keep his voice from trembling.

"I not have more money."

Ermir stopped at a red light and jerked his head around. Ahmed could feel his eyes boring into him. "That's a nice watch."

Ahmed clutched the Seamaster, as if to shield it from Ermir's greedy eyes.

"No!"

"Shut up!"

The light turned green and Ermir hit the gas hard, jerking Ahmed back into his seat.

"Let me out!" Ahmed shouted. He lunged for the door, but it was locked.

"Sit back down! You owe me!"

There was only one way to escape. Ahmed catapulted into

the passenger seat. Ermir slammed on the brakes and grabbed Ahmed by the sleeve of his hoodie. Ahmed flung open the door and charged through it with such force that he could hear his sleeve rip as he tumbled out of the van. He landed on his knees and elbows on the asphalt, but he didn't even feel the pain. He sprang back to his feet and ran as fast as he could.

Behind him, he could hear a door slam shut and tires squeal. He imagined Ermir stomping on the gas. He would slam the van into him and take his watch before leaving him for dead in the pouring rain.

"Help!" he shouted in English.

No one answered.

He turned blindly onto a quiet street, past an apartment building, to where large houses hunkered behind iron gates. One gate was open and he ran inside, around the house and into the backyard, where he nearly crashed into a brick wall.

He was coughing now and gagging and was drenched to his underwear, but the same part of him that had stopped him from jumping into the sea after his father propelled him over the wall. He dropped clumsily to the other side, scratching his face against the branches of a bush. The garden was unkempt. Even in the pouring rain, he could see that green tendrils of ivy had swallowed the walls, and weeds snaked around the trunk of a small fruit tree. The house overlooking it was dark. Ahmed slipped through the patchy grass and leaves toward the back of the house, where there was a recessed cement patio beneath an overhang.

He stood beneath the overhang, shaking as he watched the wall, half-expecting the smuggler to catapult over it. But no one came. Hot tears slid down his cheeks. At least he could feel his father's watch warm and heavy on his wrist, hear the ticking of the hand. Ahmed caught his breath, pulled up his drenched sleeve and inspected the watch for damage. It was unscathed, but in the pale light of the moonlit clouds, he could see the scraped skin on his elbows where they'd hit the concrete. He slowly became aware of the rest of his body. His throat felt dry and hurt when he swallowed. He needed water.

At the back of the patio, leading into the house, was a set of glass doors. Ahmed tried to peer through, but a curtain covered them. He quietly turned the knob and gave it a gentle push. He expected to meet resistance, but to his amazement, the knob turned and the door opened. He cautiously stuck his head inside and looked around. The room was filled with different-sized bikes, helmets, a skateboard and skis. It was clearly a basement storage space for a family. He carefully took off his sneakers and socks, then slipped inside and closed the door behind him. The blue carpet absorbed the sound of his steps, but he still walked very slowly in case someone was in a neighboring room.

As he reached the end of the storage room, he had another stroke of luck. Just outside it was a bathroom. He crept inside and turned on the tap, cupped his hands and drank. His throat burned, but he felt a little better. Just then, a white blur moved behind him.

Ahmed whipped around just in time to see a fluffy white cat look at him, then race into the next room. His heart thumping, he followed the cat into a laundry room with piles of dirty clothes lying next to a washer and dryer. It was tempting to strip off his drenched clothes and place them inside. But he continued on, tiptoeing into a room cluttered with a stack of chairs, a mattress, a rolled-up carpet and other random pieces of furniture. Ahmed slipped through a door at the side of this room and found himself in a low hallway piled high with stiff, new packing boxes. It seemed as if the family who lived here had recently moved in. Ahmed slipped in among the boxes, quietly shifting those that blocked his way. He expected to hit a wall where the hallway ended, but instead he spotted a small door. A skeleton key stuck out of it.

Ahmed turned the key and opened the door. A dank smell drifted out of the darkness. He could hear water dripping inside. He walked down two small, uneven stairs until he was below the basement, in what seemed like a subcellar. On the right was an empty room with dirt walls. Next to it was a cement room, which Ahmed figured out by touching the rough, wet walls. With his hand on the wall to guide him, he crossed the room and nearly hit his head on a low arch. Ducking beneath it, he broke through a curtain of gauzy cobwebs into a third room. It was still damp, but drier than the other two, and there was a little light from a high rectangular window, enough to illuminate a switch on the wall. Ahmed turned it on and light blazed from a single naked bulb.

At first, Ahmed thought he had discovered a crypt. The walls of the room were lined with deep cubicles. But there was nothing inside them; the room was empty except for the criss-cross of cobwebs. Clearly, no one had been down here in weeks, even months.

Ahmed realized what he was thinking, but he pushed the idea away.

Someone would find him; he would be arrested for breaking into the house. But the idea wouldn't leave him. He had no money, no phone. He had nothing—just a fake passport and a watch, not even bus fare to get back to Parc Maximilien. He swallowed and felt the pain of swollen glands. There was the bathroom outside for water and waste, and even an alcove in the wall beneath the little window that was just big enough to hide in if someone came.

What if he stayed here, just for a night or two?

Ahmed quietly retraced his steps out of this hidden wing of the basement to the laundry room. He pulled a towel out of the heap of laundry to dry himself off with and a blanket to sleep on. Then he crept back to the little door off the utility hall and closed it behind him. As he leaned against the door, his knees felt weak and wobbly. He staggered back to the crypt, stripped off his wet pants and torn hoodie and collapsed onto the blanket.

CHAPTER SIX

"You forgot to write your name again," Madame Pauline said. "How is your teacher going to tell it's yours?"

"The awful handwriting?"

"Max!"

The School of Misery wouldn't have been half as bad if Max had been able to zone out afterward, eating pretzels and playing *Minecraft*. The problem was Madame Pauline, the old Flemish woman his mother had hired to keep an eye on him till she came home from work. Madame Pauline was fluent in French as well as Dutch and English, and full of opinions in all three languages, including that "this *Mindcraft*" would rot his brain. She kept him busy, mostly studying for *dictée*, the weekly spelling test that was basically impossible since in French various words that were pronounced the same were in fact spelled differently.

Max started writing his name. But just as he reached the end of it, the doorbell buzzed. The unexpected sound made his hand jump, completely ruining his *x*. *X* was the hardest letter of all to write in French cursive, and it was Max's luck that he had to write it constantly.

"*Effaceur,*" said Madame Pauline, handing him an ink-erasing pen like a nurse ready with a scalpel. Max could barely write a sentence without it. Then she got up to see who was at the door.

Max whited out the messed-up *x* and started correcting it with the fountain pen. But the paper tore and he remembered that he was supposed to use the special felt pen on the opposite end of the *effaceur*.

There's this amazing invention called a computer, Max imagined telling a crowd of Belgians. *You can type and then erase with the push of a button!* He crumpled up the paper and tossed it onto the floor—he would have to start again—then wandered out into the entry hall to see who was at the door.

Madame Pauline was talking to a trim man around his father's age in a dark-blue uniform and matching cap, a gun holstered to his hip and the words "*Police/Politie*" on the arm of his jacket.

Max froze. Why was a cop at his house? Had something happened to his parents or Claire? A catalog of dark thoughts flashed through his mind—car accidents, heart attacks, mass shootings (they didn't seem to have any in Belgium, but his parents certainly worried about them back home). Madame Pauline didn't seem terribly alarmed, though—she was chatting in French with the cop, a rare smile on her face. Max realized it was far more likely that his family had just violated some strange, silly Belgian rule—like putting their garbage out in the wrong color bags (there was some strict code that Max's parents never quite understood and were always fighting about).

The cop stepped inside the foyer and took off his blue cap. He was balding, and the remaining hair was shorn close to his scalp. He looked up at the medieval-looking bronze lantern in the entryway with an appreciative smile before he seemed to notice Max. The corners of his dark eyes crinkled.

"La famille How-Weird?"

Max nodded uncertainly. Were they all being charged with some crime?

"You prefer English?"

"Yes, sir," Max said. He'd never called anyone "sir" before, but he'd also never had a police officer show up at his door.

"I am Inspector Fontaine. I am here for the composition of the house."

Max looked at Madame Pauline. Whatever this was didn't sound like the tragedy he had imagined.

"He wants to see if who your parents say is living here lives here," she explained. "It is required to get your identity cards from the commune."

"Oh," Max said as relief flooded through him. The commune was the local town hall that issued official documents—like identity cards and parking passes. "But I'm the only one home right now."

Inspector Fontaine smiled. "I will just talk to you then." He looked back down at his pad. "You are Max How-Weird?"

"Yes."

"And your parents are Michael and Elizabeth How-Weird."

"Yes."

"And your sister is Claire How-Weird?"

"Yes."

Max almost expected Inspector Fontaine to ask *And your cat is Teddy Roosevelt How-Weird?*, but instead he said, "And no one else is living in this house?"

Max shook his head. "Not that I know of."

Inspector Fontaine assumed a serious expression. "We have to make sure there are no illegals. It's a grave problem here in Brussels."

"All over Europe!" Madame Pauline added. "Those Muslims just keep flooding in."

The way Madame Pauline talked about "those Muslims" made Max uncomfortable. When his mother dropped him off at the School of Misery in the morning, she talked mostly with the European mothers dressed in work suits and heels like her, but she always smiled politely at the mothers in headscarves and full-length coats. Farah's mom was one of them, and Farah seemed like one of the nicer kids in his class. She always helped him when he seemed confused about what page he should be looking at or where he was supposed to put his tray at lunch.

"What Muslims?" Max asked.

"The Syrians, the Iraqis, the Afghanis," Madame Pauline said, ticking off on her fingers. "Haven't you seen the news? They're flooding Europe. It's worse than the Africans. They don't want to fit in."

She made a clucking noise.

"If you come to our country, you must follow our way of life, our laws," Inspector Fontaine said.

Madame Pauline nodded vigorously. "Exactly!"

Even though Max knew they were talking about Muslims, he felt as if the warning also applied to him. He was from a different country. He didn't really want to use a fountain pen and have recess in the rain. He hoped the interview was over, that Inspector Fontaine would leave. But Madame Pauline was just getting started.

"Europe used to be safe before they arrived."

"Islamic State is a real problem," Inspector Fontaine agreed. "We must keep watchful."

The cop stuck his head into the dining room and peered around. Max wondered if he thought a terrorist might be hiding there. Inspector Fontaine's eyes traveled over the wood paneling and the crystal chandelier, then over to the living room with its enormous picture window looking out on the garden. He took a step into the dining room toward it, drawn in by something, it seemed to Max, that only he could see.

There was a commotion as Teddy Roosevelt careened out beneath the side table and flew in a panicked white blur into the hall. *Looks like you found one,* Max was tempted to say. But he had a feeling Inspector Fontaine wouldn't appreciate the joke.

"That's my cat," he said instead.

Inspector Fontaine reached out like he might like to pet Teddy Roosevelt, but Max could already hear the cat's paws pattering down the basement stairs so he could hide among the packing boxes in the hall. Inspector Fontaine smiled.

"My grandfather, Henri Fontaine, used to own this house. My best friend, Georges De Smet, lived next door. And I'm still friends with Hugo LeClerq, who lives behind you."

At that moment, Max understood that, in the same way that he still considered his house in Washington, D.C., to be his house even though another family was living in it, the police officer considered Max's house to be his.

"They don't make houses like this anymore," Madame Pauline said.

"No," Inspector Fontaine agreed. "They are expensive to maintain, though. My father sold it after my grandfather died, and the current owners rent it out to foreigners with big jobs at the European institutions."

He smiled at Max, as if they both knew he was one of these wealthy foreigners, then walked over to the living room window and looked out at the garden. It was wild and overgrown: a tangle of ivy, roses and rhododendron bushes. Max liked it even better than the prim, old house. Inspector Fontaine spoke to his own reflection. "The garden needs a trim."

Again, Max had the impression that it was Inspector Fontaine who really owned the house.

"I'll mention it to the parents," Madame Pauline said.

This seemed to satisfy Fontaine, at least enough to return to his memories. "Georges and Hugo and I were all in *Scoots*."

"The Belgian Boy *Scouts*," Madame Pauline explained to Max.

"Fantastic group!" Inspector Fontaine said. He turned to face Max. "You know Tintin of course?"

Max nodded. As far as he could tell, Tintin and the Smurfs were the sum of Belgium's contributions to world culture. His father had given him a couple of the comic books about the Belgian boy reporter before they'd moved.

"Hergé, the man who drew him, was a *Scoot*. It gave him great *confiance*."

"Confidence," Madame Pauline translated.

"You, *Mex*, should join it."

Max gave a halfhearted smile. He'd done the Scouts for a few years back in America, but the thought of spending even more time speaking French and trying to figure out what he was supposed to be doing—while orienteering in the rain—held zero appeal.

"It would do him good," Madame Pauline agreed. "I'll make sure the parents know."

Inspector Fontaine smiled and handed Max a card. On it was his name and police station extension. "Any trouble, you call me. Albert Jonnart is a special street for me. And I still keep an eye on this house."

"Thank you, sir," Max said, even though he suspected Inspector Fontaine's interest was less in protecting his family than in meddling, with Max especially.

Reluctantly, it seemed to Max, the police officer walked back toward the door. On the way, he stopped to pick up the crumpled paper Max had left on the floor and tossed it back on the table.

CHAPTER SEVEN

Ahmed really hadn't planned on staying in the cellar more than a day or two. But the morning after he arrived, he woke up feverish, his throat so sore he could barely swallow. For three days, he shivered and sweated and slept, curled up on the blanket. The voices of the family drifted down in a dream-like murmur from someplace above him. At first, he thought he was hallucinating, but then he realized that they really were speaking English. But he couldn't tell their accent—were they Canadian, British, American?—and their voices were too muffled and their speech too fast for him to make out what they were saying. Still, it was comforting to hear the family going about their day—the mother's shouts and the rush of footsteps, doors opening and closing, the clatter of dishes. If Ahmed closed his eyes tight enough, he could almost imagine that he was back home in Aleppo.

Only late at night, when the house was still, did he dare sneak out to the bathroom to refill the plastic cup he'd found there with water or to empty the bucket he used to relieve himself into the toilet.

One night, in a feverish daze, he peeked behind the tall red shades hanging in what he had come to think of as the furniture room. He could tell from the play of light that they concealed recessed windows, and he wanted to look out at the street. When he pulled them aside, he was surprised to find a row of potted orchids on the sill, with withered green leaves and shriveled silvery gray roots. Ahmed poked his finger into the bark potting. It was bone dry. His eyes welled with pity, but he was too sick to help them.

On his fourth day in the wine cellar, Ahmed's chills and fever finally subsided, and he realized he was ravenous. He waited until the middle of the night, then crept upstairs into a cold tile hallway and through a stained-glass door. He found himself in an enormous living room with ceilings higher than any house he'd ever seen before. It felt like a palace. The fluffy white cat, who was cleaning himself on a marble windowsill, stopped to give Ahmed an insolent look, but the house was silent, the family seemingly asleep.

In the dim light, he could see framed photos on a mantelpiece. He tiptoed over, curious to see who lived in the house. Most of the photos were of a teenaged girl with long, blond hair and the confident, direct gaze of an adult, and a younger boy with unruly brown hair. Ahmed laughed at the boy's unnatural smile, the smile of someone who clearly hated having his picture taken. It reminded him of how every year during Eid al-Fitr, Baba would pose him and his sisters on the couch in their holiday best, always in the same order, and take picture after picture. Ahmed's eyes would smart from the flash, and in between shots he would jump up or make faces, annoying his father but making Nouri and Jasmine laugh. How hard it had been to sit still and stare into the camera when the whole city smelled of the anise sweet bread that marked the end of the Ramadan fast.

The memory made his stomach growl. But he paused for a moment longer in front of the largest photo. Taken against the backdrop of a beach at sunset, it featured the whole family—the mother, who looked like an older version of the girl, and the father, husky and beaming, his arm around the boy. These people looked nothing like his family—they were sunburnt Europeans wearing Western clothing—and yet the protective way the father embraced the boy made Ahmed miss his own father so much he had to turn away.

He stepped softly through the dining room and into the kitchen. He could hear his own breath, raspy and fast, and it seemed to him that the family could probably hear it too. He spotted a bunch of bananas hanging from a hook. It was a sin to steal, but he didn't have the strength to figure out his next move, not without food. He couldn't think clearly anymore, and when he tried, panic and grief overwhelmed him: Baba was gone; he was alone, lost, with no money or even a phone. He had to get control of himself, and the first step was to quiet the racking hunger. But how not to be a thief?

On the counter, he spotted a square pad of notepaper and a pencil. That was it! He would keep track of everything he took and someday pay the family back. Even though he knew it was unlikely he would be able to do this anytime soon, his intention made him feel better. He tore off a piece of paper and picked up the pencil, then stuffed them in his pocket. Then he grabbed a few pieces of bread from the middle of a loaf and a banana and raced back down the basement stairs.

Back in the cellar, he devoured the bread and banana. They didn't fill him up, but at least he felt a little calmer, especially after he listed them in Arabic on the notepaper. He slipped out of the cellar to the orchids in the furniture room. They really were in bad shape—someone had given them too much direct sun and too little water. But Ahmed remembered how carefully his grandfather had always checked the ailing orchids people brought to his nursery. "People give up on them too soon," he'd always say.

"You just need a little help," Ahmed whispered to them in Arabic. He carried them one by one to the bathroom, dunked their roots in lukewarm water in the stopped-up sink and let them drain. Then he found a razor blade in a tool kit and cut down each orchid's spike so it could focus its energy on the leaves and roots. Finally, he lined them back up in front of the windows.

Wrapped up in the blanket on the cellar floor, he thought, *I'll make a plan.* But it seemed enough to tend to the orchids and then fall asleep, exhausted by his adventure upstairs.

The next morning, Ahmed listened to the hum of the family's voices, the tinkling of bowls and spoons from the kitchen above. He knew what they looked like now, so he could imagine them hunched over their breakfast.

Finally, he heard a heavy door slam shut. He waited to be sure the house was quiet, then tiptoed upstairs. He peered out into the tiled foyer—there were no book bags or briefcases, and the coat hook was empty. The kitchen was in a state of disarray—dirty bowls piled in the sink, half-finished mugs of coffee. The family had rushed off to school and work. It appeared that all they had eaten was boxed cereal. There was no flatbread and sweet tea, certainly not the chickpea *fateyh* his mother made with its flavors of garlic and cumin. Ahmed shoved the memory away. He drank the unfinished coffee, ate mushy spoonfuls of leftover cereal. He took a couple more slices from the middle of a loaf of bread, then poked around in the fridge, taking a carrot, a spoonful of jam and a pickle from a large jar. He figured these were bits of food the family wasn't likely to miss, but he still noted every bite.

As he headed back to the basement stairs through the dining room, he became aware of a sound he hadn't heard in a long time—the happy shouts of children playing. It was the same sound in every language. He followed the noise to the living room and looked out the picture window.

On the other side of the wall, next to the yard he had run through several nights earlier, was a school. He could see a tall green fence, and on the other side of it, kids' heads and a football flying through the air.

When we get to Europe, Ahmed, you'll go back to school.

His father had made him this promise. He'd made it the night before they'd boarded that overcrowded rubber dinghy, when the boat still seemed large and the sea was calm and the future seemed to stretch its fingers eastward to pull them to safety.

Ahmed pressed his forehead against the window. It was hard to see much more over the wall, but he didn't need to. He just listened.

Something soft brushed against his leg. Ahmed started, but then realized it was just the cat. He reached down and petted its fluffy white head. The cat purred and rubbed against him. Ahmed thought about the orchids. They would eventually need more light than what they were getting through the recessed basement windows. If he left now and they remained where they were, they would die.

Anyway, there was no point in running off just yet. He needed time to make a sensible plan. He needed to make sure he was completely healthy first. Perhaps he could really figure out a way to pay back the family for the food he'd taken from them.

But deep down, he knew he was making excuses to linger. He didn't want to go anywhere anymore. He felt safer being nowhere.

CHAPTER EIGHT

"Michael, you left the toilet seat up again!"

"No, I didn't!" Max's father shouted.

Max looked up from his Cheerios. His breakfast cereal supply—a dozen boxes shipped by sea with the furniture—had lasted all of six weeks, and now his parents' angry voices were ruining his last bowl.

"You did it," said Claire, who was sitting on a stool beside him in the kitchen. She didn't even bother to look up from her phone.

"I don't go down there."

"Well, Dad says he doesn't either."

Max shrugged. "Look, if they weren't fighting about this, they'd be fighting about something else."

He knew she couldn't argue with this. Their parents had been fighting constantly. If it wasn't the toilet seat, it was something else ridiculous—who'd left the basement door unlocked, who'd forgotten to get the car registered, who'd bought the wrong floor wax for the cleaning women, who'd eaten the last banana.

Without looking at him, Claire rolled her eyes. "I wonder why."

"What's that supposed to mean?"

"You stress them out."

"Well, maybe that's their fault," he shot back. "They're the ones who put me in a French school! At least you get to speak English."

Claire gave an exaggerated sigh, like Max was being really dense, then jumped down from the stool and jammed her bowl into the dishwasher.

You could at least talk to me, he wanted to say, *because I can't talk to anyone else*. But instead, he shouted, "Claire didn't rinse her bowl!"

Swinging her blond ponytail around, Claire gave him a withering stare. Max knew he was being a jerk, but he didn't care.

"Claire!" his mom called from the other room. "I've told you a hundred times, you need to rinse here! These European appliances—"

Claire stomped over to the sink and gave the bowl a sloppy rinse. But the brief pleasure Max felt at getting Claire in trouble faded as she stormed out of the kitchen, leaving him alone. In fact, he felt worse, and the shameful, angry taste stayed with him as he veered around dog poop on the way to school.

The day didn't get any better. Madame Legrand handed back his last *dictée*. He'd scored 13 out of 77, a score so low it almost didn't seem possible. And who in their right mind scored a test out of 77? After lunch, he stood around in the rain, pretending he could understand the "Do you speak English?" gang. Their real names were Jules, Louis and André, and Max hung around with them at recess, but it wasn't like they could really communicate much.

A soccer ball—or a football, as Max had learned the rest of the world called it—rolled to a stop in front of him. Max pretended not to notice, but then he heard Oscar shout "*Mex!*" so he kicked it back. Even though Max kicked it in his general direction, Oscar made a point of groaning loudly, as if Max couldn't do anything right.

"When you're tempted to act, count to ten and think first," Ms. Krantz had advised him when they had discussed impulse control. So Max counted to ten and thought about pushing Oscar into a big pile of Belgian dog poop.

The only decent part of his day was when Madame Legrand assigned Farah to help him correct his *dictée*. She pulled her chair up to his desk and smiled sympathetically at the marked-up paper.

"French is difficult," she said, simply and slowly so that Max understood. She pointed to a crossed-out mess of vowels. "I make this mistake too, and French is my first language."

Max felt like throwing his arms around her in gratitude.

"But look, you have *gentil* right and *étudie*, even the accent. And you just started learning!" she said, as if scoring 13 out of 77 was actually some sort of achievement.

Max didn't really believe her, but it still felt good to hear praise. He smiled and said, "*Merci.*"

Later, on the way home from school, Madame Pauline announced more depressing news. She had convinced his parents to sign him up for the Scouts—or "Scoots" as she insisted on calling them. Max already hated the word. It took every ounce of self-control for him not to correct her.

"You'll get a uniform," she said, as if he didn't already hate having to wear a uniform to school.

"Great," Max muttered.

"You'll probably already know some of the boys. They try to arrange the groups by school."

Max felt even worse. "There isn't an Oscar in my group, is there?"

Madame Pauline shrugged. "I haven't seen the list. Is he a friend?"

"More of the opposite."

He expected Madame Pauline to express concern, but she seemed entirely unfazed, as if every Belgian kid had a bully personally assigned to them.

"Hopefully he's in your troop then. You can't do *Scoots* together and not become friends."

You want to bet? Max thought. There was only so much Oscar could do to him at school. But in the woods . . . He imagined Oscar purposely leading him down the wrong trail, pushing him into a mucky pond, tying him to a tree and leaving him in the middle of some creepy, wet Belgian forest. He just had to hope that Oscar thought Scouts was as lame as Max did and would never join.

CHAPTER NINE

As he regained his strength, Ahmed learned the family's routine: on weekday mornings, they were out of the house no later than 8:15, and no one was home till the midafternoon. This left him a good chunk of time in which to move the orchids upstairs to the living room for some better light, take a shower, gather some food and record it on his list, wash his clothes, pet the cat and even run up and down the stairs for exercise.

Just before the Seamaster struck ten, Ahmed would stop what he was doing and stand by the back door of the living room. Like clockwork, rain or shine, the children came out in the schoolyard for a twenty-minute mid-morning break. Listening to the voices on the other side of the wall, he could close his eyes and imagine Jasmine was there, hopping from one chalk square to another during a game of *hajla*.

Afterward, he would talk to the orchids. He remembered how his grandfather used to hold conversations with the roses in his nursery. "They like to hear your voice," he used to say, "to know you are there."

So Ahmed told them about Baba—not about the night at sea or the war, but about life in Aleppo before the war.

"He always used to join our football games in the street. He didn't care about being the only adult. He would cheer and shout louder than the rest of us. And when Nouri was little, he used to let her pull his beard and play with his lips even when he was trying to talk to his friends. He never told her 'Go away' or 'Stop.'"

"Jasmine and I used to go to the market with him, and he always gave us a few sips of fresh milk before he took it home to Mama to boil. Once I hit Jasmine for drinking too much milk. He was very angry. I told him it wasn't fair, that she was taking more than her share. 'Allah judges what is fair,' he said. 'You must judge what is kind.' I still remember how ashamed that made me feel."

At 3:35, the boy returned from school with a woman who sometimes spoke French. At 5:30, the girl's voice joined theirs, and at 6:30, the walls would shake as the front door opened and closed several times and the voices of the English-speaking parents replaced the French woman's. The family normally went to bed by eleven, which gave Ahmed another opportunity to go upstairs around midnight and eat some leftovers or take a banana. After updating his food log, he always said good night to the orchids. Even in their half-dead state, they were something existing with him. What was it that his grandfather used to say?

"Those who enjoy flowers enjoy the beauty of the world created by God."

But Wednesdays were hard; school was only a half day, and at seven thirty, the cleaning lady came. Ahmed could hear her greet the family, and then her footsteps would come down the basement stairs to fetch the vacuum, which roared on and off overhead for the next five hours. At twelve thirty, she carried the vacuum back down to the basement, and shortly after, the boy arrived home. Stuck in the cellar, Ahmed did push-ups and squats or reviewed old football matches in his head to pass the time, but the hours dragged by. Weekends were even trickier—sometimes the family was out all day; other times, someone was always home. He tried to stash extra supplies for the weekend, but he was afraid of taking too much, and by Sunday, he was often restless and hungry.

By late September, Ahmed knew it was time to go. He had outstayed a welcome he didn't even have. But he still didn't have a plan. Even if he had had money, he knew he could never trust another smuggler. The only idea he could come up with was to sneak onto a train heading to Calais.

One morning, when the family was at work and school, he opened the door to the patio for the first time and stepped outside. The sky was a dazzling blue, and florescent-green parakeets improbably flitted over the garden. He wondered if they had once been pets. His mother had kept a parakeet. He pictured her stroking its silky green head. He could almost smell the laurel soap she washed with. He could almost hear the soft lilt of her voice as she sang the lullaby *Rima tnam—Rima, Sleep*—to Nouri.

There would be no garden in Calais. He had recently seen photos of the Jungle in newspapers the family left in the recycling bin. It appeared far worse than Parc Maximilien—tents packed into muddy, garbage-strewn fields between a highway and the edge of the city, and people cooking over open fires. With winter coming, the conditions would only get worse. Ahmed imagined sleeping outside and shivered. It had grown colder since he had last been out. He didn't even have a jacket—he hadn't needed one in the summer.

What if he stayed in the cellar through the winter?

It's a stupid idea, he told himself. *Someone will catch me.*

But he'd been hiding in the cellar for a month, he reminded himself, and no one had. He began to think about the idea more practically. He'd need his own store of food, especially for the weekends. And money to pay for it. There had to be solutions to these problems.

The shouts of the schoolkids erupted over the wall. Ahmed knew it was just their recess, but it seemed like a sign. What was it Baba had once said to him as they'd walked home from Friday prayers at the mosque? It had always been their special time together, when his father talked to him like he was already a man.

When there is no way, Allah will make a way.

CHAPTER TEN

The pimply teenaged Scout leader pointed at Max.

"Et toi?"

And you?

Max could feel the other boys looking at him. They were sitting in a circle in one of the gray, damp forests outside of Brussels and he was supposed to choose a spirit animal, but his mind had gone blank. It was hard enough coming up with goofy stuff like this in English, but in French, it was impossible. He didn't know how to say any cool animals—eagle, mountain lion, bear.

"*Crapaud!*" Oscar shouted.

The other boys tittered, and Max felt his face turn red. He had no idea what animal a *crap-o* was, but he was sure it wasn't a compliment.

"Tote?" the pimply Scout leader said, poking his tongue in and out at Max.

"Toad," Max muttered.

He wished Inspector Fontaine had never showed up at his

house. The "*Scoot*" meetings lasted five hours every other Sunday, a major chunk of Max's weekends. The uniform was dorky—he had to wear a red-and-green scarf, a royal-blue oxford shirt and Bermuda shorts no matter how cold it was. He had to sing a bunch of goofy songs he couldn't quite understand but that seemed to have something to do with promising to be friends and help his fellow Scouts. Which was impossible with Oscar as one of his troop mates.

THREE HOURS LATER, Max stumbled out of the woods and collapsed into the passenger seat of his family's new Volvo.

"Drive," he ordered.

His father obediently hit the ignition with a grin and pulled back onto the road. The sun was streaming through a break in the clouds, but the bruise-colored ones blowing in told Max it wouldn't last long. That was Belgium; the weather was always changing—usually for the worse.

"So you loved it?"

Max unplastered his head from the window and glared at him. "This place sucks. Can we just go home?"

"We're going home."

"I mean home to America."

"Come on, Max. It can't all be awful."

"Well, it is. School, Madame Pauline, *Scoots*, everything."

His father didn't try to argue with him, which was a relief. He just drove.

The forest gave way to a fancy neighborhood of grand homes and embassy residences. They passed a fussy, overmanicured park and rejoined the tram lines. A drop of rain splatted against the windshield. A minute later, it began to pour. His father turned on the wipers.

"Max, have I told you what I'm doing at work these days?" his father said.

Max shook his head. He'd been so focused on his own life that he'd never asked.

"Something called resilience plans. According to the NATO charter, every country needs to have a plan for how to help itself in case it's attacked until allies can step in. It's important for every country to be resilient in the face of adversity—to fight on, not just give in."

Max bristled. "So I'm supposed to be resilient."

"All I'm saying is that you can't let a few problems set you back."

"This is not *a few* problems."

"Okay, big problems then, huge ones. Look at the Belgians. During the First World War, the Germans invaded them with an enormous force. Not only did the German Army have ten times the number of troops, they also had machine guns and mustard gas and zeppelins—weapons that the Belgian Army had never encountered before. The Belgians should have been wiped out in weeks, but they fought for years, harder than anyone expected. They even flooded their own land to keep it from the Germans."

Water as a weapon, like something out of *Aquaman*. Max

was tempted to ask more about this. He loved talking to his dad about military history. Back home, they had toured Civil War battlefields together. But he was too angry to give him the satisfaction of showing interest, so he just turned on the radio. An old American song, "(Sittin' on) The Dock of the Bay," was playing, and it made Max even more homesick. His father had some nerve to suggest that his attitude was the problem rather than his parents' lousy decision to come to Belgium in the first place.

The next afternoon, as he scratched away with his fountain pen, Max decided to ask Madame Pauline about the Belgians' defensive flood.

"Did it really happen?"

Max knew it had—his father wouldn't make up something like that—but he also knew acting doubtful would rile up Madame Pauline even more, distracting her from *dictée*.

"Of course!" Madame Pauline stared at him indignantly. "The Yser was a low-lying region. When the situation became desperate, the Belgians opened the canals and flooded the German trenches. We Belgians have always fought fiercely. Even during World War Two, there was always a resistance movement—"

Max sensed an opportunity to keep her talking. "How about here in Brussels?"

"In Brussels especially! Consider the name of your street."

"Albert Jonnart?"

"Jonnart," Madame Pauline corrected, even though to Max's ear, she said it exactly the same way he had. "Do you know who he was?"

Max shook his head.

"He lived here during the war, when the street was called Jean Linden, after the orchid grower. Tropical orchids aren't native to northern Europe, and it wasn't easy at first to keep them alive here."

Max didn't say that they still seemed hard to keep alive, at least for his mom. She had bought them compulsively soon after they'd arrived in Brussels, only to have all the flowers shrivel and fall off the stems a few weeks later. When school had started, she'd gotten rid of them and bought the cloth orchids instead.

"Jonnart forged work papers so Belgians wouldn't have to go to Germany and work for the Reich. And he hid a Jewish boy, a classmate of his son, named Ralph Mayer. Ralph was the only child of a Jewish couple who had fled to Belgium from Germany during the 1930s. When the Germans invaded Belgium, Ralph's father asked Jonnart to protect the boy. So Jonnart hid him in his house."

"Like Anne Frank," Max said. He had read her diary the previous year in school. "How old was he?"

"I don't know exactly. Not much older than you, maybe Claire's age. Jonnart's son, Pierre, and Ralph were classmates at College Saint-Michel, the secondary school."

"What happened?"

"The Gestapo found out and arrested Jonnart. They sent him to prison, then to a labor camp in France, where he died. It's why they renamed the street after him."

Ralph must have died too, probably in a concentration

camp like Anne, Max thought. The story was so sad that Max almost wished he hadn't asked about Albert Jonnart. But then he would still be struggling to figure out the difference between *toi, trois* and *toit.*

"Did he live here, at number thirty-six?"

Madame Pauline shook her head. "He was at number fifty."

Max wondered where Albert Jonnart had hidden Ralph. When they'd moved into this house, Max's father had shown him a wing of unfinished rooms behind a door off the basement, including an old wine cellar. It was too damp and mildewy to use—even to store the moving boxes, which his parents had instead stacked up outside it—but it seemed like the kind of space where you could hide someone. He opened his mouth to ask, but Madame Pauline was onto him.

"Enough, Max," she said firmly. "We need to get back to *dictée.*"

CHAPTER ELEVEN

The following day, Ahmed searched the ground floor until he found a ring of identical keys in a cluttered kitchen drawer. He tried them out on the basement door, then slipped one off the ring and into his pocket. So long as he had a key, there was no reason he couldn't leave the house. He would just be careful to sneak out when the family wasn't home and to keep an eye out for neighbors when he slipped back over the garden wall.

The money problem was a harder one. He could beg for change on the street, but the idea seemed far too dangerous—the police might ask him for documents. During his search for an extra key, he'd found a couple two-euro coins in the bottom of a cup of pens and pencils, but he felt a prick of conscience at the thought of taking not just food, but money.

Still, the more he looked, the more change he seemed to find—coins scattered on the mantel, on the laundry room floor, beneath the cushions of the living room couch. The English-speaking family seemed wealthy, at least wealthy enough to be careless with their change. He decided he would only take small change and always add it to the list of what he had taken so he could eventually pay them back.

The next day, when the family was at work and school, Ahmed gathered up the coins, unlocked the basement door and slipped over the garden wall to the neighbor's yard and the street. He had borrowed a sweatshirt he'd found in the laundry pile, but he still shivered as he walked purposefully around the block and down the hill, where he spotted a supermarket. Ahmed bought crackers, tinned fish and beans. On the way back, he passed a newspaper kiosk, and, before he could stop himself, spent his remaining money on a football magazine. Even though he couldn't read the French, he knew the names of some of the players and could look at the scores and photos. Then he scurried back to the house, his shoes squelching over piles of wet October leaves.

The days began to fall into a rhythm: mornings doing various chores or talking to the orchids; the occasional trip to the grocery store; taking long naps or poring over the football magazine when the boy came home; nights prowling the house for leftovers or loose change.

One morning, he poked around in the packing boxes and found an inflatable camping mat. He imagined how much softer it would be than his blanket on the floor. It was growing colder inside too, and an extra layer between him and the cement would insulate him. It was unlikely the family would need it, at least until spring, but Ahmed still added it to his list.

That night, he started saying his prayers again, standing atop the mat and facing southeast toward Mecca. He had silently mouthed the familiar words with Ibrahim, but now he raised his voice.

"Allahu Akbar—"

The chant coursed through him and he remembered Baba kneeling on his prayer rug bordered in red and white flowers in their sitting room in Aleppo. The image soothed him, as did the repetition of the words "God is greater."

At first, in between prayers, he'd deflate the mat, roll it up and hide it in the alcove. But it was a lot of trouble to blow it up again, and after a while, he started leaving it out. It gave the room a homier feeling, but the chipping cement walls depressed him, especially on the days he couldn't go out.

One afternoon, he tore out the posters from his football magazine, borrowed some tape and taped them to the wall. The next morning, as the cat slept beside him on the living room couch and the orchids sunbathed on the windowsill, Ahmed went through the local flyers and glossy magazines in the recycling bin. Then he cut out his favorite pictures, including a superhero with a trident and golden scales and a strange drawing of a man with a birdcage for a body, and added them to his gallery.

The first week of November, the family went away. The cleaning woman came by every couple of mornings to feed the cat, but otherwise Ahmed was free to come and go as he pleased. On Wednesday, he discovered a halal butcher in the next neighborhood and decided to try to make his mother's *kibbeh*. The butcher only spoke French, but he helpfully adjusted the amount of ground lamb on the scale to the little Ahmed could afford. At the local health food store, Ahmed spent fifteen minutes looking for bulgur because he was too afraid to ask; he knew he looked nothing like the mostly older European customers. But he finally found it and, without making eye contact, handed the last of his change to the cashier.

Back at the house, he realized he had only a vague idea about the recipe and how to cook at all, but there was no one to stop him, so he chopped and mixed, humming away to himself. He felt it was going well until, a half hour later, the onions burned and the balls of lamb and bulgur fell apart in the pan. He ate the mess with a lump in his throat, thinking about his mother and how he would never taste her *kibbeh* again.

By the end of the week, he was relieved to have the family back, if only to hear their voices. He didn't even mind when they yelled or fought. His parents had argued too sometimes, usually when they thought he and his sisters were asleep. He remembered one argument over whether Ahmed was spending too much time playing football and not enough on schoolwork. At least when he heard the English-speaking family's voices, he knew he wasn't alone.

In all his expeditions upstairs, even when the family was away, he never went past the first floor. There was something about this rule that made him feel he had an understanding with them. He didn't go into their bedrooms, and they didn't go into his. So long as everyone followed this rule, he felt safe.

CHAPTER TWELVE

Max wished the fall break in Paris could have lasted another week. He had celebrated his birthday there, eating steak and fries at a restaurant near the Eiffel Tower that looked like a movie set. The city had impressed him far more than Brussels; he had particularly enjoyed walking with his dad through the underground tunnels of the Catacombs, which were piled high with skulls and had been used by resistance fighters during the Nazi occupation. But now that it was Sunday night and he was back in his own bed in Brussels, Max couldn't sleep. From time to time, this happened to him—usually when he was nervous about the next day of school.

Max didn't believe in ghosts, but sometimes, tossing and turning in his bed, he'd hear the floorboards creaking, a light footstep. He knew it was probably just Teddy Roosevelt, but he liked to imagine that the house was alive, shifting its old bones or sighing with the weight of its dark wartime history. Anne Frank had seemed like a story from a long-ago time and faraway place, but there was something about living on the street where Albert Jonnart had hidden Ralph that made the war seem more recent.

His parents' angry whispers drifted up the stairs. He couldn't quite make out the subject of their latest fight, but he was certain it was something silly, like his mother claiming they had five extra house keys and his father swearing there were only four. Over the past month, Max had already counted three fights entirely about bananas, which seemed like three fights about bananas too many. His father would accuse his mother of eating the last one, then she would accuse him, and on it went in endless circles that nearly made Max want to tromp back to the School of Misery, where at least when people were being ridiculous, he couldn't understand them.

As the whispers grew louder, morphing into tense voices, he overheard his mother say, "We should have sent him to the American school."

Max sat up, strained to hear.

"Give him a chance," his dad said. "It's barely been three months."

"Do you hear him saying anything yet? Come on, Michael. He's not the same kind of kid as Claire."

"Which is exactly the reason we put him in a French school. It's only November. Give him time."

"Maybe we should have stayed in Washington—"

"You're just second-guessing yourself. He seemed lost there—"

Lost there? Max wanted to shout. *I'm way more lost here!* He plugged his ears. He couldn't take any more.

When Max finally took his fingers out of his ears, his parents had stopped arguing. But even after they turned off their lights, Max lay awake. Claire was right. *He* was stressing them out. And it was his mom he agreed with: the Belgian school was a disaster, and not the kind that it just took a little resilience to overcome.

Max slipped out of bed and down the stairs, past Claire's and his parents' darkened rooms, to the first floor. He sat on the couch by the picture window in the living room and looked out into the garden. No wonder Inspector Fontaine had liked it. A misty rain was drifting sideways over the holly bushes, almost like snow. There was a strange beauty to the twisted silhouette of the leafless pear tree. A cat slinked along the wall. Max's cheeks felt damp with tears, as if the clouds had moved inside. He lay back and closed his eyes.

Slam!

Max sat bolt upright. Downstairs, a door rattled closed. The confusion of sleep melted away and he realized he wasn't in his bed on the third floor, but on the first floor. The rain had stopped, and in the eerie silence, moonlight sliced across the living room. Max stood up, breathing fast. Was someone downstairs?

He crept over to the basement door, opened it and stood at the top of the stairs, listening. All was silent. He switched on the light. The halogen glow settled his nerves. Maybe the noise had come from upstairs after all—just someone closing the bathroom door? He took one step down, then another, until he was standing on the terra-cotta floor of the laundry room.

There was a bang, and Max jumped as a box in the little hallway off the front room tumbled to the floor. Before Max could race back up the stairs, Teddy Roosevelt dashed out, panicked by the avalanche of cardboard.

Max chuckled.

"So it's you," he said.

The cat stared at him with his green eyes, then bounded up the stairs.

Max was about to follow when he remembered the little door at the end of the hallway. He felt a sudden urge to open it and peek in. He picked up a flashlight from his father's tool kit and shifted the boxes so he could squeeze past them until he reached the door. It seemed odd that the boxes had been arranged so that the door could be opened without upsetting them. Perhaps his parents had stored something inside after all? Curious, Max reached for the skeleton key.

CHAPTER THIRTEEN

The sound of a key turning in the lock startled Ahmed. He jerked around in panic. As the weeks had passed, he'd grown careless, sneaking around more at night, closing the cellar door a little too loudly. But no one had ever come to his home—funny how he'd come to think of it like that—and it had seemed like no one ever would.

But now, as he heard the lock turn, Ahmed realized that this understanding had just been in his own mind. He gathered up his blanket. The door began to creak open. He dove into the alcove and squeezed himself as far back as he could, but there was nothing he could do about the camping mat or the pictures on the walls. As the beam of a flashlight passed across the cellar, he covered himself with the blanket, squeezed his eyes shut and prayed he wouldn't be found.

CHAPTER FOURTEEN

The beam of Max's flashlight illuminated an eerie sight: a picture taped to the top of one of the wine cellar cubicles. Max could not stop staring at it. The picture was of a man—or at least he thought it was a man—but the center of his body was a birdcage. One dove perched inside it while another rested, as if in solidarity, on a platform outside.

As he took a step closer, Max felt squishy canvas beneath his feet. He looked down and noticed his dad's camping mat. He wondered why his father had laid it out in front of this strange picture.

Max shined his light into the back of the wine cellar. The hair on his neck prickled. There were two more pictures taped to the wall—one of Ronaldo, the famous forward for Real Madrid, and the other of Aquaman racing through the water with his trident. There was no way his father would ever have put up pictures like that.

Max waved his flashlight back and forth across the cubicles, but he didn't find anything in them until he reached the next to last one. Inside it was a half-eaten banana.

Max took a deep breath to calm himself and tried to think of some explanation: his father could have come down here while eating a banana and accidentally left it. Maybe Max just hadn't noticed Aquaman and Ronaldo before, and a boy in the last family who'd rented the house had put them up?

"Hello?" Max said.

No one answered. He still felt creeped out. Time to leave and ask his dad what was up with the wine cellar in the morning.

He pointed his flashlight one last time at the picture of the cage man. The door of his cage looked open. Why didn't the dove inside it fly away? Why did the dove outside stay? The picture was like a riddle Max couldn't answer.

Just as he was about to turn away, his eyes fell on the alcove. He shined his light inside. It went back deeper than he had imagined. In the back, he made out a balled-up blanket. He reached in and tugged at it, but it wouldn't budge. Max gave it a hard yank. This time it fell down a little and a pair of eyes peered out.

Max stumbled backward. He was about to shout for help when the blanket rustled and a man emerged. He was muscular, with thick, dark eyebrows and the shadow of a mustache.

"Please," the man said. "No tell!"

His voice cracked and Max realized that he wasn't a man at all, but a boy, like him. He had soft, frightened eyes and smooth cheeks. What Max had taken for a mustache was the lightest wisp of fuzz above his lips. The shout died in Max's throat. The boy's dark hair was shaggy, as if it hadn't been cut in a long time. He had tan skin and spoke with an Arab accent. Max knew what he was. The boy had to be what Inspector Fontaine had called an illegal.

"Where did you come from?" Max asked. He realized his voice was trembling. Even if the illegal was a kid, he was bigger and stronger than Max was.

The boy looked around like he was trying to decide whether to reveal this.

"Syria," he finally said.

This was one of the countries Madame Pauline had mentioned the day Inspector Fontaine had come to verify who lived there. Max stared at the boy, wondering how he had ended up in Brussels by himself. But the boy seemed to interpret his curiosity as suspicion. He fell to his knees and looked up at Max, grasping his hands together. "Please, no tell! They send me to center. I no trouble! Please!"

Max had no idea what center he was talking about, but the desperate look in the boy's eyes made him answer before he could stop himself.

"I won't."

"Thank you, thank you," said the boy. He rose to his feet. But he didn't look directly at Max, and Max had the feeling he didn't quite believe him. That was fair enough. Max wasn't sure he believed himself.

"Who are you?" he asked. "And how did you end up here?"

"Ahmed," said the boy.

Max waited for him to answer the second question, but Ahmed didn't say anything more, so Max filled the silence by introducing himself. "I'm Max. I'm American. I just turned thirteen. How old are you?"

"Fourteen," said Ahmed.

Ahmed looked older than fourteen, but Max didn't challenge him. Maybe he wanted Max to think he was younger so he would seem less intimidating.

"Those are your pictures?" Max said, pointing to Aquaman and the soccer player.

"Yes."

"You like soccer—I mean, football?"

Ahmed's lips curved shyly upward. "Go, the Red Castle."

Max figured he meant the Red Devils, the Belgian team, but he didn't correct him. There was something reassuring about the boy's goofy smile.

"You like football too?" Ahmed asked eagerly. "Ronaldo? Messi?"

"Yeah," Max said, more to be polite than anything else. "You like Aquaman also?"

Ahmed looked at the picture. "He, I not know. But he good swim? That his power?"

"Not just that," Max said. "He can live under the ocean."

Ahmed's smile widened. Max realized his heart had stopped hammering; his muscles were no longer tensed. He leaned against the cellar wall, feeling almost relaxed.

"You're the one who's been stealing our bananas."

The boy's smile instantly vanished. "No stealing."

Max realized he had offended him, which seemed a little ridiculous because Ahmed was basically stealing. But it wasn't like Max's parents couldn't afford a few extra bananas, and they seemed perfectly able to fight about things that Ahmed had nothing to do with. "No, I just mean . . ." Max realized he couldn't explain without offending him again, so he pointed to the picture of the cage man. "Who's that?"

Ahmed shrugged. "I like."

"Me too," Max admitted. "How long have you been here?"

Ahmed hesitated, his eyes flickering. Max couldn't tell if he didn't understand the question or didn't want to reveal the answer.

"Do you have a family? Mother? Father?"

Ahmed looked down at the floor. "No."

For a split second, Max felt Ahmed's loneliness like it was his own.

"Can I bring you anything?" he heard himself say.

Ahmed shook his head. "No need."

"Are you sure?"

And then something strange happened. Ahmed walked him to the little door back up to the basement, like Max was *his* guest and he was escorting him out of *his* house. Then he waved Max after him into the room where Max's parents had piled their extra furniture.

"Come—" he said. "Something I wish show you."

Was this a trap? But if Ahmed wanted to hurt him, why would

he lure him out of the wine cellar to where his parents could more easily hear them? Max followed Ahmed to the front window. Ahmed raised the shade. A dozen pots, most with green leaves, rested on the sill. Twisted, gray roots snaked over their sides like fingers.

Ahmed straightened up and looked directly at Max.

"I care of them."

So his mother hadn't gotten rid of the orchids; she'd just stuck them down here, hoping they'd recover out of sight. Max wondered if she felt the same way about him—that he was just another disappointment to hide away in the Belgium gloom.

"But my mom must check on them?"

Ahmed shook his head. "Nobody come. Never."

She had forgotten about them. Max stared closely at the orchids.

"They're not dead, are they?" Max asked.

Ahmed shook his head. "Still alive."

He gently let down the shade, then stared at the floor. The only thing he seemed to want was for Max to go back upstairs and forget there was a boy living in his wine cellar. But that seemed impossible. Max stood for an awkward moment longer until Ahmed turned and walked back to the wine cellar. Max quietly followed him, but only when Ahmed had reached the little door did he speak.

"Good night," he said.

"Night," Max replied automatically.

Ahmed closed the door between them. Max stood for a

moment in the hall, staring at the moving boxes without seeing them. A stranger was living in his house, an illegal immigrant, almost certainly a Muslim. What if he was a terrorist? What if now that he'd been discovered, he decided to kill everyone in the house? Max thought of his family asleep upstairs, unprotected and helpless. He should run upstairs and call the police.

But then Max thought about the orchids. What kind of terrorist took care of the houseplants? There was something homey too about how he had arranged the camping mat and pictures. Ahmed—he had a name, Max reminded himself—was just a boy, a boy who liked soccer and comic book heroes. He had lost his parents, he was alone and he seemed far more frightened than dangerous.

The compassion Max felt calmed him. It seemed highly unlikely that Ahmed would harm anyone. Max would just be stressing out his parents more by telling them. Besides, they didn't always tell *him* everything.

By the time Max tiptoed upstairs past his parents' room, he had made up his mind. He would try to get some sleep and decide what to do about Ahmed in the morning.

CHAPTER FIFTEEN

It took several minutes for the boy to leave the passageway, several minutes in which Ahmed rolled up the mat, stuffed his remaining supply of food into a plastic bag and tore down his pictures. There was only one decision that made sense: as soon as the boy went upstairs, he would leave. True, Max had promised not to tell, but why would he keep such a promise? Ahmed was a stranger; he had invaded his home and clearly frightened him by leaping out of the alcove and begging for mercy. He should never have revealed that he was from Syria. From everything Ahmed had heard in the camps, Americans were even more frightened than Europeans of people from the Middle East, lumping them all together as fanatics and terrorists.

By the time Max's footsteps disappeared up the basement stairs, Ahmed was ready to go. The wine cellar looked exactly as it had the day he had first discovered it. There was no trace Ahmed had ever been there, and it saddened him to realize how easily he could be erased.

He opened the little door and listened. There were no sounds from upstairs. But that didn't mean that Max wasn't telling his parents. They could be listening to the story, his father getting ready to jump out of bed or his mother on the phone, calling the police. He scurried over to the furniture room to say a quick goodbye to the orchids. He was glad Max knew he had cared for them—giving something, rather than just taking from his family. But he doubted Max could take care of them as he had. Ahmed felt a tug in his chest. He reached out and took the healthiest orchid with him.

Ahmed scurried through the laundry room and back into the room of bikes and skis. He unlocked the door, then slipped out to the patio. The night was much colder than he had expected. He could see his breath, and his fingers tingled. He wished he'd bought himself a coat, or at least taken the blanket—the family would never have missed it. But he wasn't a thief. He'd even left the coins he'd found most recently, as if to prove this. It was a foolish point of pride on such a bitter night. He didn't even have bus fare.

This grim realization led to another as Ahmed's gaze fell on the plant in his numbing hand. He couldn't take it with him. It was near freezing; the cold would kill the orchid within hours. He had to put it back inside. But what if Max's father was already in the basement? Ahmed imagined his heavy footsteps on the stairs, a gun in his hands (Americans in movies were always carrying guns). He should just ditch the orchid and run for it. But instead, he stood rooted to the spot. After everything he'd lost, how could he feel weepy about a stupid orchid? Maybe, he thought, because a stupid orchid was all he had left.

He gently pushed open the door and stuck his head back inside. The basement was dark, which seemed a good sign. He slipped inside, crouched down behind a bike and listened. There were no footsteps, no shouts, no sounds from upstairs at all. He gently put the orchid on the blue carpet. Maybe Max's mother would notice it and give it a second chance. Now, it was time for him to go.

But he continued to crouch behind the bike. What if Max really had kept his promise? It didn't seem as if anyone was coming down—at least tonight. After a few minutes, he crept back outside into the yard and looked up at the house. There were no lights on. Surely, if Max had told, there would be lights on.

It seemed foolish to leave in the middle of the night. Better to come up with a plan, get some sleep and wait till morning, when it wouldn't be quite so cold. Ahmed put the orchid back on the windowsill in the furniture room, then tiptoed down to the wine cellar. He unrolled the camping mat and wrapped the blanket tightly around him. Before he could think of a plan for tomorrow, he fell fast asleep.

CHAPTER SIXTEEN

After a restless night, Max woke with a start, thinking of Ahmed. In the light of day, his promise seemed impossible. He couldn't just pretend Ahmed wasn't there. Even if he was still angry at them, he had to tell his parents. Better to be up-front and let the adults handle the situation.

On the other hand, look what good trusting adults had done for him—he was trapped in Belgium! Plus, the promise he'd made to Ahmed tugged at him, and when he finally went downstairs, it didn't seem like the right time to bring the matter up. His mother was fighting with Claire over a party she had announced she was going to Friday and his father was struggling to pay a bill in French and Teddy Roosevelt had thrown up on the fancy wood floor. His family barely seemed to notice him except for Claire, who took a break from yelling at his mom to yell at him for finishing the last of the milk.

"Max, tell Madame Pauline to pick up some milk for us on the way home," his mom said as she stuffed papers into her briefcase. "I don't have any cash. Michael, where do we keep all those coins? I swear it's like play money! Tell her I'll reimburse her when I pay her at the end of the week."

"Okay," Max said, but he wasn't even sure she heard him. He wondered if Ahmed had something to do with the missing coins too.

He thought about saying something when his father walked him to school. The sky was brightening over the town house roofs, and the calm on the street invited conversation. But instead, Max looked for number 50, Albert Jonnart's house. He found it right past the small lot with the tangle of raspberry bushes and the sign in French that warned "This is private, not a garbage." It was the only semiattached house on the block and had an impressive gabled roof that reminded Max of two flights of stairs that met in the middle. Max guessed from this that Albert Jonnart must have been a pretty important person to be able to afford such a house. And yet, he had given up his life to hide a boy who wasn't even Belgian.

"You're quiet this morning," his father remarked. "What's on your mind?"

"Nothing," Max said. He hesitated before adding, "Syria, actually."

"Syria?" His father raised his eyebrows.

"I saw something about it," Max said vaguely. "What's happening there?"

"There's a civil war."

His father launched into a complicated explanation of how

the war had started and its three sides and the roles of other countries like Russia and the United States. But what stuck with Max most was what his father said about the refugees—how millions of Syrians had fled the violence and were crowded into makeshift camps across the Middle East and Europe, afraid to go back.

"It's a terrible situation, especially with winter coming. Women and children sleeping outside in tents. Some of them have injuries from the war and others have lost family members and are traumatized."

Max was sure that this was why Ahmed was alone—his parents must have died in the war.

"Isn't anyone helping them?"

"Sure. Groups like the Red Cross, the International Rescue Committee and Doctors Without Borders; governments too. But they're overwhelmed—the last time there were this many refugees in Europe was after World War Two. Plus, since the Islamic State is in Syria, people worry that some of them could be terrorists—"

"Like Madame Pauline," Max said. "She thinks they're all terrorists."

"Oh, Madame Pauline," his father said, shaking his head woefully. "Look, maybe a few of them are. But not most."

Max felt encouraged. His father seemed sympathetic about the refugees' plight. This was his chance to bring up Ahmed.

"Are there camps here in Brussels?"

"There was a big one at Parc Maximilien this summer," his father said. "But the city closed it down in September and sent everyone to reception centers."

Center, that was the word Ahmed had used.

"Are they . . . nice?"

"They're overcrowded."

"Maybe we could host a refugee here. Our house is big enough—"

His father stopped in front of the School of Misery and ruffled his hair. "You're a good kid, Max. But we can't do that."

Max pulled away.

"Why not?"

"I'm an American contractor. It would be way too political for me."

"But what's political about helping someone?"

"Look, Max. Taking care of another person is a huge responsibility, and we're only here another eight months. Besides," he added with a grin, "can you imagine what Madame Pauline would say?"

Max hid his disappointment with a smile, then trudged into the School of Misery. He should have known not to count on his father. His father didn't really think he was a good kid anyway. He thought he was a lost one.

AT SCHOOL, Max tried hard to concentrate, but it was even tougher than usual not to let Madame Legrand's words blend together as he tried to decide what to do. It seemed foolish to encourage Ahmed to stay in the wine cellar. Max's parents would turn him over to one of the centers if they discovered him. And what about Inspector Fontaine, who claimed to be keeping an eye on the house? It would be even worse for Ahmed if the cop discovered him living in a house that Inspector Fontaine seemed to consider his own.

At recess, as the "Do you speak English?" gang cracked themselves up imitating various teachers, Max kept glancing over at his house. He wondered what Ahmed did every day while he was in school. Did he go through Max's room? Max had never noticed anything missing or moved around, but he left everything all over the place anyway—dirty laundry, his iPad and other electronics, books, comics, fantasy board games. He had never cared about being messy, but now he felt a little ashamed when he thought about how all that stuff, carelessly strewn about, must look to Ahmed.

It suddenly occurred to him that Ahmed could have fled as soon as Max had gone. In that case, Max realized, he wouldn't have to make any decision at all. But this possibility only made him feel worse. He imagined Ahmed trudging through the rain, holding a handwritten sign like the beggars on street corners and in the metro, pleading for change.

A shout interrupted Max's thoughts. His eyes focused back on the schoolyard to find Oscar staring at him, the soccer ball jammed under his big foot.

"Arrête de me regarder comme ça!"

To his surprise, Max realized he understood. *Stop staring at me like that.*

The "Do you speak English?" gang stopped laughing. The soccer game ground to a halt.

"*Je ne te regarde pas,*" Max said.

I do not look at you.

Oscar jutted out his chin.

"*Si tu me regardais!*"

Yes, you were.

Max realized it might have seemed to Oscar like he was staring at him when he was really looking at his house. But he certainly wasn't going to explain this, especially when the kid seemed to have it in for him. Max knew he should count to ten, but instead he took a step forward.

Jules, the most good-natured of the "Do you speak English?" gang, put an arm around Max and tried to turn him around.

"*C'est un idiot,*" Jules said under his breath.

Oscar is a jerk.

But Max pulled away.

"*Et alors?*" he said, staring straight at Oscar.

Max wasn't even sure this was the right expression for "And so what if I was?" but maybe just butchering the language was insult enough. Oscar's nostrils flared.

"Maybe you understand, stupid," Oscar said in English. "No boy love here."

Max could hear his heartbeat whooshing in his ears. It didn't matter whether or not the other kids understood, or even whether they thought he was gay. It didn't matter that he was breaking school rules or that his parents had warned him to never, ever hit anyone again. He'd had enough of Oscar's bullying. With a running start, Max rammed into him.

Oscar had several inches and a good twenty pounds on him, but Oscar's foot was on the ball and he lost his balance. Still, he managed to sideswipe Max's nose with one huge fist as he fell. The pain stunned Max only for an instant, then it blinded him with fury. He leapt onto Oscar and began walloping him.

"Mex How-Weird!"

By the time Max recognized his full name shouted in her French accent, Madame Mansouri, one of the aides, had shoved through the circle of kids gathered around them. She pulled Max roughly toward her. Oscar clutched his stomach and began to holler in such rapid-fire French that Max could understand only the angry jabs of his thick finger in Max's direction.

Max realized he was in serious trouble. Oscar hadn't won the battle of fists, but he could definitely win the battle of words. Who even knew what he was saying—maybe that Max was a crazy American who had been bullying *him*. It was the incident with the eighth grader and the bike all over again.

But just then, a voice from behind him cut in.

"Non, c'est pas vrai."

No, it's not true.

Max turned to look at his defender. It was Farah.

"Oscar was the one being cruel to Max," she continued, speaking in a slow, calm French that Max could understand. "He wanted Max to attack him."

There were murmurs of agreement from Jules and several others.

Madame Mansouri loosened her grip on Max's arm and turned to Oscar. "Oscar, is this true?"

"*Non*," Oscar said. But he made the mistake of not meeting her eyes, and at this she let go of Max's arm and shouted at both of them. Max couldn't completely understand what she was saying, but he caught something about rules and about how next time they would be sent to *la directrice*, the principal. Then she made them shake hands and look each other in the eye, which Max thought was a fitting punishment, at least for Oscar.

When the bell rang, Max rushed to line up behind Farah.

"*Merci*," he said.

Farah shrugged. "It was nothing," she said in French.

Max struggled to find the French words. "I wish to know . . . why he detest me."

Farah turned around to face him. "It's not you. Oscar's father died in third grade, in a car accident. Everyone was very nice to him, I still try to be, but he's been mean ever since."

Max felt a flicker of pity. "He has a mom?"

"Yes," Farah said. "She's a secretary at the commune. She lets him do whatever he wants. And he does whatever he wants here at school. You were brave to fight him."

Max stared at her in amazement. No one had ever called him brave before, certainly not for following his crazy impulses. He suddenly wondered if they were so crazy after all. He let the French word—*courageux*—sink in. Maybe he wasn't smart like Claire, maybe he would never be the best at anything. But he knew the difference between cruelty and kindness; he knew how to protect a friend.

His thoughts circled back to Ahmed. Perhaps there was another way for him to be brave; not by using his fists, but by acting like Albert Jonnart and simply doing the decent thing. He would follow his first impulse. He wouldn't turn Ahmed in. He would try to help him.

It was probably already too late. Ahmed had sensed his fear and hesitation; he was most likely long gone. But Max couldn't be sure—not the rest of the afternoon as Madame Pauline relentlessly drilled him on French verbs. Not as he searched online in his bedroom for the picture of the man with the cage torso. Not even after Claire and his parents came home and started arguing again about the party Claire wanted to go to. During the fight, Max tried to sneak down the basement stairs—with the excuse that he needed to use the bathroom—when Claire heard him.

"He's the one leaving the toilet seat up!" she said with a note of triumph in her voice.

"Max!" his mom said. "I told you to put the seat down."

"Sorry!" Even if Ahmed had left, it seemed best for everyone to believe he was the culprit.

"And he probably pees all over it!" added Claire. "Like he does upstairs!"

It wasn't till everyone had gone to bed that Max was finally able to find out if the boy in the wine cellar was still there.

CHAPTER SEVENTEEN

Over the past few years, Ahmed had learned the language of knocks—something-horrible-has-happened-to-someone-you-know knocks, get-out-before-I-throw-you-out knocks, it's-time-to-go-now's-your-only-chance knocks. Which is why, at half past eleven, when he heard a knock on the little door, he let out a deep breath. It was a gentle knock, a knock that said, "I come in peace."

Ahmed ducked under the arch and opened the little door. Max stood there in his pajamas, holding a blanket and a pillow, a paper bag resting on top of them.

"I wasn't sure what you liked to eat," he said, looking down at it. "I mean, besides bananas."

For the second time in the past few days, Ahmed felt his lips turn in the direction of a smile. "Thank you," he said.

Then he took the bag and stepped aside to indicate that Max should enter.

"There's a turkey sandwich and a juice box and some health-food bars. They're kind of gross, but they're supposed to be full of vitamins."

Ahmed couldn't follow what Max was saying, but he nodded as if he understood. And in a sense, he did, at least Max's tone, which was nervous but kind.

"I also brought a pillow and another blanket," Max said as he followed him back into the cellar. "It seems kind of cold down here."

"Thank you." Ahmed crouched down to lay the pillow and blanket on the camping mat. "Sit?"

Max plunked down on the mat. He seemed more relaxed now, his legs crisscrossed beneath him. "I was worried you'd left," he said.

Ahmed didn't tell him how close he'd come. How he would have left before dawn had he not accidentally slept in, roused only by the family's voices above him. How the moment the front door had slammed shut, he had showered, dressed and repacked his provisions, adding more bread and an orange from upstairs. How at the last minute he had carried the orchids upstairs and how he had ended up talking to them over the shouts from the schoolyard:

"If the boy told, someone would have come for me already. But can I trust him?"

We trust you, he'd imagined the orchids saying. *Trust him—at least for another day. Besides, it's cold and it's going to rain.*

Ahmed opened the bag and took out the sandwich. It had cheese and some kind of meat in it. He poked it with his finger, trying to decide what to do.

"Do you not like turkey?" Max asked.

Ahmed was relieved he didn't have to explain about halal. The less he said about his religion, the better.

"No."

"I'm sorry. I didn't know. You can take it out."

Ahmed reached out to hand back the slices. "You want?"

"Oh, no," Max said, waving him off. "I'm fine."

It seemed rude to eat by himself, but Ahmed was hungry. He took a bite, chewed.

Max watched him with a satisfied expression. "I'm glad you didn't leave," he said after a minute.

"No place to go," Ahmed admitted.

"That center you mentioned, it's really that bad?"

A lump of crustless bread and cheese stuck in Ahmed's throat. He shook his head vigorously. "Like prison. Wait with many boys, then they send me back."

"They won't send you back! I looked it up. Syrians can stay."

"No papers." It seemed less suspicious, Ahmed thought, than telling Max he had false papers. But Max still looked confused. He probably thought moving to a new country was as easy as showing up. Life was easy for Americans. He tried again to explain. "No papers, then no name, no birthday, no home country. Everyone want to be Syrian. No one believe me. They send me to Turkey . . . Please, no tell."

"But you're just a kid—"

Ahmed put down the sandwich. His appetite had vanished. They seemed to be back to where they had started—Max on the verge of betraying him, Ahmed begging him not to. He wished he could blame the orchids. *You said to trust him.*

But Max must have read his face because he held up his hand. "Relax. I promised I wouldn't tell. And I won't. I'll help you. But we're only here till next July, and besides, you can't spend the rest of your life down here. Maybe we can talk about it another time?"

Max was certainly persistent. Ahmed didn't want to promise, but he also didn't want Max to act without his permission. "Maybe," he said without enthusiasm.

Max's face relaxed; this answer seemed to satisfy him.

"What else do you need?"

Ahmed could think of a hundred things he needed, but he said nothing. He didn't want to be in Max's debt. And he also worried that Max might get caught taking things for him.

"That's your only pair of clothes," Max said into the silence. "You don't even have anything else to sleep in."

"Please," Ahmed said. "No need."

"It's no big deal," Max said. "I'll come again tomorrow night."

He stood up and looked around the cellar as if taking inventory of what Ahmed did and didn't have.

Ahmed stood up too.

Max pointed to the cage man, which Ahmed had taped back up again.

"It's Magritte."

Ahmed didn't understand. "What?"

"The artist—his name is Magritte. I googled him. He's Belgian."

But what meant more to Ahmed than the artist's name or nationality was the fact that Max had bothered to look up the picture in the first place. The image had stuck with Max the same way it stuck with him. He wondered if Max had also noticed that the man was sitting on a cliff, above the sea.

"A book," Ahmed suddenly said. "You bring for me? I read a little English."

Max nodded. "What do you like? I have a ton—comic books, science fiction, history. You've been to my room?"

Ahmed shook his head. He didn't know how to explain his rule about not going past the first floor. "You pick for me."

"Sure," Max said. He was clearly happy to be asked for something.

Ahmed walked him back to the little door. As he opened it, he noticed that the left side of Max's nose was red.

"What happen?" he asked, pointing to it.

"I tripped. No big deal."

Max shrugged, but his eyes darted away. It wasn't a very convincing lie, Ahmed thought. But it reassured him: Max knew something of the world after all.

He followed Max around the boxes into the hall, but halfway there, Max stopped and turned around.

"You're Muslim, right?"

Ahmed froze. He could tell from the way that Max asked the question that he'd already guessed he was. So why did he want him to say so? Ahmed's stomach clenched. Max must be having doubts about helping him, helping a Muslim. He was probably worried he was a terrorist. But Ahmed couldn't lie, not about this.

"Yes," he said. "It's why I not eat meat. It needs be halal."

"What's that?"

"Halal is Muslim rules for how animal killed."

"I don't know much about being Muslim," Max admitted.

Ahmed wondered if he knew anything—he probably thought Islam was just some violent religion that was all about attacking non-Muslims. He wished he could tell Max how his father used to take him along when he handed out rice and sugar to the poor, lecturing him on the importance of charity, how it was one of the pillars of their religion. But he didn't think he could tell Max about his father—not yet.

"Very important in Islam is to help poor and strangers. Muhammad, our prophet, say the best Muslims is those who be useful to others. This is in our holy book, the Qur'an, the words God revealed to Muhammad."

Max nodded, his expression thoughtful. "I don't really believe in God. But sometimes I think someone needs to."

Ahmed's throat tightened; he was afraid he might cry. So he just turned away with a whispered "Good night."

CHAPTER EIGHTEEN

The next day was Friday the 13th of November, but it wasn't until that horrible evening that Max even noticed the unlucky date. As soon as he got home from school, he went to work. First, he looked through his books and comics, trying to pick a couple of perfect ones for Ahmed. *Aquaman, Volume 3: The Throne of Atlantis* was an obvious choice. But he had a hard time choosing the second book. He had the idea it should be a subject Ahmed could relate to, but uplifting as well. Anne Frank's diary didn't end well, so he nixed that. Dead parents were another subject he wanted to avoid, but almost every fantasy book seemed to start with a dead parent.

And so he went backward in time through his bookshelf till he found one of the first books he'd ever read by himself. It was called *Boy Heroes of the War Between the States*, and it had been written in the 1950s. Max had gone through a huge Civil War phase in third grade. His father had remembered enjoying *Boy Heroes* himself as a boy and had found Max an old, water-stained copy on eBay. A few of the stories were sad, but there were triumphant ones too, ones that showed that kids could be as courageous as adults. The book had made a deep impression on Max. After sliding the book and comic into a tote bag, he went through his dad's old clothes and found a pair of pajamas he had never seen him wear and that his father was unlikely to miss. He added a spare toothbrush, never used, and a travel-sized tube of toothpaste.

Just as he had hoped, his parents went to bed early—as they usually did on Fridays, exhausted by the week. In another stroke of luck, Claire went to sleep early too, complaining of a sore throat. At ten thirty, he crept down to his parents' bedroom and peeked in. The only light emanated from his father's phone, which blinked on with messages or news alerts—he had clearly forgotten to switch it to do not disturb. He was a heavy sleeper, though. There was no light at all coming from beneath Claire's door.

Max became aware of soft footsteps in the hall below. The front door creaked open. Max's stomach tightened. Where was Ahmed going? Was he leaving? Max raced down the stairs and was about to whisper his name when Claire lurched around, her long blond hair swinging after her, and stared at him. She was in her coat, wearing eyeliner and lipstick, and holding a small beaded purse in her gloved hand.

"Don't you dare tell Mom and Dad," she hissed. "I'll kill you."

Then she quietly closed the door behind her.

Max stood frozen in place, his heart still pounding. Had she wondered what he was doing, coming down late at night, carrying a tote bag? But then he realized that she was only thinking about herself and whether he would tell. She was sneaking out to the party, of course. His parents had never agreed to let her go. A small part of him was tempted to tell—how refreshing it would be for her not to be Miss Perfect anymore. But then his parents would go after Claire and be up half the night fighting with her, and he wouldn't be able to visit Ahmed. Plus, for a long time after, his parents would be on the lookout for anyone sneaking around at night.

It was better, anyway, to have her owe him a favor than to start a war. As he fixed Ahmed a peanut butter and jelly sandwich in the kitchen, Max laughed softly to himself—how many secrets were there in this house? How many kids wandering around at night? He almost felt sorry for his parents, unaware of the crazy hidden universe around them.

His mood was buoyant when he knocked on the little door. It seemed contagious too, because when the door opened, Ahmed smiled. Max held open the tote bag.

"Bananas, peanut butter and jelly, two books—"

But before he could finish, he heard his mother's voice from upstairs. "Oh my god!"

The smile dropped off Ahmed's face. Max shoved the tote into his hand. By the time he was back in the hall, Ahmed had already closed the cellar door behind him. Max tiptoed up the basement stairs, his stomach clenched. Had something happened to Claire? He pictured her mugged and beaten. He snapped himself out of these dark thoughts. She had left barely ten minutes earlier. It wasn't very likely she was in trouble already—that is, unless she was in a different type of trouble. His mother was fully capable of a cry like that over simply finding Claire missing from her bedroom.

He grabbed a banana from the kitchen and ran upstairs, this time not even bothering to mute his footsteps.

"What happened?" he said, bursting into his parents' room.

They were both sitting up, the light on, looking at their phones.

"Quiet!" whispered his mom. "You're going to wake Claire."

Max let out a breath he hadn't realized he was holding. Whatever was happening had nothing to do with her.

"You're the one who shouted," his father said to her.

"Well, you're the one who left your phone on."

"What happened?" Max interrupted.

"There are terror attacks happening in Paris," his father said. "In a bunch of places. They're holding hostages at a concert hall."

"God, all those kids," his mother said.

"What kind of terrorists?" Max asked.

"Muslim ones," his mom said. "They were shouting 'God is great.'"

Max felt like he couldn't breathe. What if Ahmed was sympathetic to terrorists? What if he was helping them?

"Max, are you okay?" his mom asked.

"Most Muslims aren't terrorists," he murmured.

"Of course not." She hesitated, seemed to choose her words carefully. "They're peaceful, decent people. Like that girl . . . at school—"

"Farah."

"Right, Farah." His mother smiled as if the thought of Farah made her happy before her expression turned serious again. "But Islamic extremism is also a real problem."

"And not just in Europe," his dad added. "In the Middle East and Asia too."

His mother's voice started rising. "These were innocent people just going to a concert—"

"You're going to wake up Claire," his father said.

Claire! Max had to warn her. What were the chances his mother would check on her? She was upset; people were being killed. At some point, his mother would want to peek in as she slept.

"Where were you anyway?" his mother asked.

Max held up the banana. "Getting a snack. I've got to pee now. Be right back."

"Look at this," his mom said, holding her phone out to his dad.

Max ran upstairs, grabbed his phone and started typing as fast as he could.

MOMDAD UP TERROR ATTACK PARIS GET HOME B4 MD REALIZE UR GONE

He hit send. Then he ran back down to his parents' room. They were both still glued to their phones.

"Any more news?" he asked.

"The police haven't gone into the Bataclan yet," said his dad. "The terrorists must have suicide vests. The police must be worried they're going to blow themselves up."

His father's voice was tense, and the fear in his mother's

eyes as she scanned her phone frightened Max. It was horrible to imagine the people trapped inside the theater with the suicide bombers, not knowing whether these very moments would be their last. Max tried not to think about it. He focused instead on keeping his parents talking so they wouldn't get up and check for Claire.

At last, his phone vibrated.

FRONT DOOR

"I'll be right back," he said.

Neither of them said anything. His mother looked like she was about to cry over what she was reading on her phone.

Max ran downstairs and opened the door. Claire slipped past him. She had somehow managed to wipe off all her makeup. She kicked off her shoes and hung up her coat, then peeled off her jeans and stuffed them into the bottom of the bin of hats and scarfs. Only then did she stop to look at Max, not with a scowl but with a look that was calm and clear-eyed. He felt like it was the first time since they'd moved to Brussels that she really saw him.

"Thanks," she mouthed. Then she waved him upstairs, tiptoeing behind him while he stomped heavily.

"What are you doing, Max?" his mother said in a loud whisper. "You're going to wake up Claire."

Claire ducked in front of him through the door of his parents' bedroom, yawning. "Too late. He already did."

"I was checking to make sure the door was locked," Max said, following behind her.

"What happened?" Claire asked, rubbing her eyes as if she'd just woken up. Only if Max looked closely could he see the smeared gray makeup near the creases.

"Terrorist attacks in Paris," said his dad. As Claire sat down beside their mother, Max's dad moved over and patted the empty space next to him. Max walked to his side of the bed and sat down. His fear melted into shame. How could he think even for a second that Ahmed was involved in anything like this? True, he was Muslim, but he'd talked about charity, not violence. He had been nothing but gentle.

"Don't worry, Max," his father said. "No one's going to hurt you. This is happening in Paris, okay? You're safe here."

His mother wrapped her arms around Claire and kissed her hair. His father put an arm around him. But all Max could think about was Ahmed, sitting alone in the wine cellar, with no one to tell him he was safe.

CHAPTER NINETEEN

It wasn't until late the next night that Ahmed heard the gentle tap on his door. In the twenty-four-plus hours since Max's mother had shouted and Max had rushed away, Ahmed had stayed inside the cellar, not even leaving to use the bathroom, relieving himself in the bucket instead.

To pass the time, Ahmed looked at the books Max brought him. It was easy enough to follow the Aquaman comic. The pictures helped: there was Aquaman on the Throne of Atlantis; there he was leaving to join the Justice League; there was the evil Lord Orm holding the world at ransom and stealing away Aquaman's throne. The other book had more words with a few photographs. It seemed to be about boys at war a long time ago, but Ahmed's English wasn't good enough to understand it, and he didn't like the photos of the boys holding rifles bigger than they were or weighed down by large drums. There was a haunted look in their eyes—of weariness and resignation—that he recognized.

As soon as he heard the knock, Ahmed hurried to the door. He felt bad for not wearing the pajamas Max had given him, but at any moment he still expected to have to flee, and it seemed ridiculous to run through the city in pajamas. But Max didn't seem to notice. He entered quietly, carrying a tote bag and a small cooler.

"What happen?" Ahmed asked.

Max didn't quite look him in the eye.

"There were a bunch of terrorist attacks in Paris."

"How many people kill?"

"More than a hundred."

Max didn't say anything more, but Ahmed understood everything. The terrorists were most likely Islamic State, trained in Syria. Some of them had likely gone back and forth from Turkey to Europe and might have even pretended to be refugees. They probably seemed a lot like him—young men without documents traveling alone.

"Very bad," he said.

Max nodded, but he didn't seem to want to discuss it further. He held up the cooler. "I brought you some other things to eat," he said. "Yogurt, veggies, no meat. Also some more books."

"Thank you," Ahmed said.

As he led Max back into the wine cellar, he allowed his thoughts to reach their inevitable conclusion. The Europeans would blame the refugees. It didn't matter that many of them were fleeing Islamic State themselves. They were all Muslim. To the Europeans, they were all the same. He needed to make it clear to Max that he had nothing to do with this.

"Did you like the first books?" Max asked.

"I like Lord Orm," Ahmed said. Too late, he realized how it might sound to Max that he liked the villain. "Not like. He is bad."

"No," Max said, seeming to understand. "He's Aquaman's half brother. Did you know that?"

Ahmed shook his head.

"They had the same dad, but Lord Orm is completely human."

"Human?" Ahmed repeated, not sure of the word.

"Like . . . um . . ." Max paused. "Like not magical. Ordinary. Like us."

Ahmed shook his head. "But I not like Lord Orm. I not like this bad men in Paris—"

"Stop," Max said, holding up his hand. "I know." His face was slightly red, as if the conversation embarrassed him, but Ahmed wondered if he was also embarrassed because these fears and doubts had crossed his mind.

"Did you read the other book?" Max asked.

"A little," Ahmed said, mainly not to sound rude.

"I was a slow reader," Max explained. "My sister, Claire, read the first four *Harry Potter* books in first grade, and everyone was worried because I still wasn't reading chapter books in third. But then I got this book and it just . . . I don't know. I liked it."

Ahmed didn't follow. Afraid Max would expect a reply, he decided to tell the truth. "That book too hard. I cannot read."

"Oh," Max said, his cheeks coloring as if he was the one admitting this. "Your English is really good, though. Where did you learn it?"

"My father."

The word hurt to speak.

"He spoke it well?"

"He was English teacher."

"What happened to him?"

Ahmed glanced at the picture of the man with the cage body balanced atop the cliff overlooking the sea. He felt exactly like this man, on the brink of a precipice. He was sure that if he answered, he would topple into the sea.

"You teach me better English?" he asked instead. "So I read this book?"

Max looked surprised. Then his eyes crinkled with a smile. "Sure. We can read it together. I'll bring you a dictionary too, so you can look up words and see what they mean. In the meantime, you can check out these others. This one is about the boys who invented Superman—you know who he is, right, the superhero from another planet?"

Ahmed lifted one fist to the sky. "Nabil Fawzi!"

Max shook his head. "Who?"

"This is his name when he is just working guy."

"You mean Clark Kent!"

"No Clerk Cant! In Arabic, Nabil Fawzi."

"It's a bird, it's a plane, it's Nabil Fawzi?" Max fell over sideways laughing. "Maybe in Arabic it's got a ring to it—"

Ahmed realized he was laughing too. He tackled Max and pinned him to the floor.

"Okay, okay!" Max cried. "Nabby Fonzi! Nibble Fuzzy!"

When Ahmed finally sat up and released Max, his stomach ached from laughing.

"What else you bring me?" he asked in his most imperious voice.

"I hereby present—" Max took the next book from the bag with a flourish. "*The Calculus Affair*, one of the better Tintins, or as you call him in Arabic—"

"Tintin."

"You sure it's not Abdul Abdul or something?"

Ahmed gave him a playful shove.

Max placed the book on Ahmed's head, then took out one more.

"And last but not least, my dear, considerate parents gave me this one before they announced they were forcing me to move here. No words, just pictures. It's about this man who arrives in a new city alone—"

Ahmed smiled. "Brussels?"

"It's not a real city, though, I suppose it's more like New York."

"Where you live?"

"No, I'm from Washington, D.C."

"It is like Brussels?"

Max laughed. "No way. It doesn't rain all the time for one thing. And people are friendlier. At least most of them. Here, I'll show you some photos—"

Ahmed hunched over Max's phone as Max scrolled through pictures of his friends and silly selfies. Even though Max's house and neighborhood looked fancier, his life really didn't seem that much different from Ahmed's before the war—hanging out with cousins and friends, goofing around.

"You have any photos of your family?" Max asked.

Ahmed shook his head. They'd all been on his phone.

Max paused on a photo of two boys perched on their bikes. Kids with backpacks were streaming out of a brick building behind them.

"This your school?" Ahmed asked.

"Yep."

Ahmed's stomach clenched with longing. He glanced over at Max, surprised to find him staring at the photo with equal intensity.

"That's Kevin and Malik. And the bike I destroyed."

He pointed to Kevin's blue mountain bike.

"Destroy how?"

Max looked at Ahmed like he wasn't sure he wanted to get into it. Then, with a big exhale, he launched into the story. He laughed when he told it, acted like it hadn't been a big deal, but Ahmed could tell otherwise from the way he fiddled with his hands.

"Everyone was mad at me," Max said. "But I was just being a good friend."

He said this defiantly, but at the same time he peered at Ahmed as if he needed him to confirm this.

Ahmed didn't hesitate. "You are good friend, Max."

CHAPTER TWENTY

Every night over the next few days, Max brought Ahmed food and other supplies, including the English dictionary he had promised. Then Max listened to Ahmed read from *Boy Heroes of the War Between the States*. The first chapter was about Johnny Clem, who joined the Union Army at age ten and, at age twelve, during the Battle of Chickamauga, shot the Confederate colonel who had demanded his surrender. Max had found Johnny's story thrilling, but Ahmed seemed unmoved. Max figured this was probably due to the difficulty of the language: they had to pause often so he could explain to Ahmed what a word meant or how to correctly pronounce it. But it also crossed Max's mind that Ahmed had actually been in a war. As he imagined the story through Ahmed's eyes, it seemed sadder and less glorious: a boy who'd begged to join the army after losing his mother in a train accident and then ended up shooting a man with a tiny musket sawed down to his size.

During these visits, Max purposefully avoided telling Ahmed the latest news: how the chief planner of the Paris attacks had turned out to be Belgian, how he had traveled back and forth to Syria. How three of the other terrorists, including the only one still at large, had lived in the Brussels neighborhood of Molenbeek, a short walk from Parc Maximilien and just three miles away from Max's house.

An edginess had descended over the city. It was impossible not to feel it, even at school. Waiting for the sliding door to the courtyard to open in the morning, parents huddled together, talking quietly. Max noticed a few of them eyeing the mothers in headscarves, their polite smiles struggling to camouflage their unease.

In class, Madame Legrand handed back the latest *dictée*. Max had received a 34 out of 77.

"Almost half," Farah said in French when she joined him at his desk to help correct it. "Not bad!"

Max wished he could make some joke about how she was grading him on the largest curve ever, but that was way beyond his French. "Thanks to you," he said instead.

"I can read your writing too."

"My handwriting, you say, was bad?"

Farah blushed. "No . . . not."

Max grinned to show he was just teasing. "I know. Bad in America too. But on the computer I write good. You need a computer. Modern."

She burst into an easy laugh that made Max feel clever—even in French. He wondered if she could ever hang out after school, perhaps to help him with his homework. He wanted to hear her laugh again. But he had a feeling that Madame Pauline might not appreciate Farah as her replacement.

"Farah," a voice called out from behind them.

Max stiffened. Oscar had been avoiding him since their fight, but Max didn't like the mischievous tone of his voice.

Farah turned around and gave him a stern look. "What?"

"You know any of those terrorists they're looking for?"

Farah turned back around without answering, but Max shot Oscar a look.

"What?" Oscar said innocently. "You know she lives in Molenbeek."

Before Max could spring out of his chair to grab Oscar, a shadow fell over the table.

"Oscar!" Madame Legrand barked.

Oscar slumped down in his seat, but his narrowed eyes made Max think he was still gloating.

Before dismissal, Madame Legrand reminded the class that the school welcomed children of all religions and believed in treating everyone with respect.

On the way home, Max told Madame Pauline what his teacher had said, hoping to work up to inviting Farah over. But she just responded with a loud snort, as if Madame Legrand was the real fool.

"You think these people pouring in respect *our* culture? They want us to support them, but they don't want to become anything like us.

"You'll see, Max," she added darkly. "One day, Europe is going to be theirs."

Max sighed. He didn't want to risk Madame Pauline sharing an opinion like this with Farah. He wanted Farah to like hanging out with him, not think he or his parents thought this way. Madame Pauline wasn't alone in her opinion. After Paris, Max had started reading the newspapers online. Politicians across Europe and the United States were blaming the refugees for the attacks—or at least the open borders that allowed them in.

The next afternoon, Max was home, reading a British editorial calling for stricter identity checks and border controls, when the doorbell rang. He closed his laptop and rushed downstairs just as Madame Pauline opened the door. A familiar voice echoed up from the foyer.

"*Bonjour, Mex,*" said Inspector Fontaine, looking up to where Max had stopped short on the stairs. "Or should I still say hello?"

"*Bonjour, Monsieur,*" Max said. His heart was hammering, but he tried to keep his voice steady. Even if Inspector Fontaine knew about Ahmed, maybe Max could still warn him.

"Tu parles un peu français maintenant. Bravo!"

"I just speak a little," Max said in English.

"You make the effort. Not everyone does."

Max nodded. He couldn't tell if the cop was playing with him or whether it was possible he didn't know about Ahmed.

"You must be busy," Max said, trying to suss out why he was here.

He slipped down the stairs, desperately trying to think of a way to warn Ahmed. But the only idea he could come up with was to shout, "Run, Ahmed! Police!" and this seemed just plain idiotic, a good way to both incriminate himself and make sure half the Brussels police force went racing after Ahmed.

Inspector Fontaine took off his cap and brushed his sleeve against his forehead, wiping away drops of rain. "Oh, yes. Bad business."

"You need to get rid of these people," Madame Pauline scolded.

Only a small twitch of the inspector's eye betrayed his annoyance. "If only it were so easy, Madame. The European Union won't agree to bar the door, not yet anyway. But I have resolved to get tough. If I catch any of them breaking even the smallest law—"

"Aren't some of them just kids?" Max asked before he could stop himself.

Inspector Fontaine gave him a pitying look, as if he didn't truly understand. "Islamic State recruits children, Max, boys your age, even younger."

"Islam is a violent religion," Madame Pauline added.

Max almost mentioned what Ahmed had said about the importance in Islam of helping people. But she probably wouldn't believe him, so instead he just said, "Most Muslims don't seem violent."

"Until they are radicalized," Fontaine said. Then, before

Max could reply, he held out a piece of paper. "I was passing by, so I thought I'd drop this off."

Was this some elaborate police game? Max opened it up. A man's name was written inside next to a phone number.

"What is this?" Max asked.

Inspector Fontaine smiled in a self-congratulatory way. "A gardener. You give your parents that number." He strode into the dining room and pointed out the window. "Tomek will trim the garden back into shape. Fall's the best time to plant bulbs . . ."

But Max barely listened as he prattled on. Had Inspector Fontaine really come by just to pass on the name of a gardener? It bothered him too that the cop knew that Max's parents hadn't hired someone. Had he just assumed they wouldn't get around to it or was he watching, perhaps from the neighbor's house?

"Thanks for this," Max said, holding up the piece of paper. "*Merci.*"

Inspector Fontaine hesitated, continuing to look out at the garden. Max almost felt like he was fishing for an invitation to stay. But Max didn't offer one.

"I must be going," Inspector Fontaine finally said.

But as he walked himself back to the hallway, he stopped by the basement door and poked his head in. Max felt his legs crumple.

"Your cat likes to hide down there, I bet!"

Max couldn't even speak. He just nodded.

Inspector Fontaine chuckled softly, as if remembering Teddy Roosevelt's panicked flight. "I used to play hide-and-seek there."

Then he walked himself to the door.

"*Bonne journée*," he said, seeing himself out.

The moment the door slammed, Max let out a deep breath.

But Madame Pauline just shook her head. "It's no wonder this city is crawling with terrorists when the Brussels police are more worried about gardening!"

CHAPTER TWENTY-ONE

That afternoon, Ahmed heard a faint knock followed by a rustle as a piece of paper slid beneath the cellar door. He scrambled over and opened up the note.

"Do not go out," it read. In loopy script, it was signed, "Max."

Someone had come to the house. Ahmed had heard the doorbell ring, an unfamiliar voice and footsteps overhead. It was a man's voice, and once he had seemed close, perhaps near the basement stairs. Whoever it had been had frightened Max. But the man had gone, or at least Ahmed thought he had, because he'd heard the front door slam.

Ahmed obediently stayed in the cellar. He tried to keep himself busy by looking at the new books as he waited for Max.

It was almost midnight when Ahmed heard the gentle knock. He opened the door to find Max carrying the usual tote bag loaded with food, books and other supplies.

"What happen?" he asked.

Max handed him the bag, then closed the door behind him. "A cop stopped by."

Ahmed shook his head at the unfamiliar word. "Cop?"

"Police officer. Don't freak out."

Ahmed's arms felt limp. He put down the tote. He didn't know what "freak out" meant, but he had a feeling it had something to do with the way his stomach started to toss and turn, like he was still at sea.

"I don't think he knows you're here," Max said.

Ahmed didn't feel very reassured. "Don't think?"

Max sat and patted the camping mat next to him. Ahmed sank down beside him. If a policeman was snooping around, he was no longer safe.

"He's the same guy who came to check who we were so we could get our residency permits," Max explained. "His grandfather used to own the house, so he's kind of obsessed with it."

"Great," Ahmed muttered.

"Don't worry, he's mainly focused on the garden. He wants my parents to clean it up."

"It needs cut," Ahmed agreed glumly.

"He dropped by with the name of a gardener. I really don't think he knows anything. But just in case he was still hanging around, I didn't want you to go out."

Max had done the right thing. But Ahmed still felt "freaked out." It wasn't good that the police officer had a special interest in the house. And if he'd played in it as a child, he probably knew about the cellar. He tried to calm himself: if the police officer had really suspected Ahmed was there, wouldn't he have already checked?

"I stay inside," Ahmed said.

"Maybe for a few days," Max agreed. "It's raining anyway." Then he reached for *Boy Heroes*.

Ahmed sensed there was something else Max wasn't telling him.

"Have they caught all terrorists at Paris?" he asked.

Max paged to the chapter they were on. "I don't think so," he said without looking up.

So that was it. There was a manhunt. The authorities were probably looking for them all over Europe, including Belgium.

"Want to read?" Max asked.

But as Ahmed tried to read about John Cook, a fourteen-year-old Union musician (he played the bugle, which Max explained was a kind of horn), his mind wandered. With a manhunt going on, he might have to stay inside for more than just a few days. This wasn't terrible—he had blankets now, and books, plenty of food and company from Max. The orchids were looking better—a few had even grown a new leaf—but the days were growing shorter, and Ahmed knew that if they were to recover fully, they needed more light.

John Cook had just thrown down his bugle to carry a wounded officer to safety when Ahmed stopped reading and looked up at Max.

"The orchids not have enough light. Will you bring me lamp for them?"

"Like a desk lamp?"

Ahmed couldn't help but laugh. "No, fool, grow lamp. Special lamp for flower. Like sun."

Max grinned. "What am I, your personal shopper? All right, all right. I'll see what I can do, Your Highness."

"Not so high here in cellar."

"It's a turn of phrase. How do you know so much about orchids anyway?"

It wasn't the first time Max had asked him about his life, but it was the first time Ahmed felt like answering.

"My grandfather, father of my mother, has flower store."

"He's alive?"

Ahmed looked down as he realized his error. "Had."

Max didn't say anything, and Ahmed knew he wanted him to continue. But telling the story of his family to another person, who could read his eyes and ask questions, was a lot different than telling a flower.

"Will they bloom again?"

Ahmed paused, then spoke truthfully.

"I don't know."

CHAPTER TWENTY-TWO

On Saturday morning, a week after the Paris attacks, Max woke to find his parents still in bed, watching armored vehicles and soldiers with assault rifles patrolling the city center on the local French-language news.

"What's going on now?" he asked.

"The city's under lockdown," his dad explained. "The police think one of the Paris terrorists is here, and they're doing raids across the city to find him."

"We're not supposed to go out," his mom added.

"Even for food?" Max said.

"They said to stay out of stores, anywhere people congregate," his mother said. "They've closed the metro, and they're canceling all public events today. This guy is armed and he could take hostages."

"I heard," said Claire, wandering in from her room. "People are tweeting the most awesome cat pictures."

"Cat pictures?" Max asked.

Max expected Claire to roll her eyes, but since the night of the Paris attacks, she'd been more patient with him.

"To keep police operations secret—no one's supposed to post on social media what the police are up to. So cat pictures. It's the Belgian way of showing they're not afraid."

The old Max might once have found this exciting—a dangerous criminal on the loose, being forced to hunker down inside like on a snow day but without the snow, even the zaniness of the cat pictures. But now, he was more worried about Ahmed than anything else.

"My way of showing I'm not afraid is to buy some beer," his father said, pulling on his shirt. "And maybe some chips and salsa, if I can find salsa in this crazy country."

"Michael, are you kidding?" his mom said, her voice edged with panic. "We're staying inside—all of us!"

While his parents argued over whether his father was risking his life for beer and salsa, Max ran downstairs and slipped another message beneath the wine cellar door. "Don't leave, even to the orchids," it read. As far as Max knew, Ahmed hadn't left the wine cellar since Inspector Fontaine had dropped by, but with everyone home all day and the lockdown, it was vital that Ahmed stay hidden.

"Max, what are you doing down there?" Claire yelled from the top of the basement stairs.

Max ran back into the laundry room. What was he doing? Then he remembered—the cat pictures!

"Looking for Teddy!"

"He's up here. Do you still have that Batman mask? I want to take a picture of him in it."

His mother managed to nix the beer expedition, but only because the next-door neighbors, a young French couple named Florian and Inès, who'd always seemed too busy to say much more than hello, came by with several bottles of wine. The Belgian-German family on the other side, Arnaud and Petra, also joined them, with their seventeen-year-old daughter, Simone. Everyone ate pasta in the living room, where Max's father had lit a fire, and discussed the lockdown.

"The police have embarrassed themselves," said Arnaud. "For too long, they don't pay attention to Muslim crime and extremism."

Max shifted on the brick hearth, thinking of Ahmed hiding below. He wasn't an extremist or a criminal, but what was the likelihood that anyone would believe he was innocent if he emerged from the cellar during a lockdown?

"Well, they seem to be making up for it now," Max's dad said.

Inspector Fontaine in particular, Max thought glumly.

Claire stood up. "We're going upstairs," she said as Simone followed.

"Hey, Max, why don't you join them?" his mom said.

Max knew she was trying to get rid of him so the grown-ups could talk more freely, but he was too nervous to leave. What if Arnaud or one of the other neighbors knew about the wine cellar? Max thought it was unlikely they would decide to tromp down there, but anything seemed possible in the tense, excitable atmosphere.

"I'm still eating," he said, and stuck a forkful of spaghetti into his mouth.

His mom shot a glance at his father. But his dad just shrugged as if to say, *He's old enough*, then turned to Arnaud.

"How long do you think the city will be under lockdown?"

Max listened intently. Ahmed would have to stay in the wine cellar until the lockdown was over. But surely it would be over tomorrow?

"Who knows?" said Arnaud. "The Brussels government tries to show competence with this."

Florian shook his head. "But instead it overreacts, creates *panique*."

"They've certainly done a good job of that," his mom said. She started to refill her wine glass, then stopped and looked at Max. "This is a crazy situation. Especially for the kids—"

The other adults stared at him.

"What do you think, Max?" asked Inès.

Max imagined saying, *I think you should all leave so I can go see the Syrian refugee hiding out in our basement*, but instead, he just shrugged. "I hope they find the guy."

It wasn't until after midnight, when his parents and Claire had finally gone to sleep, that Max had a chance to visit Ahmed and explain what was going on.

"They're mostly looking for the terrorist in Molenbeek, on the other side of the city," he said.

He said this to calm himself more than Ahmed, who listened quietly and without much emotion, like someone accustomed to receiving bad news.

"The policeman, does he come by again?"

Max shook his head, thinking about what the adults had said. "He's probably too busy."

To change the subject, Max pulled out his phone and showed Ahmed photos of some of the lockdown cats—dressed in army fatigues, carrying tiny machine guns or Photoshopped flying over Brussels with stormtroopers on their backs. He was relieved to see Ahmed smile.

"And your cat?"

"Teddy's aren't quite as good—"

Teddy had been a reluctant participant in Claire's photo-shoot, trying to pull off the Batman mask and bite it.

Ahmed laughed at the blurry pictures.

"He think mask is terrorist."

"Or me," Max said, revealing a scratch on the inside of his arm.

Ahmed studied the wound solemnly. "Hurt during battle with cat. Belgium honor your bravery."

Max laughed. "Next time you can hold him down."

"No, this is dangerous job only for American hero. Nabil Fawzi chooses taking picture."

By the time Max stood up to go, they had teased each other so much that he felt relaxed again.

"I'm sure the lockdown will be over by Monday," he said to Ahmed.

But it wasn't over Monday. Scouts had been canceled, and now school was canceled too; the metros weren't running, and both his parents had been advised to work from home. Again, normally, Max might have enjoyed the break. Madame Pauline couldn't come, he had no homework, and his parents, who were distracted either by work or the latest lockdown alerts, seemed happy to let him stream movies and play on his iPad all day. It wasn't even so bad being stuck inside with Claire. Instead of picking fights or battling over the remote, she made them hot chocolate and let him choose the movie.

But Max could barely concentrate, even on the latest Captain America. Police activity was spreading to more neighborhoods, including to the one directly beside his. Sirens wailed in the distance. He was half-afraid the police, Inspector Fontaine in the lead, would storm his house next. He had given his parents the gardener's name and number, but his mother had just rolled her eyes. "Dealing with that garden is the last thing on my mind right now."

Tuesday the lockdown continued, and whatever might have been fun about it was decidedly over. Max longed to go outside, to get away from Claire (he was tired of her suffocating niceness), even to go to the School of Misery. He reminded himself that Ahmed had been stuck inside far longer than four days; he imagined how it must feel for him to hear the world outside—the shouts from the schoolyard, the planes overhead, the sirens and honks and construction noises—and know he couldn't be part of it. Whatever Ahmed had seen, whatever he was afraid of being sent back to, had to have been horrible for him to prefer a life like this.

Max wasn't the only one feeling squirrely. Later that afternoon, his father announced that he needed to get out of the house, and Max begged to go with him. His mother fussed—the authorities were still saying to stay out of public places—but they were low on groceries and Max could tell she couldn't take much more of his whining.

It was a relief to get out of the house, even into the damp, chilly late-November afternoon. He strode energetically ahead of his father down the hill to the Carrefour. Usually he hated shopping, but even trying to find allspice in French for his mom and waiting in the endless beer aisle while his dad struggled to choose between Belgian beers named Black Hole, Delirium and Crazy Steam was more interesting than being locked up at home.

Max had stopped thinking about the lockdown, but as they left the store loaded down with bags, he noticed a commotion. Across the street, a young Arab-looking man was standing with his legs spread and his arms out while a police officer patted him down.

A second officer, whom Max instantly recognized as Inspector Fontaine, barked at the young man in French, "Don't move, don't move!"

Several passersby skirted the men warily.

"What's going on?" Max asked his dad.

"I don't know. Looks like they're searching for suspects. We better not mention it to Mom. She'll never let us out of the house again."

His father started up the hill, but Max stayed where he was. He couldn't stop watching. The young man was trying to explain something.

"I was just going to—"

"Where's your identity card?" Fontaine interrupted.

"I will give it to you," the young man said. "But I must move my hands."

Fontaine gave him a shove. "Then move them!"

The rest of the day, Max couldn't get the scene out of his mind, especially the anger in Fontaine's voice and the way he wouldn't even let the young man speak.

That night, Max decided to try again to find out Ahmed's story. The wine cellar was flooded with the pinkish-purple light of the grow lamp Max had bought for the orchids at a local garden store. It illuminated the spiderwebs and dust and cast shadows on the plaster walls. At night, Ahmed moved the orchids in with him for extra hours of light. He wrapped them carefully in newspaper to keep them warm and had Max bring him a desk fan to keep the air flowing. He explained to Max how to water the orchids so the roots wouldn't rot, to make sure the air temperature was above eighteen degrees Celsius, and to be careful not to place them in direct southern light in the summer, as Max's mother had. It amazed Max that anyone his age knew how to take care of something so fragile.

Ahmed had started reading chapter three of *Boy Heroes*, about Edwin Jamison, a sixteen-year-old Confederate soldier who'd fought in the Battle of Malvern Hill. It wasn't one of the more uplifting stories, but Max felt there was something dishonest about skipping it. He listened to Ahmed read how Edwin had charged bravely up a slope and directly into Union fire. But every time Max was about to interrupt and ask Ahmed about himself, he hesitated. He felt the same way he did before throwing a pebble into a pond, half-afraid to disturb what was beneath the surface.

When Ahmed reached the part of the chapter where Edwin was killed by the direct hit of a cannonball, he stopped reading to look at Edwin's photo. Max had always thought it was the best of all the boy heroes—the image clear, Edwin staring straight into the camera, his eyes wide and gentle.

Ahmed opened his mouth. No sound came out, but his eyes looked at Max like Edwin Jamison's, like they wanted to speak.

"What is it?" Max asked.

Ahmed blinked and turned away from him toward the orchids.

"Cannonball is like bomb. The people hit straight at feel no pain."

CHAPTER TWENTY-THREE

That was what his father had told him. And for nearly a year now, Ahmed had pretended to believe it.

"Who are you talking about?" Max asked gently.

Ahmed turned to Max. It was too late to keep his mouth shut, to lock the story back up inside him. A part of him no longer even wanted to.

"We live in Aleppo," he began. "You know Aleppo?"

Max shook his head.

"Biggest city in Syria, very old. Home of Jami' Halab al-Kabir, very famous old mosque. Also most big market bazaar in world."

These were familiar tourist places. He was certain that at least pictures remained of the vast tiled courtyard of the Great Mosque and its thousand-year-old minaret and the Al Madina souk, thirteen kilometers of covered shops selling everything from bolts of silk to nuts. What seemed even more lost was something that he couldn't have captured even if he knew the English words—the ordinary rhythms of life that make a place and a time feel like home. There were only flashes of memories, almost unreal now: the smell of jasmine as he walked to school; cheering the Red Castle, the city's champion football team; the pomegranate tree by the playground, pigeons perched on its branches; helping his grandfather prune the roses and water the pear and loquat trees at his nursery; Ramadan nights, after the long Taraweeh prayer; playing with his sisters and eating date-filled *ma'arouk* sweet bread; his father taking him through the twisting cobblestone alleyways of the Old City to listen to Sufi musicians chant the haunting, ancient poetry of Aleppo: *Why did you teach me to love / Then leave me when my heart became attached to you?*

"When war start, it summer, I am eleven years old. Rebels who want end to Syrian president Bashar al-Assad take over eastern part of Aleppo, and government army tries to take it back. One morning, all calm. The next there is bomb, one street from our street."

Ahmed still remembered that day. How Baba had ordered Ahmed and the rest of his family away from the windows, then rushed outside. But Ahmed had found a way to peer out, in the direction of the explosion. A cloud of gray, chalky dust hovered in the air where his friend Hassan's apartment building had been. Ahmed could hear cries and shouts as his father and other neighbors scrambled atop what remained of the building, tearing with bare hands through the rubble.

It still hadn't seemed possible, though, that the building was gone, that there was air where there should have been wall, that Hassan, whom he had seen earlier that morning carrying home a stack of bread, might be gone too. The sun was still shining, the summer air still scented with coffee, a motorcycle engine roared and Fairuz, the popular Lebanese singer, blared from a radio in the distance. Ahmed's eyes settled on a familiar orange tree in his neighbor's garden. It was the same as ever—spindly and yet sagging with fruit—and for a split second, Ahmed felt reassured that life was still this and not that—the empty space of the missing building, like a punched-out tooth. Then he noticed eyes staring back at him. Among the branches of the orange tree, a rebel soldier was crouching with a gun.

"In days after this, more bomb, more gunfire. Many people leave—take all they can in car, bus, on motorbike. So there is no enough petrol. We stay at school of my father, wait."

Ahmed wished he could describe the exodus—mattresses, carpets, children and old people crammed together in the flatbeds of pickup trucks; whole families teetering on a single motorcycle like some desperate circus act; even people on foot, carrying children and overstuffed sacks on their backs. Even without petrol, Ahmed's family could have left that way, but the school seemed safe and his father feared that the refugee camps forming outside the city might be targets too. So they had waited several days till the bombs seemed less frequent and the artillery fire more distant.

"A few days later, it is quiet, we go home. Many buildings fallen on ground, shops closed, few car on road. But our home is there."

Ahmed was certain Max could never understand the relief

they had all felt to see it still standing. It was only when they had stumbled inside, tears brimming in his mother's eyes, the girls almost giddy, that they realized that the TV, his father's desktop computer, the table and every single one of the chairs were gone, looted most likely by rebels. A foul smell drifted from the kitchen. The food in the fridge had rotted after the power went out. At nearly the same time, his sister Jasmine shouted that the toilet wouldn't flush.

"Many problems, though. No water, electric, phone," Ahmed explained to Max. "Mother, father get ready to leave—they pack photos, documents, clothes. But there is no bomb that night and everyone is tired."

They were awakened the next morning just before dawn by the call to prayer. As the sun rose, the neighborhood came creeping back—a few merchants' carts, a handful of neighbors inspecting the sandbags piled up at an intersection. The electricity flickered on, a radio blared, a baby cried. That was how it began—the illusion that life could be normal again. As his parents and sisters sat on the floor and quietly ate stale bread and fig jam, Ahmed could tell that none of them wanted to leave. When the rat-a-tat-tat of gunfire echoed through the air, they froze mid-bite. An eerie silence fell outside, as if they all were birds and a cat was passing. But as soon as the gunfire stopped, the sounds and voices returned and Ahmed and his family went back to eating.

"Father feel bad to leave his students," Ahmed explained. "We decide not to go."

They never made an actual decision to stay, though. An

emergency bag always remained packed, waiting by the door. It was more that one day stretched into another and the rat-a-tat-tat became a familiar background noise. Some stores reopened, and, with one of their remaining neighbors, they bought a generator, which gave enough energy to power the fridge. Ahmed helped his grandfather plant vegetables—squash, fava beans, potatoes—in the little garden in his grandfather's nursery that they had always filled with flowering plants. They learned to collect water when the taps worked and to bring containers to the large metal water stations when they didn't. They even learned to play inside when it seemed too dangerous to go out, Ahmed inventing games for Jasmine, who was seven, and Nouri, who was only three.

"At end of summer," he continued, "I go back to school."

It was the same school he had attended the year before, but it felt different with half the teachers and more than half the students gone. Some, like Hassan, had been killed, but most had fled to Turkey, Jordan or Lebanon. It took several weeks to figure out a new football team, what with the center having lost a leg, the left wing dead and the goalie and halfback in Turkey. There were also days when it was too dangerous to walk the five blocks to school, so his father taught him and Jasmine at home. But on the days that he could go, Ahmed was happy to be there, if only because he imagined he was safe. But that feeling didn't last long.

"That spring, school is bombed. Thank God, no one is there, but building is no more. After this, I stay home."

"Did you feel safe there?" Max asked.

"Not during bombs."

While it amazed Ahmed what a person could get used to, there was no getting used to the bombs. When they heard the vacuum-cleaner sound of a government helicopter flying in overhead, they would run to the shelter in the basement of a large building nearby. If they heard a whizzing noise, however, even Nouri knew there was not enough time and to instead run to the bathroom, the safest place in the house. They would all pile into the tub together, his mother and father on top of them, Ahmed's palms sweating and his breath short. At night, he had sickening dreams of bodies split in half. He found himself staring off into the distance more and more, forgetting what he was supposed to be doing. Nouri started to wet the bed. One day, a bomb hit his grandfather's nursery. His grandfather, fortunately, was not there; he had gone to help plant flowers at a traffic circle. But the nursery's destruction affected him almost as much as the death of Ahmed's grandmother had several years earlier.

"My grandfather has heart problem and comes live with us. Mother not want to leave him. She worry also what happen to him if we go."

Every day the electricity came back on for about two hours, and his mother was able to check her email. She read news of more roads north being closed and families stranded on the Syrian side of the border, sick from spoiled food, infested by lice and without toilets in the scorching heat. *Better to die here*, she said, *together*.

Ahmed knew she didn't really mean this. Accepting death, looking it in the face, was just a way to be less afraid.

"In 2014, my father starts secret school for his students, underground in a cellar."

Max looked around the cellar. "Like this?"

"Yes."

For the first time, Ahmed wondered if that was part of the cellar's appeal.

"And you went too?"

"Sometime I come, but most times my father say it is too dangerous for me to be out. Daesh, Islamic State, comes to Aleppo too. They want boys over ten years to fight. Not go to school. I help mother at home. Last winter is very hard. Most cold winter in long time."

The heat only worked a few hours a day, so all five of them had started sleeping in his parents' bed. Although Ahmed could see the clouds of his own breath, they'd kept warm this way. Outside on the streets, trash piled up, pipes burst and the puddles froze. The bread lines grew longer, and people quarreled to protect their spots. His father sometimes had to close his school to buy bread, waiting up to twelve hours in the chilly rain. Fewer students were attending anyway. Every day they heard more stories of government planes bombing schools and hospitals, of rebels executing entire families they suspected of collaborating with the government, of Daesh killing civilians who didn't follow their strict religious rules. His father looked at their bag, still packed by the door, and wondered aloud if it was time to leave. But his mother wanted to wait till spring. People were living in flimsy tents in the Turkish refugee camps, with no heat and very little food, and some reported it was even worse than being back home. "At least here we still have walls," his mother had said. His father couldn't argue with this; Ahmed's grandfather was sleeping more and more, and none of them really seemed in any condition to travel.

"Much sickness that winter," Ahmed explained.

Nouri became sick with a fever and a cough. Ahmed and Jasmine developed a strange peeling rash. His father suspected it was from the water, which he feared had become contaminated with sewage. But it seemed too dangerous to venture out to a doctor. After a few scary nights, Nouri had recovered. But then Jasmine got the fever, her cheeks flushed under her big, dark eyes. She was the beauty of the family, but she was also easily frightened, as if she knew how fragile anything beautiful really was. She didn't bother to try to hide her fear like he and Nouri did, pushing it away till it came back in other forms—in bedwetting and nightmares. Jasmine trembled when the bombs fell, then burst into tears. She cried over the deaths of strangers. She fed stray cats, then sobbed when snipers used them for target practice.

"One March day, I beg my father to take me out with him to buy mechanic oil. This is for car, but we use it for stove so my mother can cook special Friday meal. My sister Jasmine still getting better from sickness. She stays home with my mother, grandfather and Nouri."

Jasmine's fever had broken, but she was weak. Nouri, who

enjoyed tending to anyone who would let her, was feeding her pieces of old bread. His mother was making tea on the cookstove with the last of their oil. That was how Ahmed had left them—Nouri leaning over Jasmine, his mother crouched over the stove, his grandfather repotting an orchid with trembling fingers. He was certain they had said some words of goodbye as he left, but they were too ordinary to remember.

His father walked in front of him, always staying a few steps ahead, like a shield. Two boys were playing marbles under an archway. A burst of gunfire made Ahmed and his father start, but the boys kept playing. A hungry dog followed them for a while till his father shooed it away. They passed the abandoned bus, its windows blown out, which had been wedged between two buildings as a buffer against bullets. Then they jogged quietly past a screen of white sheets hanging from laundry lines to hide anyone passing from snipers.

"We hear plane overhead and bomb falls, very fast. I see gray cloud over my home. I start to run home. Baba shouts at me to stop. But I cannot stop."

It hadn't even mattered that there was still a plane overhead. Ahmed raced down the empty street toward home. He could smell the acrid smoke, the dust. As he reached his block, it seemed to envelop him. The early spring sun vanished into haze. He stumbled into the cloud, shouting their names: "Mama, Jasmine, Nouri, Grandfather!" But before he could clamber onto the remains of the house, someone jumped down from the top of it and tackled him. It was a neighbor, an older man named

Mr. Algafari. Ahmed had never liked him much—he'd once shouted at Ahmed for playing football under his window and frequently coughed and spat from years of smoking, but he held Ahmed with surprising strength. "Don't go up there," he grumbled in Ahmed's ear as he dragged him away.

It was only then that Ahmed understood.

"Bomb hit them direct," Ahmed whispered to Max.

Seconds later, his father had arrived, shouting. Mr. Algafari did not try to stop him from digging in the rubble. His father's wails confirmed what Ahmed already knew.

"They were—"

Ahmed closed his eyes, squeezed in the tears.

"It's okay," a voice said softly. "You can cry."

Ahmed opened his eyes and looked at Max. "My father said they feel no pain. But how could he know?"

And then he collapsed against Max and sobbed. Like Jasmine would have.

CHAPTER TWENTY-FOUR

The next morning, the lockdown ended, even though the missing terrorist was still on the loose. The police claimed that he'd most likely left the city, but Max suspected that the government officials who had approved the lockdown were just as tired of being cooped up inside as he was.

An armed police officer—thankfully not Fontaine—stood outside the entrance of the School of Misery, and even parents were no longer allowed inside thc building. This seemed to reassure his mother, who had wavered about sending him back. But she still gave him an extra-tight hug at the courtyard entrance.

Max pulled away. "I'm in more danger from this one stupid Belgian kid than I am from a terrorist," he murmured.

The crinkles in his mother's brow deepened. "You didn't tell us someone was bothering you. What's he doing?"

"Just teasing," Max lied. "It's no big deal."

His mom studied his face. "Don't take things into your own

hands, okay, Max? If this continues, tell me and I'll talk to Madame Legrand—"

Max instantly regretted mentioning Oscar. The last thing he needed was his mom stepping in to defend him.

"Really, it's nothing—"

His mom nodded like she wanted to believe him. But Max wondered if she just didn't want another problem on her hands.

"Maybe he just wants to be friends?" she said. "Some boys don't know how except by acting out—"

Max was tempted to remind her that her experience with school was like a century old, besides which she couldn't possibly understand a thug like Oscar. But instead he just smiled.

"Yeah. That's probably it."

Before he could dart away, she lunged forward and gave him a kiss. At least it wasn't as embarrassing in Belgium as it would have been in America.

"Relax," he mumbled. "I'll be fine."

His mom wasn't the only one who was nervous about a terror attack. Several kids, including Farah, were missing from Max's class—either because half the metro lines were still closed or because their parents were too worried to send them. Max wished he'd asked Farah for her number so he could text her about how weird school felt after the lockdown. Every time there was a police siren or a loud noise outside, everyone froze, even Oscar, and looked as if they were deciding whether to duck under their desks. But then Max thought about how this experience was nothing compared to Ahmed's daily life in Syria. He imagined a bomb blowing up Claire and his mother. It was too horrible to think about, even before he reminded himself that Ahmed had somehow lost his father too. Max wanted to ask him about this, but he figured it was better to let Ahmed tell him when he was ready.

As Madame Legrand reviewed how to balance an equation, Max thought about how math always had rules—equations had to balance, to make sense. But what kind of sense did Ahmed's life make? Most people would probably live and die without knowing one one-hundredth of the sorrow and tragedy Ahmed had already experienced. Where was the balance in that? Max knew one answer—he'd heard his father say it a thousand times: life isn't fair. But thinking about this just made him angry. It seemed less a fact than an excuse, a way to let others be losers and victims and to not try to change anything. But what could he do to change Ahmed's life? Right now, Max couldn't think of a single way to help with his future, much less change his past.

At recess, Max climbed up on the fence so he could peer at his house. A slanted ray of sun cut through the clouds, illuminating the garden. The vines were tangled, the bushes were overgrown and dried leaves littered the ground. What cheer there was came from bright-green birds that twittered in the trees overhead. Max pictured Ahmed in the wine cellar, as much of a prisoner as the cage man in the Magritte painting.

"What are you doing?" asked a sharp voice behind him.

Max hopped down to the asphalt, ready for trouble. But he noticed that Oscar looked tired, like he had spent too many nights up late listening to the news.

"I look at my house."

"You scared? Want to go back home?"

But Oscar's taunt was so far from the truth that Max realized it didn't bother him.

"No," he said simply.

Oscar didn't say anything. He just stood there. What did he want now? Max thought about what his mom had said—*maybe he just wants to be friends*. But he pushed it away. Oscar was probably just waiting for him to come up with another, angrier comeback so he had an excuse to take a swing at him.

But that wasn't going to happen. Oscar couldn't upset him, not anymore. Max calmly looked him straight in the face until Oscar walked away.

It was at that moment that Max made up his mind: if only for a day, he would find a way to get Ahmed outside.

CHAPTER TWENTY-FIVE

From Max, as well as from the English-language newspapers he took from the recycling bin to wrap the orchids, Ahmed knew all of Europe was on alert. Police and security were everywhere, and the idea of trying to go to Calais or anywhere else seemed preposterous. Ahmed focused on his daily routine in the cellar, and with each day that passed, the outside world seemed to fade. He practiced his English reading, tended the orchids and ate small meals, staring at the picture of the man whose torso was a cage. While Max was at school, Ahmed teased out details he hadn't noticed before: How the man was carrying a beat-up traveler's sack laced together. How a red cape, almost like a dress, obscured his face.

Sometimes, when the house was empty, Ahmed hid himself behind the curtains of the storage room that faced the garden so he could look out the window. The days had grown extremely short—Max and his family left for school and work in the dark, and the sun was already starting to set around three thirty in the afternoon, when Ahmed heard Max return home. Ahmed had never lived in a place with such a long night, but in a way he didn't mind it—he felt safer in the shadows.

One Tuesday afternoon in the middle of December, Ahmed heard the front door open, the sign that Max and Madame Pauline were home. Max had warned Ahmed to stay quiet when Madame Pauline was there, so he was surprised a moment later when Max pounded on his door, shouting his name. Was the police officer back? Had he been discovered?

Ahmed grabbed the bag he always kept packed and ran to the door. But when he wrenched it open, he found Max dressed in his jacket, holding a puffy parka and striped hat.

"What is happen?" Ahmed whispered.

"You don't have to whisper," Max said. "Madame Pauline isn't here today."

"Where is she?"

"There's a metro strike, so she called this morning to say she couldn't come."

"And your parents?"

Ahmed had noticed that Max's parents never seemed to leave him home alone, although he was certainly old enough. In Syria, kids far younger than Max cared for smaller children.

"I was the one who answered the phone, and I didn't tell them. We have two hours till Claire gets back, so we'd better get going."

Ahmed pulled away, confused. "What? Where?"

"It's a surprise."

"That police officer? What if he see me?"

Max smiled. "He works for the local police, and we're getting out of his territory. But if we do run into him, I'll just tell him you're a friend from school, okay? Just don't say too much."

"But—"

"Look, you've got to get out of here, just for a few hours. You'll be safe with me. Here, take my dad's coat and hat. It's chilly out there."

Ahmed's instincts told him to stay put, but the thought of the outside—of the ordinary world, where people lived beautiful, ordinary lives—beckoned. The lockdown was over, he told himself, and being out with a white American boy would be less suspicious than wandering around the city alone. Besides, he was curious to see what Max wanted to show him. Ahmed slipped on the coat, pulled the cap low over his forehead and followed Max up the stairs.

It felt strange to walk out the front door as if the house was his, and then to stand in front of it so openly as Max unlocked a shiny red mountain bike chained to the neighbor's gate. The afternoon light was already dim, the roofline of the block in silhouette against sunset-tinged yellow clouds. Ahmed drew in a deep breath of cold air, then breathed it out in a damp cloud.

Max wheeled the bike to the sidewalk, then swung his leg over the crossbar and took hold of the handlebars.

"Sit on the seat and hold on to my shoulders."

Ahmed did as he was instructed, and Max pushed off the sidewalk. The bike wobbled, nearly toppling them over, before Max brought his foot down on one pedal, then the other. As the bike righted itself and picked up speed, Ahmed remembered the magical rush of watching the streets of Aleppo sail by as he rode sidesaddle on the back rack of Baba's bike, one hand clutching his father's shirt.

A bump jostled him out of the past as the bike leapt off the curb and Max steered it down a one-way street. They picked up speed on the downhill, and Max stopped pedaling and coasted. At the bottom of the hill, a park with a dry fountain came into view.

"That's Parc du Cinquantenaire," Max said.

As Max steered onto a bike path that ran alongside the park, Ahmed peered through the gates at an enormous arch topped with rearing bronze horses pulling a chariot. They passed a running track, ball court and playground. It was the first time he'd really been able to tour Brussels by day. Just past the playground, he spotted a minaret, the crescent moon resting calmly atop it. Ahmed stared at the circular white building, as out of place as himself.

Max glanced back at him.

"That's the Great Mosque of Brussels. Do you want to go in?"

Soon it would be time for the Maghrib prayer. But Ahmed shook his head. What if he ran into Ermir, the smuggler, or if the police kept an eye on who went inside?

Max pedaled on across a large avenue lined with office buildings. The street was jammed and Max was silent and focused, his head constantly swiveling to watch the cars and buses that crept up alongside them. Military police, assault rifles slung against their fatigues, stood outside various official-looking buildings flying the European Union flag, with its white stars in a circle against a field of blue. Ahmed noticed each policeman, then tried not to. Max pedaled around a traffic circle and in between an enormous curving building surrounded by flags and cement barricades and another imposing building with a facade of glass windows.

"That's the European Commission and the European Council," Max said.

In an island between them were four military vehicles with soldiers sitting inside or stretched out in the back, smoking. For a moment, Ahmed felt as if he was back in Aleppo, at the very beginning of the war. But the soldiers paid him no attention. Ahmed felt almost giddy as Max glided over a bridge, past the English word "MAD" scrawled in giant graffiti letters on the side of a building, past the entrance to Maelbeek metro station. Max rang his bell at pedestrians who'd wandered into the bike lane, and Ahmed felt the thrill of watching them scurry out of the way. After nearly a month inside, he was out in the fresh air and wind, cold as it was. He tilted his head back and looked up at the darkening sky. It felt wrong when his family was dead, but he couldn't help thinking, *I'm alive.*

They crossed a large intersection jammed with cars and taxis, their headlights shining. After a few minutes, the street turned from asphalt to cobblestone, and they bumped into a square lit up by old-fashioned streetlamps. One whole side of it was occupied by a grand building with Roman columns, a domed clock tower and a cross.

Max pulled up to the sidewalk across from it and jumped down. "That's the Royal Palace," he said.

"Is that where we're going?" Ahmed asked.

Max spun around and pointed to a square classical building behind them. "No. There. It's the Magritte Museum. We can find that picture you like."

Ahmed stared at him. The whole idea of taking such a risk, of venturing out of the safety of the cellar just to go to an art museum, was extravagant, indulgent, as MAD as the graffiti.

"What?" Max asked.

"I love it," Ahmed said with a grin.

Max locked up the bike and led him into a large foyer where they had to walk through a metal detector. Ahmed's heart fluttered as he passed, imagining the guard stopping him, but the machine didn't beep. He had no metal. He followed Max into another hall to the information desk, where Max bought them tickets and asked directions. They were just ordinary tourists looking at art.

"Never been here," Max explained as they stepped into a room-sized elevator and handed their tickets to the operator. He opened the door on the top floor; through glass windows, Ahmed could see the entire city of Brussels—the fairy-tale towers, Old European squares, modern office buildings and domes—spread out before him. It was strange and wonderful to be so high after months of being so low.

"Ready?" Max asked.

They opened a set of glass doors and strode into an exhibit

hall where an illuminated plaque in French, Dutch and English told the story of René Magritte's life. Ahmed started to read the English: Magritte was born in Hainaut, Belgium, the oldest son of Leopold and Regina. When he was fourteen years old, his mother drowned herself in the River Sambre. Her body was found with her nightgown covering her face. But it was the word "drowned" that struck Ahmed like a blow.

"Do you understand?" Max asked.

Too well, Ahmed wanted to say. But he just nodded and moved on to Magritte's pictures. The exhibit was like walking through a hall of funhouse mirrors reflecting his dreams and nightmares. There was a jumbled pile of town houses, not unlike the one he was hiding in, some on their sides, some upside down like buildings in Aleppo; there was an empty picture frame on the beach with a gray sea blending into a gray sky behind it; there was a man asleep in a coffin-like wooden box, an enormous boulder balanced above him. As they wandered from hall to hall, from floor to floor, Max told him that the plaques explained that Magritte was a surrealist, an artist interested in the relationship between reality and illusion.

But Ahmed knew that this fancy term concealed something more basic: from all the pictures of women with their faces covered by cloth, Ahmed could tell that Magritte longed for his mother.

They continued down to the final floor, but found only a gift shop.

Max frowned. "Your picture's not here. Maybe we missed it?"

Ahmed knew they hadn't, but Max insisted on asking a woman in the gift shop.

After she replied in French, Max turned to Ahmed. "I'm sorry. She said it's in a private collection."

He truly looked disappointed. But Ahmed didn't mind that the picture wasn't there; what touched him was how Max had wanted the outing to be perfect.

"No sorry, please. I love this."

Max looked at his watch. "We better get back soon."

"Wait," Ahmed said. "One other thing I wish to see."

CHAPTER TWENTY-SIX

As Max pedaled down Rue Vergote, Ahmed told Max about the terrifying night with the smuggler, how Ermir had taken his phone and demanded his father's watch, how he had barely escaped the van. Then he pointed out the house whose gate he had run through three months earlier. Max tried to imagine himself in Ahmed's shoes, scrambling up the garden wall when the neighbor's light switched on, drenched and stumbling through the tangle of weeds and bushes toward the basement door. It seemed like fate now that his father had forgotten to lock it.

But it wasn't the gate that Ahmed wanted to see. A few seconds later, Max squeezed the brakes and they drifted to a stop in front of his school. From the outside, there wasn't much to see: just the cement facade of the building and windows rising up, floor after floor. The lights were still on inside for the aftercare program, but the doors were locked, and when he and

Ahmed pressed their faces up against the glass, all they could see was the brown tile foyer and the plastic bins of the Lost and Found. For the second time that day, Max felt as if he'd let Ahmed down.

But when Ahmed finally pulled away from the glass, his face was relaxed, even peaceful.

"I look at back of school for many weeks, now I can know how looks the front."

Three months earlier, Max never would have understood such an urge. If he could have left school forever, if someone had told him he could stay home all day and hang out and play Minecraft, he would have done it in a heartbeat. But that had been before the long, dull days of the lockdown, when school was closed not for a vacation or a snow day but because it was no longer safe.

"How long has it been since you went to school?" he asked.

"Real school? Three years."

Max stared at him, stunned. "When did you leave Syria?"

"A month after bomb. In refugee camp in Turkey, there is school but too many people, we no can stay. In Izmir, I help at bakery, father works construction building till we can pay for fake passport and smuggler to Europe. There is no time for school."

Max pressed his face back against the glass, pretended to try the door again. But he was really trying to hide the tears that were welling up in his eyes. He had always taken school for granted. Now he realized that even being able to hate it was a luxury. Max stared bitterly at his own reflection as the old, angry protest rose to his lips: *It's not fair!* Ahmed deserved to go to school.

It was at that very moment that the idea came to him. He spun around.

"What if you go to school again?"

Ahmed's thick eyebrows knitted together in confusion. Then he seemed to decide Max was joking because he laughed.

"No, really," Max said. "What if you start here, as a new student in January?"

Still smiling, Ahmed just shook his head. "With no document?"

"You said you had a forged passport," Max said, thinking out loud. "It got you this far; what are the chances the school would be able to tell? And the Belgian identification card for foreign kids, it's just paper with a photo. It's not even electronic. We could make one ourselves."

Max knew the idea was a fantasy, but it felt better to come up with a crazy plan than to do nothing. Ahmed must have felt the same way, because he played along.

"If I leave before dawn by back door, no one see me."

Max nodded. "And I can make sure the coast is clear—I mean, no one is looking—so you can sneak back in after school."

"But what about police officer?"

"Same plan as before. If he sees you, I'll tell him you're my best friend from school. It's a lot less suspicious than being some kid I can't explain sneaking around my garden."

Ahmed grinned. "We will become very good friends."

“Two foreign kids who don’t speak much French. It makes sense.”

Could they pull it off? Max was actually beginning to think they could. Going back to school would change Ahmed’s life in a way that really mattered. Max waved him onto the bike. “Come on. Let’s try to forge that ID.”

CHAPTER TWENTY-SEVEN

Ahmed knew they were playing a game like the ones he used to play with Nouri. "This bed is a spaceship," she'd say, after they'd all started sleeping together, "and we are space travelers going to a planet far, far away."

Jasmine would get annoyed—she liked to sleep in—but Ahmed would play along. He knew he was too old for make-believe, but he'd found himself swept up in their adventures—the bed flying around the rings of Jupiter, racing away from a black hole or an exploding star.

Since Nouri had died, Ahmed had kept his feet firmly on the ground. There were no flights of fancy—just flights across countries and cities, seas and highways, fields and mountains. But Max's crazy scheme awakened that old part of him. Back in the cellar, he studied Max's ID as if he were an expert forger. Max sat beside him, peering eagerly over his shoulder.

"It doesn't seem that hard, does it?"

The ID *was* surprisingly primitive, without any watermark or chip. But forging it wasn't entirely without challenge. "Paper needs match, letters need match, and very important, this—"

Ahmed pointed to a circular stamp over Max's photo.

Max nodded. "The official commune stamp. There must be a way to fake it, though."

It was a ridiculous game, of course. Millions of people were trying to forge their way out of the world's war zones and wastelands, desperate for the piece of paper that would give them a future. If these documents were so easy to fake, the refugee camps and detention centers would be empty, not jammed with asylum seekers. But like in his games with Nouri, Ahmed decided to pretend anything was possible—Jupiter, the outer reaches of the galaxy, even school with Max in Belgium.

"You have computer?"

"I don't think the Internet works in the basement, but my iPad's charging in the living room—"

Ahmed stood up. "What time you have?"

"Five-ten."

Ahmed knew he and Max were thinking the same thing: twenty minutes till Claire's bus. They raced upstairs, breathless. The living room was already dark. Max unplugged the iPad and they plopped down beside each other on the couch. Max flipped back the cover, and the screen glowed to life.

"Google it," Ahmed ordered. "What is this word again? For—"

"Forge," Max said, typing fast. "Looks like you can carve the seal into a half-cooked potato."

Ahmed laughed.

"Seems a little crazy, huh? This one says wax."

"Like from candle?"

"Exactly." Max hopped off the couch. "We've got to have candles."

He disappeared into the kitchen. A moment later, he returned, holding out a handful of birthday candles, a baking tray, a box of matches and a tiny hooked utensil.

"What is it?" Ahmed asked.

"A lobster fork," Max explained. "It'll be perfect for carving the wax."

Ahmed grinned. "You think like master forge."

"Forg*er*," Max corrected. "So here's the plan. I'll work on getting the paper and matching the font and all that. You'll work on making the stamp and getting a photo of yourself. There's a booth that takes ID-sized ones in the metro station. Saturday afternoon, my parents are taking us to Aachen, Germany, for the Christmas Market. That'll give you the perfect chance to sneak out. Just keep an eye out for any police officers."

Max narrowed his eyes in a critical way. "You should probably get a haircut too."

Ahmed instinctively touched his shaggy hair.

"You serious?"

Max grinned. "It kind of has a crazy terrorist look."

Normally, Ahmed would have kidded back. But he couldn't.

"Not hair, Max. School."

"Of course, I'm serious."

It was time to stop dreaming, to end such childish games. After all, Nouri was dead; she had never made it out of Aleppo, never mind to Jupiter. "But—but it not possible."

"Why not?"

Because he was an illegal Syrian refugee squatting in a basement while the police combed the city for Muslim terrorists. That was the obvious answer. But it seemed cruel to say it out loud, like telling Nouri that they weren't on a spaceship, but in a war zone.

"Even if we forge this ID, how do I just go to school? I must need parent."

"Not necessarily."

"What you mean?"

Max smiled craftily. "I was thinking about this. It's really just a voice we need. My parents enrolled me over the phone and mailed the paperwork in."

"School would not wonder if no parent bring me?"

"No one pays any attention in the morning; parents aren't even supposed to enter the courtyard right now. And in the afternoon, as long as your parent signs a permission form, you're allowed to walk home alone."

"Max, you are kind to think of this plan, but it is too much danger."

"Look," Max added. "I'm only here for this school year, then we're going back to Washington. But right now, I can be there with you. Let me help you while I can."

Ahmed's stomach dropped. How much longer could it be until the end of the school year—six months, seven at most? Then Max would leave and he would have to head to Calais, to the Jungle, by himself, the odds of making it to England stacked against him.

Ahmed thought of the orchids, lined up downstairs in a school-like row. He didn't talk to them as much as he had before Max was there. They were just plants, not human classmates. He pictured the School of Happiness in his mind. He could almost smell the chalk dust and notebooks, could almost see the head of the kid at the desk in front of him, could almost hear the teacher call his name. He imagined the alternative, waiting in the cellar for Max to come home from school. The long winter stretched ahead of him; the dank walls pressed in. Even in Calais, it would be useful to know a little French. He took a deep breath and looked back over at Max.

"But who is this person who play parent? I need trust him not to tell."

"Not him," Max said simply. "Her."

But before Ahmed could ask who Max had in mind, they heard the click of a lock. Ahmed bolted off the couch and raced down the basement stairs just as the front door opened.

"Hi, Claire, what's up?" he heard Max say in a loud voice.

Ahmed froze midway down the stairs. He heard a bag hit the floor, then footsteps approaching.

"Why are you shouting?"

"Madame Pauline isn't here," Max said. "Metro strike. So I'm home alone."

"Shouting to yourself?"

Max let out a whoop that allowed Ahmed to tiptoe down a few more steps. "Why not? I found mom's secret stash of soda in the kitchen. Want some?"

"Sure," Claire said. "You're kind of a freak sometimes. Were you hanging out in the basement?"

"No," Max said innocently.

"Then why are you standing there with the door open? And why is your face all red? Were you playing some fantasy game down there?"

"I had to pee."

There was a loud slam as Max shut the door. Ahmed took the opportunity to scramble down the remaining steps. But he didn't notice the cat till he tripped over him. Teddy hissed and Ahmed lost his balance, hitting the tiled floor. Before he could get back up, the basement door opened and the cat raced up the stairs in a state of terror.

"What's going on down there?" Claire said.

Ahmed didn't move. His heart thudded violently.

But then Claire's voice softened. "Oh, it's you," she said, clearly talking to the cat. "Silly Teddy."

"Got a Coke for you," Max called from the kitchen with barely disguised urgency. "You coming?"

"Yeah," she said.

But Ahmed didn't hear any movement above. He held his breath.

"Claire?!" Max shouted.

At last, her footsteps receded. Ahmed let out his breath with a whoosh.

CHAPTER TWENTY-EIGHT

Farah was back at school the next day, but it wasn't so easy to catch her alone. Even at recess, she stayed in a tight circle of her friends. Max glanced over at her so many times that even the "Do you speak English?" gang started teasing him.

"Who's your girlfriend, Max?" André asked.

Max turned back around. "No girlfriend."

"You like Farah, don't you?" Jules said. "Those sexy glasses."

"No," Max said. "You know what I love? Big, sexy nose, like you, Jules."

Then he tackled him.

How annoying that they thought he was *amoureux*, or in love, with Farah. But ten minutes later, when she was still locked up tight with her friends, Max decided he didn't care. He abandoned the gang and sidled up to her.

"Hi, Farah," he said. "I talk to you?"

His face felt hot, and the meaningful looks the girls gave one another were painful; he knew the minute he left they would start talking about him.

"Sure," Farah said with a shrug.

He quickly walked across the schoolyard, trusting she would follow, to a patch of dirt on the other side of the green fence. Farah's friends exploded into chatter.

Farah must have heard them, but she leaned against the fence and pretended not to.

"What's up, Max?"

He had stayed up half the night preparing for this moment: Writing what he meant to say in English, then translating it to French. Adjusting his translations after checking them online. Reviewing the proper pronunciations. Now, he let it come pouring out—all the carefully memorized sentences, all the perfectly conjugated verbs.

He tried to be like his mother, whom he'd once seen argue in court. She'd never stopped to look at her notes, had kept her eyes firmly on the judge. She had been arguing for something he couldn't understand—something to do with companies and regulations—but she had done it well, like an actor playing a role. He tried to present Ahmed's case the same way, with the same practiced calm: the school would be sympathetic to a single mother, a new immigrant with other children, too tired to come to the school. Farah just needed to speak with an accent, like Ahmed's mother would.

It was only when he reached the last sentence that his voice rose.

"Veux-tu nous aider?"

Will you help us?

Max caught his breath. He had been speaking fast, barely aware of the shouts and cries of the schoolyard, of the icy rain turning into enormous flakes of snow. His attention was focused entirely on Farah.

She looked away from him.

"Farah?"

She winced then faced him. *"Max, c'est fou."*

It's crazy.

Max felt something crack inside him. He had worked hard, harder than he ever had before. And his worst fear had come true: he still wasn't good enough.

"No, no—" he argued.

But he was off script, and the French words came to him more slowly. "We have a plan . . . We buy you a phone . . . No one never know that the number is yours."

Farah shook her head. "It's too dangerous."

He was tempted to tell her it wasn't dangerous, not the way he and Ahmed had carefully thought it out. But that would have been a lie. He could only convince her that Ahmed was worth taking a risk for.

"For three years, Ahmed no school. He is kind, smart. He wants to go."

"I'm sorry for him." A strained note crept into Farah's voice. "But you are asking me to break the law."

"I break the law too for him," Max said, thinking of Inspector Fontaine. "Because the law is not right!"

"Whether it is right or wrong, it can still get us in trouble. Me especially," she snapped. "You're American, but this is my country. I must follow the rules."

"Even if they not—?"

"I'm sorry, Max."

She glanced over at her friends, who Max figured were probably still giggling about how he had whisked her off. But he couldn't let her slip away, not yet.

"Please, Farah. Ahmed is like you—"

She looked back at him, eyes narrowed. "Muslim, you mean?"

Max shrugged uncomfortably. He hadn't really wanted to make a point of it, but he was desperate.

Farah's eyes flashed behind her thick glasses. "This boy is from Syria. My grandparents were from Morocco. There's a big difference."

Max's cheeks burned. Morocco was in Africa. It wasn't just a different country than Syria; it was on a different continent.

"So you born here?"

"Yes, I was born here!"

Her frustrated tone made Max realize how offensive his question had been.

"And my parents were too," she continued. "My mom was born in France, actually. But we're Belgian."

"I am sorry," Max said. "I should not have—"

Farah waved her hand, cutting him off. "You're not the first. There are plenty of Belgians who still see us as foreigners."

"Does your family speak Arabic?"

"At home my parents mostly speak French or Berber—that's another language of Morocco. Anyway, even Moroccan Arabic is different from the Arabic they speak in Syria. This boy likely wouldn't even understand it."

"I never know this," Max admitted.

"We are not all the same," she scolded. But there was a gentler note to her voice that made Max feel he had a chance. He grabbed her hand. He didn't care what it looked like to their friends. He had to try, one last time.

"You not the same. But you know what it like to be different. And you are brave and you care what is kind. I see. I know. Ahmed, he has no mother, no father, no family. He is scared. He is a good person. He wants nothing but the school. I cannot help him all alone. Please, Farah."

Max's voice was as broken as his French. This wasn't the elegant speech he had so carefully prepared—he sounded emotional, his pidgin French idiotic.

"Max, do you understand how dangerous this is for me? As a Muslim, I must do twice as well in school as a non-Muslim Belgian to get the same opportunities; my behavior must be twice as good."

The word "good" triggered Max's memory.

"Ahmed says is very important for a Muslim to help the stranger, the person that need."

Farah stared at him hard, almost as if his words had frozen her.

Max dropped her hand and looked down at the ground. How would he tell Ahmed that he had failed him?

He waited for her footsteps. But he didn't hear them.

"You just need me to make a few calls?" she asked quietly.

Max's breath caught. He looked up at her and nodded, pleading with his eyes.

The silence stretched out again, but this time, Max didn't press her. He waited while she took off her glasses and wiped away a melted snowflake. Her eyes looked naked without the thick frames, and Max watched her blink and stare into the distance, as if she were trying to see without them. At last, she put her glasses back on.

"Okay."

Max gave a loud whoop that made Farah's friends look over and titter.

"Thank you, Farah, you are best, more kind, many fabulous—"

"Max—" she interrupted with the amused grin he was used to.

"What?"

"I better take a look at the ID you're working on. Your French is much better, but we need to be certain there are no mistakes."

CHAPTER TWENTY-NINE

Just after four on Saturday afternoon, Ahmed slipped on the jacket and hat Max had left him, grabbed *Boy Heroes of the War Between the States* and opened the back door to the cement patio. The air was chilly and damp, as if the whole city had a cold, and it made Ahmed shiver, even in his jacket. The early winter dusk was already falling—pink clouds floated across the sky and shadows gathered in the corners of the garden. It was easy enough to slip over the wall and into the backyard of the house behind Max's. The neighbor's lights were on, and Ahmed could see people milling around inside—it looked like they were having a party. He hugged the wall and, after checking to make sure no one was coming in or out of the house, he dashed through the gate.

Ahmed scurried around the corner, past a small hospital where patients were smoking outside, their blue gowns peeking from beneath their coats. Then past the health food store and the newspaper shop and down the hill to the Rue des Tongres shopping district. The street here was lively: Customers rushed in and out of the butcher's and cheese shops, wheeling lumpy shopping trolleys behind them; red-faced men and women drank and smoked under heat lamps at Le Petit Paris café; a toothless organ grinder played a song. Enormous snowflakes, illuminated by white lights, hung over the street, and the windows of the chocolate shops teemed with gold-foil-wrapped coins, dark-chocolate saints and what Ahmed guessed must be other Belgian Christmas treats. A church bell clanged in the distance—there had been churches in Aleppo, and his family had even had some Christian friends—but it made him miss the soulful voice of the muezzin echoing over a loudspeaker as he called the faithful to prayer. It was a relief, at least, to see a few women in hijabs.

Just past the wine store was a gleaming-white hair salon. Ahmed took out a slip of paper and reviewed the vocabulary that Max had taught him. Then he took a deep breath, opened the door and walked up to the woman at the counter.

"Bonjour. Une coupe, s'il vous plait. Courte."

Ahmed half expected the woman to send him away, but she just nodded and waved him to the back. There was a brief, awkward moment as she held out a robe and he realized that he was supposed to put it on. Then she seated him in a chair in front of a large illuminated mirror. At the house, the basement bathroom had a small oval mirror that Ahmed had never really wanted to gaze into. But now, as he kept his head still and his eyes forward, there was no choice. Ahmed stared at himself.

Max had been right about his hair—it had grown long, as if it too was trying to hide him. As the hairdresser snipped away,

Ahmed felt a small pang. This was hair his father had stroked, hair that had been pasted to his cheeks by the sticky salt of tears. But as the woman cut, he realized he could see the strong line of his jaw—like his father's—his protruding ears, his round, open face. He no longer looked like a boy who'd spent the past three months in a cellar. He looked like a boy who went to school, who belonged.

At the counter, Ahmed paid the hairdresser with Max's twenty, glancing shyly at himself in the mirror. Then he walked to the corner and took the escalator to the underground passageway that Max said led to the metro station. He kept an eye out for police officers, but he saw none as he scurried along the short passageway lined with advertisements and safety reminders. Voices and footsteps blended into a soothing backdrop, overlaid with the strains of a busker's violin.

The photo booth was right where Max had said it would be. Ahmed slipped inside and closed the curtain. Taking off the parka and adjusting the collar of the shirt Max had lent him, he sat on the plastic bench and pushed three two-euro coins one by one into a slot. Then he selected *Photos officielles d'identité* on the screen.

A green light blinked on and a strange face stared back at him before he realized it was his own. He wasn't supposed to smile—no teeth in official photos, a picture on the booth warned—but he couldn't stop the close-mouthed grin that spread across his face. A minute later, a sheet of six ID-sized photos slid out of a slot. The boy in them looked friendly, happy even. Ahmed slipped the sheet carefully between the pages of *Boy Heroes* to keep it flat.

Still smiling, he walked back up the hill. The early night cloaked everything in darkness, but the lights made it festive. He gave Max's last euro to a beggar woman in a hijab, a child sleeping in her arms.

"*Barakallahu fik,*" she murmured.

May Allah bestow his blessings on you.

The familiar expression felt lucky, like the universe was chiming in on his plans, wishing him well.

As he turned the corner back onto the street behind Max's, Ahmed imagined himself making this same walk—but to school. In his dream, friends appeared and waved at him. He could hear them shout out across the street. "Did you study for the test?" "Want to play football later?"

Absently, he turned into the neighbor's open gate, imagining it was the school entrance and one of his teachers was greeting him. But at the same moment, the door to the neighbor's house opened and a trim, balding man in an overcoat stepped out.

"*Bonne soirée, Hugo!*" he said, clasping a man in the doorway and kissing him on each cheek.

Ahmed swiftly backed out of the gate.

"*Au revoir, Émile!*" the host said.

Ahmed was just in time; the trim man jogged down the stairs and nearly ran into him.

"*Désolé,*" Ahmed murmured, jumping aside as if it had been his fault. *Sorry.*

The man said something in French he couldn't understand. His tone was sharp. Just then, the door of the house opened and a woman in a red dress emerged, holding out a man's hat.

"*Inspecteur Fontaine*," she trilled playfully, waving it in his direction.

The policeman!

Fontaine swiveled around and Ahmed took the opportunity to walk away. His throat was too tight to swallow, and his temples pounded. But he continued walking calmly, slowly. He expected to hear the police officer's voice calling after him, or his footsteps as he gave chase.

But when Ahmed finally got up the courage to peek behind him, Fontaine was heading back to the house to retrieve his hat. Ahmed continued past the school and around the corner, as if he had no right to be there, as if he was just passing by.

CHAPTER THIRTY

As soon as the recess bell rang, Max waved Farah over to a corner of the fenced yard. Both Farah's friends and the "Do you speak English?" gang seemed to have accepted them as some sort of couple and left them alone. But Max still took a quick look around before he turned his back to them. Then he slipped the ID out of *Boy Heroes* and handed it to Farah.

Max was proud of the work he and Ahmed had done. Claiming he needed supplies for a school project, Max had dragged Madame Pauline to the stationery shop, where he'd matched the color and stock of the ID paper. He had found the exact font online and laid out Ahmed's information in the same way. Ahmed's photo—the neatly trimmed hair, the hint of a smile—was exactly the image Max had hoped for. Together, they had glued it to the ID, then Ahmed had pressed the commune stamp he had carefully carved into the hardened candle wax—a saint with a staff encircled by the words Woluwe-Saint-Lambert.

Max tried to read Farah's face to tell if she too was impressed, but she studied the ID without emotion.

"The accent is wrong," she finally said in French, pointing to the word *Nationalitè*. "It should go the other way."

Madame Pauline was always scolding him for lazy copying. It had never seemed very important—Max figured that the teacher usually knew what he meant. But this was different.

"Thank you," he said gratefully.

Farah turned the ID over, looking at it again, first the cover, then the inside with Ahmed's name, nationality and a made-up national number. Finally, she stared at Ahmed's photo.

"He looks nice."

"He is nice," Max assured her.

Farah reached out to hand the ID back to him. "Except for the accent, it looks good."

But Max barely had time to enjoy the compliment when a big hand yanked the ID out of hers.

"No, it doesn't."

Max whipped around. Oscar stood behind them, peering at Ahmed's ID with a malicious grin. Max grabbed for it, but Oscar held it out of reach.

"Give that back!" Farah demanded.

But Oscar just rubbed one of his big fingers over the commune stamp. "It's a fake."

"No it's not," Max shot back. But no sooner had he said this than he remembered that Oscar's mom worked at the commune.

Oscar rolled his eyes. "Yes, it is and I'm telling."

Max couldn't believe his own stupidity. Oscar had been waiting for a chance to take his revenge. Max felt his hands ball into fists.

Oscar turned to Farah. "Who is this guy anyway?"

Max noticed her jaw tighten, but she didn't answer.

"Some terrorist friend of yours?"

"This boy is not a terrorist!" Farah hissed. "He is a war refugee! He lost his entire family. He just wants to go to school! Like us!"

Max waited for the burst of laughter that would be his signal to pound Oscar as hard as he could, but Oscar didn't laugh. He lowered his arm and studied Ahmed's photo. His eyes narrowed, like he didn't like what he saw. But at the same time, Max heard a small whoosh of breath, a little wistful sigh. It reminded Max of the way Oscar had stared at him after the lockdown. Could his mom be right?

"Please, Oscar," he said gently. "Ahmed is nice."

Oscar looked up from the ID and rolled his eyes. "*You* say he's nice."

But Max noticed he didn't walk away. If Oscar really wanted to tell, he would have. He had the evidence in his hand. He didn't need to argue about it. A crazy thought occurred to Max. What if they could convince Oscar to help? He had access to the commune through his mother, and he didn't seem to care about breaking rules. He might even be able to get them a real stamp.

"You want to meet him?" Max asked.

"Max?!" Farah whispered.

But he ignored her, keeping his gaze on Oscar.

Oscar shook his head. “I’m telling.” But he sounded less certain than before.

Max took a gamble. “Maybe you are scared.”

Oscar took a menacing step toward him. “I’m not scared. I’m just not an idiot like you.”

“Then meet him,” Max said calmly. “Farah and me go with you. And if you think he is a bad person, you tell on us.”

Oscar looked from him to Farah as if he was trying to figure out the trick.

“When?” he finally said.

Max pointed across the wall. “Tomorrow, after school. In my backyard.”

CHAPTER THIRTY-ONE

Ahmed crouched behind the holly bush in the back of the garden, waiting for Oscar. He was surprised by how determined he felt, especially since he had nearly changed his mind about the whole plan after running into Inspector Fontaine.

The night after he'd bumped into the cop had been a restless one. *What if Fontaine catches me? What if Farah betrays me? What if, what if?* The song of fear was a familiar one. And so too was its chorus: *The world does not care about you.*

But Max did. And it was this thought that steeled his nerves as he waited in the chilly rain behind the holly bush. If Oscar told, he would have to say goodbye—not just to his cellar hideout, but to Max.

At last, he heard the back door open and voices speaking French—first a girl's, Farah's, of course—then Max's, then a gruffer boy's voice he didn't recognize. This had to be Oscar's. Ahmed listened to the thuds of a football being kicked around. Madame

Pauline was probably still watching from the picture window. But when the ball came sailing past him and rolled to a stop in front of the wall, Ahmed knew that the nanny had gone to the kitchen. This was the signal they had agreed on.

As footsteps came his way, Ahmed straightened up, but he had been crouching for so long that when the large, sandy-haired boy stepped in front of him, he was still hunched and stiff. The boy drew himself up as if to accentuate the difference. But he wouldn't look him in the eye.

"This is Ahmed," Max said.

Ahmed stuck out his hand. *"Bonjour."*

Oscar lurched back. Ahmed realized he had frightened him and put down his hand.

"I speak a little English," Oscar said flatly.

Ahmed smiled as politely as he could. "Easier to me."

But only Farah smiled back. Ahmed wondered whether to offer her his hand too. It wasn't the Muslim custom between girls and boys, but Max had said she was a Belgian. It was Oscar who unknowingly saved him from this awkward situation by leaning right in his face.

"If you lie, I know."

Ahmed looked him in the eye. "I not lie, I tell you only true."

Oscar's pudgy face remained stony. "Who are you and how did you get here?"

"I am Ahmed Nasser," Ahmed began. "I come from Syria to escape war. I come by sea, to Greece. My family all dead."

He paused there, in part because the words caught in his

throat, but also in the hope that Oscar would feel some pity. But the boy looked on with the same hostile expression.

"Why you come to Belgium?"

"Man I go with has family here."

Oscar crossed his brawny arms over his chest, then said something in French to Max.

"He said that this doesn't give you the right to be here too," Max said.

"I not know where to go," Ahmed admitted. But before he could explain further, Oscar interrupted, speaking in French to the others.

Farah glowered.

"What?" Ahmed said to Max.

Max shifted uncomfortably. "He's saying how the police are worried the terrorists could attack schools and how does he know you're not trying to go to school to attack it."

"I no terrorist!" Ahmed said. "I hate these peoples, like you."

But he could tell from Oscar's narrowed eyes that his words were unconvincing. He had to find a way to change the conversation, to reach Oscar before it was too late. "My mother, sisters, grandfather die in bomb. My father—"

Max leaned forward with interest. Ahmed knew he'd never told him the story. But he felt unable to, as if saying it out loud would confirm that his father's death was real.

"What happen to him?" asked Oscar.

For the first time, Ahmed realized, he sounded genuinely curious. But then he remembered something Max had told him: Oscar's father had died too.

He had to tell the story. And not just in a simple sentence or two but with all the small, important details that would put Oscar on that deflating dinghy with him.

"From Turkey to Greece, we take boat—"

As best as he could in a language that was not his own, he described the waves, the seawater rising around his feet, the woman's cries, the baby in the sling, not knowing how to swim, his father placing the inner tube around him, then jumping overboard to save them, the wave that swept him away.

The rain fell harder, but no one seemed to care.

"At Lesbos, Greek island, we pull to shore. Ibrahim says I must come with him, that he promises my father this. I refuse. I stay for some days, sleep near beach. I hope for my father. Ibrahim is patient. He wait with me."

Every night, the flimsy, overcrowded boats arrived and rescuers on shore helped drag them in, pulling out screaming children, sobbing women, glassy-eyed men, and handing them blankets, bottled water. Ahmed always ran down to the beach to help in the hope his father might be there. But with each passing day, Ahmed knew there was less of a chance of ever finding his father—or even his body.

One night there was a storm, and the next morning dawn brought a ghastly tide: a half-dozen drowned children. They lay on the rocky beach in contorted poses, still wearing their sneakers, clothes with the emblems of Western sports teams or cartoon characters and the flimsy life jackets that had failed to save them. It was impossible to cry for them all, so Ahmed cried for none of them. Perhaps they were the lucky ones, freed from fear and pain, from loss.

"When I stop to hope, I look at sea. I wish to join him."

"But you can't," Oscar said gruffly.

Ahmed looked at him. It was the first time during the story he'd spoken.

"I know."

By that day on the beach, it was nearly August—the days were growing hotter, the sun searing his face as it reflected off the water. Despite Ahmed's grief, he was constantly hungry—with hundreds of new refugees arriving each day, the volunteers making sandwiches and handing out water were running out of supplies.

"I go with Ibrahim and his family to Kara Tepe camp. After some weeks, we are allowed on ferry to Athens. I go. But I feel nothing. I think nothing. Only about my father, you understand?"

For a moment the others were silent, even Oscar.

"Your father was brave," Max said at last.

Oscar kicked the wet ground and said something in French.

"Oscar!" Farah said. While she unleashed a torrent of French, Ahmed turned to Max for an explanation.

Max's cheeks colored slightly. "He said your father was stupid for dying. For leaving you."

Ahmed held up a hand, and Farah stopped mid-tirade. "He is right."

Oscar looked him in the eye. "Why you want school?"

Ahmed thought for a moment. There were so many ways to answer—because his father had been a teacher, because he wanted to learn. But one answer seemed truer than the others, and he had a feeling Oscar would understand it.

"I feel in the world alone."

Oscar turned to Max, said something in French and walked back to the house. Farah narrowed her eyes skeptically, but Max smiled.

"What he say?" Ahmed asked.

"He told me to come to the commune with him after school tomorrow," Max said. "And to bring along your passport and extra ID photos."

CHAPTER THIRTY-TWO

The commune of Woluwe-Saint-Lambert was a large yellow brick building with a distinctive clock tower. Max had been to it several times with his parents. As if they were ordering a sandwich, they had to take a little paper ticket printed with a number. Then they had to sit on hard plastic seats in the cavernous central hall, waiting for their number to flash on a large monitor. Only then could they approach the clerks, who sat like bank tellers on the other side of a windowed wall, issuing documents with the stinginess of dentists giving candy.

The experience, however, was entirely different with Oscar by his side. Oscar didn't say much on the bus down Avenue Georges Henri—he seemed almost shy—and for a moment, Max worried that Farah was right and he was planning to turn them in ("The police station is near the commune," she'd pointed out). But as soon as they stepped off the bus, Oscar headed straight into the commune. He swept past the ticket machine, grunting a "*Bonjour, Madame*" to the cranky old woman at the information desk, who replied, "*Bonjour, Oscar*" in a tone actually approaching friendliness. He marched past the people in the plastic seats clutching paperwork and anxiously watching the monitor. Then he rapped on a door in the center of the windowed wall marked NO ENTRY, EMPLOYEES ONLY.

"*C'est moi, Oscar!*" he hollered.

A second later, the door opened and a bearded man whom Max recognized as one of the clerks greeted Oscar and waved them in. The door closed behind them with a click, and Max found himself on the other side of the windowed wall. The clerks' area was larger than it looked from the other side of the wall, with rows of computers and filing cabinets and a lounge where the clerks could retreat for their endless lunch break. A woman's voice rang out from one of the windows reserved for native Belgians.

"*Bonjour, petit chou!*"

Max's lips twitched as he suppressed a laugh. He'd heard the French term of endearment before, but it was hard to imagine Oscar as a "little cabbage." The small, plump woman who rushed up to them fit the description far better herself.

"*Bonjour, Maman,*" Oscar replied, his cheeks reddening with what Max felt was the proper degree of embarrassment.

"And this is your friend, the American, the one you're always talking about from school and Scouts," she said in French, turning to Max.

"Hello, Max, hello," she said warmly in English.

"*Bonjour, Madame,*" Max said. Oscar had obviously prepared her for his arrival, but what surprised Max was the *toujours,* or always. Had Oscar been talking about him before this week? She seemed too enthusiastic for Oscar to have told her the true nature of their relationship.

"Oscar speak English," she said, beaming at Oscar. "His father teach him. Me, not so well."

Oscar scowled at her. "You sound stupid. It's 'taught.'"

Oscar's mother blushed and gave a laugh.

"See how smart he is?" she said in French.

Max nodded, but he felt sorry for both of them.

Oscar's mother looked at a clock on the wall. "I have a half hour left. But you two can sit in the lounge—"

"Monsieur Dupont closed up," Oscar interrupted. "Can't we play on his computer?"

Oscar's mother heaved a sigh that told Max that she'd prefer they didn't. "You know I'm not really supposed to let—"

"He doesn't care," Oscar said. "He plays solitaire half the time on it himself."

"That's not true," his mother said.

By this time, Oscar had already plopped in Monsieur Dupont's seat and turned on his monitor.

"She always let me," he whispered to Max in English. "I've been playing on these computers for years. Take a chair."

The battle lost, Oscar's mother retreated back to her window beside the bearded man. She pressed a buzzer, and Max could hear a ping outside as the next number appeared on the monitor. Seconds later, she was talking with someone on the other side of the window in French too rapid for Max to follow.

"You have photos and passport," Oscar whispered.

Max pulled *Boy Heroes* out of his backpack and flashed it open to the page where he had stowed Ahmed's fake Syrian passport, the extra ID photos tucked inside it.

"Good," Oscar said.

He had opened the solitaire window and rapidly played a few cards before switching windows. A screen came up asking for a password, and Oscar typed something. A second later, a list of names came up with dates of birth, addresses and identity card numbers beside them.

"How do you know how to do that?" Max whispered.

Oscar shrugged. "I hang out here a lot, so I watch and learn."

He scrolled through the *N*'s until he reached the name "Nasser."

"It's good he has a popular surname. What is his mother name?"

Max looked at the passport.

"Reem. R-E-E-M."

Oscar moved his cursor down the list of Nassers.

"There is a Rima, R-I-M-A. Close. Date of birth four December, 1992."

Max was surprised by how swiftly he was able to do the calculation in his head. "She's twenty-four. Ahmed's fourteen. She cannot give birth to him at ten."

Oscar quickly changed Rima to Reem, then 1992 to 1982. Then he pressed Save. "Anyone could make this errors," he said innocently.

Max couldn't help breaking into a grin.

"What?" Oscar said.

"Nothing," Max said. "It's just . . . you're a natural."

"Natural?"

"Like, you're really good at this."

"Criminal mind," Oscar said, sounding pleased with himself.

"You know that term?"

Oscar's lips flickered as he fought a grin. "I watch *CSI: Miami* in English—you know this show?"

Then he highlighted and pasted the revised entry, hit copy and switched screens to a file marked "Identification Documents for Foreign Minors." He opened a new template, took out the ID that Max and Ahmed had forged and copied the information. After he'd printed out the new ID, he glued on one of Ahmed's photos and wedged the document into what looked to Max like a large stapler and pulled down the handle. When he handed it back to Max, the commune seal was imprinted over Ahmed's photo. The ID looked as authentic as Max's.

"Oscar, enough computer," his mother called from the other side of the room in French.

The clerk with the beard said something to Oscar's mom. Max couldn't make out the words, but he sensed from the way he cocked his head in their direction that he wasn't pleased that they were still playing on it.

Oscar ignored them. He deleted the template and opened another file marked "*Composition de ménage.*"

"Aren't we done?" Max said quietly in English.

Oscar shook his head. "You need this too."

"What is it?" Max asked.

"The document that shows all the people in Ahmed's family home. The school ask for it."

His parents must have turned this in without mentioning it to him. Max realized how much they'd needed Oscar. But he didn't know how to express this other than saying, "Thanks."

Oscar smiled. "We give him other family?"

Max nodded. "Younger brothers and sisters. Excuses for his mother not to come to school."

"Names?"

"Jasmine," Max said before he could stop himself. "Nouri, the baby."

Oscar typed in the names and made up some birthdays. "But no father."

"No," Max agreed.

Oscar printed this document out as well. Then he took out an inkpad and a rubber stamp. He had just stamped it with the official commune mark when the door opened.

"*Bonjour, tout le monde!*" said a familiar voice from behind them. *Hello, everyone!*

Max shoved the document into his bag, then swung around. Inspector Fontaine was walking toward them.

"*Mex How-Weird,*" he said sternly in French. "You should not be back here."

Max's stomach dropped. Had Oscar tricked him? Perhaps he had just been pretending to help. He turned back to Oscar, who was playing solitaire and looked entirely calm and unbothered by the police officer's presence.

"I'm here with . . ." Max stuttered in French. "Oscar and I go to school . . . He—"

"We're friends," Oscar interrupted matter-of-factly.

Was this true? Max prayed it was. He reminded himself that Inspector Fontaine worked with the commune. If his home visit was necessary for the approval of IDs and other documents, then he had a legitimate reason to be here.

"The friendship of boyhood," Inspector Fontaine said wistfully in English, leaning against a filing cabinet. "I told you, *Mex*, that I played in your garden with boys I am still friends with, though we are old men now."

He chuckled, perhaps at the idea of himself as old. Then his eyes fell on Oscar and he took a step forward. "Are you winning?"

Max suddenly noticed that he could see the tip of the *Composition de ménage* file still open at the top of the screen. There had been no time for Oscar to delete it. He had to distract Inspector Fontaine before he noticed.

"We still haven't found a gardener," he said.

The police officer's brow crinkled as he looked toward Max. "Oh no? Tomek didn't work out?"

"No," Max lied. "My parents are going to find someone though."

"Well, it is winter," Inspector Fontaine allowed. "But you must tell them not to delay too long."

When Max glanced back at the computer, the file edge had

vanished. Max was ashamed of having doubted Oscar. He truly was a first-rate criminal mind.

Oscar's mother closed her window and scurried over to Officer Fontaine.

"Hello, Émile. I told him not to use the computer," she said apologetically in French.

Max waited for Fontaine to transform into the same ferocious cop he had seen on the street with the young Arab-looking man, but the police officer merely shook his head. "Always breaking the rules, Oscar. You must listen to your mother."

"Sorry, *Inspecteur*," Oscar said, turning off the computer.

Inspector Fontaine pulled a bundle of papers out of his messenger bag and handed them to Oscar's mother. "For tomorrow," he said.

Then he turned back to Oscar and Max. "Play outside, boys. The world is much more interesting than a screen."

CHAPTER THIRTY-THREE

The documents were perfect, almost foolproof. Oscar had done a phenomenal job, better than even a professional forger. But Ahmed knew that none of this mattered if the School of Happiness didn't have a spot for him.

On the Thursday before the start of the holiday break, Ahmed slipped over the garden wall and onto the street. He crossed the big avenue with the American name—Brand Whitlock, Max had told him, for the U.S. ambassador who had arranged food drops during the First World War—and walked to Oscar's apartment building. He knew he was at the right apartment when he saw Farah's shoes lined up outside. He knocked on the door and Max answered.

"Good timing, we just got here."

"*Bonjour, Ahmed,*" came Farah's voice from inside.

"No Oscar mom?" Ahmed asked as he pulled off his sneakers.

"I told you, she come home after five!" Oscar hollered in English from inside.

"He's just nervous," Max whispered.

Ahmed understood. He lined up his shoes next to Farah's, then followed Max down the hall to a combined dining/living area. Photos of a man Ahmed presumed to be Oscar's father decorated every wall. He was a big man, like Ahmed's own dad, and he looked too strong to no longer be alive.

Oscar disappeared into the kitchen and Ahmed sat down across from Farah, who was perched on a loveseat, staring at a mobile phone. As Oscar awkwardly played host, dumping four bottles of orange Fanta on the coffee table, Ahmed noticed Farah's lips moving silently.

"You okay?" Max asked her in French so simple that even Ahmed understood.

She nodded, then pointed to a piece of paper that listed the members of Ahmed's household.

"Mother name—Reem Nasser?" she asked in English. *"Oui?"*

It had been wise of Max to use his mother and sisters' real names—Ahmed wouldn't have to remember made-up ones. But he still winced to hear his mother's name spoken out loud. "*Oui*, Reem."

Farah said something to Max in French.

"She said maybe it's too difficult for you to listen?" Max translated.

"No, no," Ahmed protested. "I want be here."

But as Max presumably translated this for Farah, Ahmed continued to peer at the document. It was like a glimpse into an alternate reality in which the bomb had never struck and his mother and sisters had made it to Belgium with him. He wished he could add his grandfather's and father's names, make his ink-and-paper family complete. But then he shook off the fantasy. The document was counterfeit in the worst way. There was no alternate reality. There was only this one.

He tried to follow the conversation Max and Oscar were having with Farah. They seemed to be coaching her on what she should say, but she waved them off and picked up the phone. Ahmed noticed her finger trembling as she typed in the first few numbers.

Ahmed turned to Max. "Please translate her. She need not do this. I am not want to harm her honor—"

"Her *honor*?" Oscar cut in. "Is this some crazy Muslim talk?"

Max's eyes shifted uneasily. "He just means—"

But Oscar wouldn't let him finish. "That he does not want her to get in trouble, but with us, it's okay—"

"I want no one to have trouble!" Ahmed interjected.

Farah had stopped punching in numbers. Oscar and Max switched into French, and Ahmed was briefly left out of the conversation. He wished he could explain how, at least back home in Aleppo, a girl Farah's age wasn't supposed to meet with boys outside her family by herself.

Farah glared at Oscar, then turned to Max and, with a knowing glance, spoke firmly.

Max translated: "You are kind, Ahmed, to worry about me. But where is my honor if I do not help a brother?"

It had been a long time since anyone had called him a brother, since Jasmine and Nouri were alive. Ahmed's voice caught.

"*Merci.*"

Farah narrowed her eyes and finished typing in the number. As he watched her, Ahmed recalled a passage from the Qur'an: *Allah knows well the mischief-maker from the reformer.* They weren't really doing anything wrong. She lifted the phone to her ear.

A silent moment passed, then another.

Even Oscar leaned in anxiously.

"Maybe secretary no there?" Ahmed finally said.

Oscar looked at his watch. "She should be."

"*Bonjour, Madame.*"

Farah's hand shot up to silence them. Ahmed could barely breathe. Max and Oscar seemed equally frozen.

"*Je m'appelle Reem Nasser.*"

Farah's voice sounded different, lower and more nasal. It shook slightly but in a way that Ahmed hoped made her seem sympathetic. Ahmed could only understand a few words and phrases of what she said next: *mon fils* (my son); *il s'appelle Ahmed* (his name is Ahmed); *dix Juillet, 2001* (July 10, 2001—his birthday). Her accent sounded like an Arabic one, although not particularly Syrian. But how many Belgians would be able to tell the difference?

In the pause that followed, Ahmed felt almost physically ill.

"*Non, Madame,*" Farah said. Then she began to argue. Ahmed

couldn't understand what she was saying except for the phrase "*de Syrie*," from Syria. He looked frantically over at Oscar.

"The secretary thinks you are too old for class six," Oscar whispered. "But Farah is telling her that you did not go to school for three years—"

He stopped and pointed to Farah, whose voice had softened.

"*Oui, Madame*."

Farah reached out for the household document and his ID. The secretary was clearly asking about his immigration status, whether he had Belgian residency.

"*D'accord, Madame, merci*." Another silence followed. Farah held the phone away and mouthed something in French to Max and Oscar.

"She's going to talk to the principal and check for open spots," Max whispered in English.

Ahmed curled himself into a ball, holding his knees against his chest. He closed his eyes and listened to Max tapping his fingers against his empty Fanta bottle. The minutes seemed to drag on.

At last, he heard Farah's voice.

"*Merci, Madame. Je comprends. Au revoir, Madame*."

She hit a button, put down the phone and smiled at Ahmed. Was it good news or was she smiling to soften the blow? He was too afraid to find out.

Max scooted to the end of his chair. "*Et?*"

And?

"*Tu peux y aller*," Farah said quietly, still addressing Ahmed.

Ahmed was sure he hadn't heard her properly, that she was saying he couldn't go, that the School of Happiness didn't have room. "*Aller?* Go?"

"You're in!" Max shouted.

They were all looking at him, waiting for a whoop of joy, a word of thanks, a smile. But all Ahmed was able to do was hide his face in his hands.

CHAPTER THIRTY-FOUR

There's a new kid starting in my class after vacation," Max announced on the way home from school.

"That happens sometimes," Madame Pauline said absently.

It was the day before Christmas break, and even Madame Pauline seemed distracted. But Max felt it was important to lay the groundwork for Ahmed's public debut.

"He's from Syria."

Madame Pauline stopped. Max had known this would get her attention.

"They're letting him in *now*?"

Max felt even more annoyed than usual. "It's not like he's a terrorist."

"How do you know?"

Car lights were already turning on in the early December dusk. Madame Pauline narrowed her eyes at them, as if they too might contain potential suspects.

"Because he's . . . he's like me. He's into football and stuff."

She shook her head and resumed walking. "This is why the terrorists just waltz in here. Too many Europeans have this naive attitude: *They're just like us*. But they're not!"

"But refugees aren't terrorists," Max argued as they turned onto his street. "They're escaping terror. They want the same things we do—to go to school, to work, to have a home."

"At what price to the rest of us? Our values? Our society? Our lives? Terrorists are posing as refugees to get into Europe. I don't want to frighten you, Max. But something is going to happen here in Brussels, like it happened in Paris."

Max wished he could tell her she was just being paranoid. But he knew that she wasn't the only one still worried. The reason they had gone to the Christmas Market in Aachen was that his mother was afraid that the one in the Grand Place might be a terrorist target. But it still seemed wrong to blame Ahmed for any of this.

Number 50, Albert Jonnart's house, was coming into view. Max wondered if Jonnart had been scared. He must have known the risk to himself and his family of hiding the boy. But he'd still done it.

"How did they catch him?"

Madame Pauline's brow furrowed. "Who?"

"Albert Jonnart. I mean, how did they know he was hiding someone?"

"Oh, the Jonnart story," Madame Pauline said, sounding slightly disappointed to abandon her favorite topic. "Ralph was sneaking out at night to visit his parents. They were living with a couple of other Jewish families on Square Vergote."

The coincidence made Max shiver. "That's at the end of the street where my school is!"

Another similarity occurred to him. "Ralph was kind of a refugee too, wasn't he?"

Madame Pauline looked at him blankly. "What do you mean?"

"You said his family fled Germany. So they were refugees too, like the Syrian kid."

"That's not the same," Madame Pauline said flatly. "There have been Jews in Europe for centuries. They're Europeans."

"Hitler didn't think of them that way."

"They weren't trying to blow anyone up. These people are different, Max."

It annoyed Max that she couldn't—or wouldn't—see the connection. Maybe if she met Ahmed? But he was worried she'd be more likely to turn him in.

"So how'd the Gestapo find out about Ralph?"

"A neighbor, a Nazi collaborator, saw him going back and forth and told."

"That's horrible!" Max said.

"This is why more Jews weren't saved. Albert Jonnart was exceptionally courageous. It was hard to get away with a thing like that."

Max's stomach tightened. What he and Ahmed were about to do was arguably even harder. They weren't just hiding Ahmed; they were forging his way into school. For a split second as they climbed the stairs to his house, Max wondered what they had done. There were so many lies to keep straight, so many people to fool. Just the other day, Claire had said he should get checked for a tapeworm because he kept raiding the kitchen at night. But Ahmed had to go to school. Max had promised him. There was no turning back now.

CHAPTER THIRTY-FIVE

Early on the morning of Monday, January 4, in the pitch-black darkness, Ahmed scaled the garden wall and dropped into the neighbor's yard. His eyes stung with exhaustion; he'd barely slept, but at least it had been easy to wake up early and change into one of Oscar's old uniforms. As he raced across the yard to the front gate, his backpack rattled softly with the school supplies Farah and Max had bought him. He kept an eye on the neighbor's house, but it remained dark.

Past the School of Happiness, at the end of the block, was a small square. Trees ringed the side closest to the school. Ahmed took cover there, crouching in the shadows. Through the patchwork of leafless branches and clouds, he could see a few stars.

"Nouri, Jasmine," he whispered. "I'm going to school."

Did one of the stars wink back at him, or was it just his imagination?

On the other side of the square, he could hear the hum of

cars, the brakes of a bus, the occasional honk of a horn. Traffic was picking up. Long minutes passed and more noises struck up out of the orchestra pit of darkness—the tinkle of a dog's leash, the crash of a glass bottle in a recycling bin, the clack of footsteps and the murmuring of voices. As the night sky paled, kids began to trudge past the square. The little ones were with their parents, but some of the older ones walked by themselves or in groups, their shoulders slumped beneath backpacks.

It was time.

Ahmed took a deep breath, then slipped into the stream of kids heading toward the School of Happiness. No one paid him any attention. He was just another kid making his way to school. Being ordinary had never felt so special.

Ahmed surged toward the open door. Standing sentry were two young women, aides whose job Max had said was to make sure no strangers slipped into the school. Ahmed was sure to attract their attention—they had never seen him before, and he was much bigger than most of the primary school students. But he and Max had come up with a plan. Ahmed checked his father's watch, then bent down to tie his sneaker.

At 8:13, a shoe grazed his heel.

Ahmed looked up at Max without recognition.

"Sorry," Max said. "*Pardon.*"

Ahmed jumped to his feet. "You speak English?" he asked.

"Yes," Max said, pretending to look surprised.

"I look for my new class. Madame Legrand?"

"That's my class!" Max exclaimed. "Are you the new kid? The one from Syria?"

Ahmed almost laughed at Max's overacting. "Yes. I am Ahmed."

Max grinned. "Max," he said. "Come on, I'll take you."

He grabbed Ahmed's arm and whisked him inside.

"*Bonjour, Madame,*" he said to one of the aides, then pointed to Ahmed. "*Ahmed est nouveau.*"

New.

The aide smiled at him. "*Bienvenue, Ahmed.*"

Welcome. It was a word Ahmed had seen in the French books he'd been studying, but this was the first time someone had said it to him. He smiled back. "*Merci.*"

"*Merci, Madame,*" Max gently corrected.

He waved Ahmed after him, squeezing through the crowded passageway into the courtyard. Ahmed looked around in every direction, trying to take it all in. The language, the clothes, the faces of the other students—all were different than back home. But the feeling of being lost in a confusing swirl was one he was used to after six months in Europe. At least here, at school, there were universal rules he understood.

A football flew through the air toward him. Ahmed instinctively trapped it.

"*Pas mal,*" shouted Oscar from across the courtyard. *Not bad.*

Ahmed slipped off his backpack and dribbled the ball around. He hadn't played football since he'd left Syria, but his favorite moves came back easily. He could feel eyes on him, kids watching. A boy he didn't know tried to kick it away, but Ahmed dribbled the ball diagonally, then faked him out. There was an appreciative murmur from some of the other kids.

A bell rang and everyone scooped up their bags and scurried toward a door off the courtyard. Ahmed's audience was gone, but he knew they had noticed him, and it felt good to be noticed not as a refugee or a potential terrorist, but simply as a good footballer. He had nearly forgotten this about himself—after his father had died, being good at football had hardly seemed important. But at school, the skill counted for something. *He* counted for something.

Madame Legrand didn't seem particularly happy about having another nonnative French speaker in the class; she sat Ahmed all the way in the back, at a desk that smelled faintly of musty old sandwiches. But Ahmed didn't care. The desk was his. He neatly stacked his new notebooks and folders inside it, lined up his pens and erasers, sharpened his pencils, enjoying the woody smell of lead and shavings.

Madame Legrand wrote something on the board. Ahmed took out one of his notebooks and opened it up to the first, blank sheet. It reminded him of what he'd missed most about school: how each year, you started fresh. Gone were last year's marked-up notebooks, worn-out pens, bent folders filled with work that wasn't always your best. What mattered wasn't who you were. It was who you could be.

The morning flew by as Ahmed diligently copied everything on the board. Even though he didn't understand most of it, it felt good just to write it in his notebook to decipher later. Math required no translation, and neither did the gentle string of words that Madame Legrand said to him as she checked his work. Her praise made him glow from the inside, like a house that had been waiting for someone to turn on the lights.

Lunch returned him to a state of confusion. He had no idea where to sit—Max had warned that there were assigned seats—so he just stood around until an aide directed him to a table where he knew no one. He had just started to unwrap the soggy peanut butter sandwich Max had packed him when Farah appeared, trailing the aide behind her. Farah dragged him to another section of the cafeteria, where she filled up a tray with soup, vegetables, potatoes and pudding and handed it to him. Then she pointed him to an empty seat at her table. He found himself surrounded by girls. This might have unnerved him were it not for the flavorful steam rising up from his tray that was making his stomach rumble. He couldn't remember the last time he had eaten a full, hot meal at a table. He dove in, forgetting all about the girls. Only when he had scraped clean his soup bowl and plate and was stuffing the last of the pudding into his mouth did he look up and notice them staring. He stopped midbite, put down his spoon and daintily wiped his mouth with his napkin so they wouldn't think he was a complete savage.

At recess, he was immediately drafted into a game of football. There was no invitation—not in words, anyway—just the ball rolling toward him, the shouts of kids he didn't know, the arrangement by some prior order into teams. Despite the chill, he found himself sweating. His breath came hard; he was out of shape after months of mostly lying around the cellar, but it felt good to run. He found himself calling out names, hearing his own—*Ahmed, Ahmed!* At first it was just Oscar, shouting for a pass, but then he heard other voices. It was like a dream, with Max on the edges, cheering as if each goal Ahmed scored was his own.

Back inside the classroom, some of the boys called him by name. Madame Legrand pulled him aside and gave him a book of French verbs, writing down the pages he should study. She seemed to have decided that he was worthy of her attention. She also handed him a sheaf of forms—"*pour ta maman*"—including the card his mother had to sign so he could walk home alone. Ahmed obediently nodded.

Too soon, it seemed, the bell rang and everyone gathered up their books and bags and lined up in the hallway, waiting for Madame Legrand to lead them down to the courtyard. It was fortunate that Ahmed was last, because as they rounded the ground-floor landing, it was easy for him to peel off the line unnoticed and dart into the hall. He found the janitor's closet at the end of it—unlocked, as Max and Oscar had said it would be—and slipped inside. On this first day, without the signed card, he couldn't just walk out by himself without an aide stopping him.

He knew he'd have to wait a long time—according to Max, the school didn't close till six p.m., when the aftercare program ended. The closet smelled like wax and cleaning supplies, but at least it was warm. He squeezed himself into a corner, behind a row of buckets and mops, put on a headlamp-style camping flashlight Max had given him and began to study the book of French verbs. He recopied his notes, looking up the words he didn't know in his dictionary, then made a list of words to memorize. He carefully filled out a math worksheet. The work, the simple task of it, kept him calm.

Two hours later, he had nearly finished it all when he heard footsteps outside.

Ahmed switched off his headlamp just as the door flew open. A small woman in a white uniform swung a bucket and mop into him. He stifled a yelp. She turned around, wedged a cleaning product onto a shelf. Ahmed tried not to move a muscle. She turned on the light. If she turned back toward him, she would certainly see him. But with a mutter, she turned it off and closed the door behind her.

It took Ahmed several minutes to stop shaking. He was almost certain she hadn't seen him—it was a good thing he had been sitting down—but what if she came back?

For the next half hour he sat in the dark, afraid to turn the headlamp back on. A sliver of light allowed him to make out the hands of his father's watch, and only at 6:15 did he dare move, creeping to the door, opening it slowly, peeking out. The hallway was dark and deserted. The doors, Oscar had warned, would be alarmed. It was Ahmed himself who had come up with a solution. He scurried down the hall to the closest classroom.

With the softest of thuds, he dropped out the window. A minute later, veiled by the darkness of the winter night, he scrambled over the wall. He waited by the holly bush till a flashlight blinked once in the living room window, Max's signal for all clear. But as he raced across the garden, he thought he saw a silhouette in a second-story window. The figure vanished and he hoped it was just the drapes, playing tricks on his mind. He unlocked the door and tiptoed back into the cellar.

Ahmed collapsed on his mat, still shaking. But there was no question in his mind of what to do. He would be back at the School of Happiness tomorrow.

CHAPTER THIRTY-SIX

"Madame Pauline told me she's very pleased with your progress in French," Max's mother said one night over dinner. "Do you feel like it's getting easier?"

"Yeah, I guess so," Max said between bites of what had become their traditional Friday-night dinner—a rotisserie chicken from the local halal butcher ("I want to try one," he'd told his mom one day) with mashed potatoes and *haricots verts*, the slender French string beans. He always tried to eat less so there would be more leftovers for Ahmed.

"She said January is usually a turning point, but that you really seem motivated now," his mom continued.

Max smiled, but not because he felt he'd earned the praise. What Madame Pauline took for his sudden enthusiasm for French was really Ahmed's. Ever since he'd started school, Ahmed had thrown himself into learning the language like his life depended on it. Every night, he checked his homework against Max's and was full of questions. Max had found himself paying more attention to Madame Pauline and asking her Ahmed's questions about irregular verbs or complicated tense structures. He talked more in school and at Scouts, trying to practice. He wished he could give Ahmed some credit.

"You know who's doing really well?" he said. "The Syrian kid."

Claire's head jerked up. "What Syrian kid?"

His parents had a strict no-devices rule at dinner, but Max knew she'd been peeking at her phone under the table. He didn't say anything, though.

"There's a new kid in my class," Max explained. "Ahmed. He's a Syrian refugee. He missed a lot of school because of the war."

"How old is he?" Claire asked.

Her interest surprised Max. She usually just tuned out when his parents forced him to talk about school.

"Fourteen," Max said.

"A fourteen-year-old sixth grader?" his mother said.

Max was tempted to remind her that he was a thirteen-year-old sixth grader.

"He's doing really well," Max said. "And he's super nice. He works really hard."

His mother shifted in her chair. "I didn't mean to sound critical. I'm glad the school took him in. I feel sorry for them, for all the refugees. These soldiers and army trucks everywhere have just been getting to me."

Max understood how she felt. It wasn't just Fontaine. Ever since the lockdown, it seemed like policemen and soldiers were everywhere—outside the metro stations and farmers markets, patrolling the street corners, sitting in the camouflage-painted trucks or milling about on patrol outside any even vaguely important or official building. But they unsettled Max for an entirely different reason: one day, they might notice Ahmed, figure out who he really was.

"They're just keeping us safe," his father said.

"And we are safe," his mom said, a little too heartily for Max to believe.

"Where does he live?" Claire asked.

"I'm not sure," Max said vaguely.

His mother smiled at Max. "Well, wherever he lives, you should invite him over."

"Okay."

But Max regretted mentioning Ahmed. Now he'd have to make up some excuse for why he couldn't come.

LATER THAT NIGHT, after his parents' light had been turned off, Max heard a soft knock on his bedroom door.

He jumped out of bed and opened it fast, imagining it was Ahmed.

Claire slid past him into his room, then closed the door behind her.

"Can we talk?"

Max's stomach tightened. She almost never came up to his room, and he wasn't sure he liked it now.

"Sure."

Claire paced back and forth, then stopped and looked at him. "That Syrian kid, is he living in our house?"

Max stared at her as if he'd never heard anything so ridiculous. "What?"

"I saw someone in the garden a few weeks ago."

This wasn't good. But it wasn't undeniable proof either. He needed to keep calm.

"I don't know anything about—"

"You've been sneaking around—"

Max shrugged. "So have you."

"*Once.* I sneaked out *once.* I hear you going up and down all night, Max. Food is disappearing, the toilet seat in the basement keeps popping up, then there's that afternoon you were home alone and you didn't want me near the basement door. I didn't put it together, but then I see someone sneaking around the garden and the next thing I know this Syrian kid shows up at school—"

He could continue to deny it, but Max could tell she wasn't going to let it go. He was half-afraid she would march down to the basement and drag Ahmed out herself, just to prove he was lying.

Max locked his eyes on her. "You can't tell."

"I knew it! I knew you were up to something!"

"His name really is Ahmed, and he's living in the wine cellar."

"The wine cellar!"

"We've fixed it up. It's not so bad—"

Claire bugged out her eyes at him.

"How long has he been down there?"

Max did a quick count on his fingers. "Five months."

"Five months! Are you crazy?"

"You can't tell, Claire! You owe me."

"I didn't, did I?" she snapped.

But Max still didn't trust her. His only hope was to convince her. He softened his tone. "His parents are dead and if anyone finds out he's here, he'll either be deported or sent to some horrible refugee orphanage."

"How long were you planning to keep him down there?"

"Till we go back."

"And then what?"

"I don't know. I was going to figure something out."

Claire collapsed onto his bed. "This is insane."

Max sat down next to her. "I know, but he's all alone."

"There's got to be some adult who could help him—"

"Who? Mom and Dad feel sorry for refugees, but you know they'd never take him in—"

Claire acknowledged this with a sharp exhale. "They just do what's right for themselves."

Max had a feeling she was talking more about the move to Belgium than about Ahmed, but he needed her on his side.

"Exactly."

For a moment, neither of them spoke.

"I remember seeing pictures of refugees who'd drowned trying to get to Greece," Claire finally said. "There was one of a really little kid, facedown in the water. It was like the world didn't care."

Max nodded. "Maybe adults don't care. But we do."

They sat silently side by side.

"You're a lot craftier than I thought," Claire finally said.

"Thanks," Max said sarcastically.

"No, seriously. How did you enroll him at Bonheur?"

But before he could answer, she held up her hand. "Actually, don't tell me. I don't want to know anything more about it."

"You don't even want to meet him?"

Claire thought about this for a minute.

"No," she finally said. "I'm staying out of it."

"But you promise not to tell, right?"

"I told you I wouldn't. But this is your brilliant mess, not mine."

It was the first time, Max realized, she had referred to anything he'd done as brilliant. He tried not to let it bother him that she'd also used the word "mess."

CHAPTER THIRTY-SEVEN

One afternoon in the middle of February, Ahmed took a plastic chair from the basement and carried it out into the garden. Even though it was still cold and raw, the light was lingering a bit longer now, and on a rare sunny day, like this one, it was just possible to imagine spring.

Five weeks had passed since Ahmed had started school, twenty-five days, and now it was a holiday week. As far as Ahmed could tell, the holiday, Carnival, was about dressing up in fanciful costumes and parading around (at least this was what the youngest children at the School of Happiness had done). "Everyone pretends to be someone they aren't," Max had explained.

Ahmed stretched out his legs and watched the parakeets. With a smile, he thought about how he too was celebrating this strange, upside-down holiday—at least in spirit. Max and his family were in London and he had been playing their roles—cooking himself simple dinners in the kitchen, stretching out on the living room couch with his French books, rubbing Teddy under the chin or throwing around his toy mouse. The orchids sunbathed in the living room during the day and beneath the grow lamp at night. A few healthy new spikes had emerged. Ahmed knew from Max what days and times the cleaning woman was coming to feed Teddy and always made sure they were back in the cellar by then. He still avoided the upper floors, where the family slept, but otherwise, he pretended the house was his own.

Ahmed had brought his French verb book outside with him. He had resolved to study for at least six hours every day of the break. But the book lay unopened on his lap as his thoughts drifted. His father would have been so proud of how he was doing at school. He cheerfully did whatever extra work Madame Legrand suggested; raised his hand, especially in math; and had become a favorite of the lunch aides for never wasting food. Max, Oscar and Farah were naturally his closest friends, but he'd made a few more, including a couple of boys who wanted him to join their after-school football club. Ahmed had declined—the club cost money and he enjoyed having his afternoons free. Now that "his mother" had signed a pass so he could leave school on his own, he would either study with the others at Oscar's apartment or by himself at the library until it was dark enough to sneak home.

"Toi, là-bas!"

You, over there!

The harsh voice made him jerk upright. His eyes locked on Inspector Fontaine's face, peering at him over the wall.

"Qu'est-ce que tu fais?"

Ahmed rose so fast that he knocked over the chair. He was too panicked to understand. But some instinct told him not to run. Inspector Fontaine scaled the wall and with a practiced leap, jumped down.

"You speak English?"

Ahmed nodded.

The policeman strode toward him.

"What are you doing here?"

Ahmed opened his mouth, but no words came to him.

The cop was coming closer, close enough to reach out and grab him.

"I know the family is not home."

"I am—" Ahmed looked around, frantically trying to think of a reason for him to be there. His eyes landed on the overgrown bushes and the wild tangle of ivy on the walls. Suddenly, he remembered what Max had told him about the cop's obsession with the garden.

"Howard family . . . pay me to clean garden."

He shrank back, still expecting the cop to grab him. But Inspector Fontaine stopped his charge and let out a bitter laugh.

"Finally!" he said. "They find a gardener. But do they pay you to sit?"

"I am just to start," Ahmed said. He glanced back, grateful that a rake and shovel had been left in sight by the basement door.

"I have seen you before."

Ahmed turned back to find Fontaine's eyes narrowed.

"I go to Ecole du Bonheur," Ahmed said, pointing toward the school. "I am friend, *un ami de* Max."

"So you do speak some French?"

"I am new. I am learning. My English is—"

"Where are you from?" Inspector Fontaine interrupted.

Ahmed thought it unwise to lie. "Syria."

"Ah, and so the Americans have given you a job. They should take more of you into their country. But they love to start wars, not solve the problems they cause for the rest of the world."

Ahmed didn't know what to say to this, so he said nothing.

Inspector Fontaine sighed. "At least they finally take care of the garden. It was once not like this. This was my grandfather's house, and he kept the garden himself. I spent my boyhood playing here. But what do you know about gardens? How old are you?"

"Fourteen," Ahmed said. "My father and grandfather keep a garden."

Inspector Fontaine gave a snort. "They should be doing the job then."

"They are dead."

Fontaine's expression softened, but only for a moment.

"So the family gave you a key." The police officer shook his head as if he thought Max's parents very naive. "What's your name?"

"Ahmed."

"Better you work, Ahmed, and not become a radical like the boys in Molenbeek."

"I am not like that," Ahmed assured him. "I like garden."

"I like to check up on it."

Fontaine gave Ahmed a meaningful look, as if to remind him that he would be keeping an eye on Ahmed as well. Then he gazed out over the garden. "It was a beautiful garden once. I cannot imagine that you know how to take care of it. There are no gardens like this in Syria."

Ahmed was tempted to say, *How do you know?*

"My grandfather had garden store," he said instead.

Inspector Fontaine raised an eyebrow as if he didn't believe him. "*Bon chance,* Ahmed, good luck. But if I see you being lazy again, I will tell them to hire the Pole."

Ahmed nodded, then walked down to the basement door and grabbed the rake. When he turned back, Inspector Fontaine had hopped back up on the wall. He sat there for a moment, surveying. Ahmed, poised with the rake in hand, did the same.

"I told Madame *How-Weird* I would look in," the cop called out. "Tell her next time to let me know you're going to be here."

"Okay," Ahmed said.

He was still trembling when he got down to work. But the funny thing was, he really did have ideas about how to bring the garden back to life.

CHAPTER THIRTY-EIGHT

Surprise!" Max said.

His parents stood in front of the picture window in the living room, gazing out at the garden. The bushes were clipped and trimmed, the old leaves raked up, the ivy thinned, the flowerbeds weeded and turned. Max studied their expressions—they looked surprised all right.

"Is this what that note in the door was about?" his father asked.

Max nodded. The note had been a clever way for Ahmed to alert him to what had happened. In addition to thanking Max for the gardening job, he'd also let him know that Inspector Fontaine had been surprised to find him in the garden so they should make sure the cop knew next time that they had given him a key. Even if Inspector Fontaine himself had read it, he wouldn't have found the note suspicious.

Max noticed Claire staring at him intently, trying to figure out the scheme. "Ahmed was looking for some work," he said, "and I knew you were getting sick of that cop bugging you about the garden, so—"

His father's brow wrinkled. "Ahmed?"

"The new kid from my class, the one from Syr—"

"How did he get into the garden?" his mother interrupted.

Max shrugged. "I gave him a key."

"Max! You can't just give a stranger a key to the house!"

"He's not a stranger. I told you, he's in my class."

And he lives in our basement, Max imagined saying. But from the way his mother was looking at him, Max knew that there was no way he could ever tell her that. He turned to his dad, hoping for a better reaction.

"Your mother's right, Max."

For once, Max thought bitterly, *they agree on something*.

"We were gone for an entire week," his father continued. "You gave this boy the run of our house."

"He's not *this boy*," Max said. "I told you—he's my friend. And he was just fixing up the garden."

But his mother had begun to stalk around, as if checking to see that everything was still in its place.

"It's just because he's a refugee!" Max shouted. "You think he wants our stupid stuff—?"

"Max." His father's voice was low but stern. "This isn't about him being a refugee. You can't just let someone we've never met into our home without telling us. It's a betrayal of our trust."

"Isn't that a little dramatic?" Claire said.

"Claire—" his father warned.

"Fine," she said, holding up her hands in a "don't shoot" position. "I'm out."

Then she went upstairs, leaving Max to face his parents alone.

"I'm sorry! I just thought I was doing you a favor!"

His voice broke and his eyes filled with tears, as if he really believed the lie. But it was something else that was making him cry—the truth of his father's words. He had betrayed his parents for months now, and for Ahmed's sake, he would continue to do so. It was wrong and right at the same time.

"Look, Max," his father said. "I know you meant well."

"And I'm sure Ahmed is a nice boy," his mom added as she wandered back into the living room. Max sensed from the calmer tone of her voice that she had reassured herself that everything was still there. "I still want to meet him. But you need to get that key back from him first thing tomorrow and *never, ever* give someone access to the house without asking us first."

Max could just make another copy of the key for his parents and pretend it was the one he'd given Ahmed. There was no need to tell Ahmed how his parents had reacted. He hadn't told Ahmed about Claire knowing either. It felt very grown-up to protect someone by not telling them the entire truth. But Max wasn't sure he liked it.

"Okay," he said quietly. "I get it."

CHAPTER THIRTY-NINE

Every morning, as he left for school ever earlier to beat the sunrise, Ahmed expected to run into Inspector Fontaine. But with Max's family back from vacation, the police officer kept away. Even so, Ahmed considered changing his route. One night, in the early hours of the morning, he investigated other ways of getting out of the garden to the street. But this involved sneaking through multiple gardens, raising the risk of being spotted, and only confirmed his suspicion that the LeClerq's yard was still the quickest and safest way out.

Still, Ahmed worried. It had been easy enough to pass himself off as the gardener on a clear afternoon. But would Inspector Fontaine believe him on a rainy predawn March morning? The police officer began to haunt his dreams, trimming the garden with a pair of large clippers. He would come closer and closer to where Ahmed was hiding. Ahmed would try to run, only to realize his feet were rooted to the earth and he had turned into an orchid.

"You can't grow here," the cop would say, grabbing Ahmed by the stem, his clippers gleaming.

But Ahmed could live with nightmares. At least when he woke from them, he no longer had the sinking feeling that waking life was worse. Three months into school, it was as if he'd always been there—the aides at the gate greeting him in the morning, the other boys waiting for him to kick off the football match at recess, the stack of increasingly thick French readers in his desk. Best of all, at night, he always checked his homework and discussed his day with Max.

"Your room is a total disaster," Max said on one of these nights.

"Disaster?"

"A mess."

Ahmed looked sheepishly around the cellar. Piles of paper—mostly used to practice French—were scattered across the floor next to a banana peel and a stack of comics Max had given him. Since starting school, he'd been busier than ever, but he realized the disorder was also a sign that he felt comfortable.

"You were so neat, I was beginning to wonder if something was wrong with you," Max said.

Ahmed grinned. "I know. It is hard to believe I am not perfect."

Max shoved him. Ahmed shoved him back. Then they teased each other about girls and teachers until they were laughing so hard they had to clap their hands over their mouths so they wouldn't wake Max's parents.

But one afternoon a couple of weeks into March, a problem emerged that had nothing to do with Inspector Fontaine.

"Ahmed, may I talk to you?"

Ahmed looked up from his math worksheet to find Madame Legrand waving him up to her desk. There was nothing unusual about this—she often called him up to correct a mistake on his French homework or slip him an extra worksheet or book. It pleased him that even without the cue of her gesture, he understood her French. His long hours of study were starting to pay off.

"Oui, Madame."

It was only after he'd trotted past Max, Farah and Oscar to the front of the room that he noticed the white slip of paper in her hand. It was the sign-up form for the parent-teacher conferences at the end of March, before the spring break. His "mother" had signed the form saying she couldn't come.

"Tell your mother she has to come," Madame Legrand said, handing the form back to him. "It's important."

For the first time, Ahmed wished he didn't understand the French. He gave a half nod and took the form, but hesitated.

"It's hard for her, Madame," he said.

It made it worse somehow that Madame Legrand's expression softened.

"Why?"

Ahmed swallowed, trying to think of an answer. Could the imaginary Jasmine or Nouri be sick? It would have to be something serious—the parent-teacher conferences were still two weeks away. Or should his mother herself be ill? But he didn't want Madame Legrand to worry that he wasn't being taken care of and alert the authorities.

"Max, eyes on your work!" Madame Legrand said.

Ahmed glanced around just in time to see Max look back down again. He clearly had figured out what was happening. But at least his bold stare had distracted Madame Legrand. With a sigh, she turned back to Ahmed.

"Tell her I can come to her if it's necessary."

Ahmed forced himself to smile, as if he were grateful for this kind offer.

"No, Madame," he said. "It's not necessary."

He carefully folded the paper and walked back to his desk.

AFTER SCHOOL, Max held an emergency meeting in the garden. Unlike the last time they had all gathered there, Ahmed didn't hide behind the holly bush, but instead followed Max, Oscar and Farah through the front door. It felt strange to enter the house this way, to meet Madame Pauline, who for so long had been only a disembodied voice, to eat kiwi slices and meringue cookies with the others around the dining room table. The nanny looked the way he had expected—grim and colorless, like the weather—and she stared at him and Farah unapologetically. Teddy was far more welcoming, rubbing against his shins and even jumping up into his lap. Ahmed worried that the cat's familiarity might give him away, but it only seemed to amuse Madame Pauline.

"Well, the cat likes him," she muttered under her breath in French.

After the snack, they went out to the garden to kick around Max's football. Madame Pauline watched them for a bit through the picture window. As soon as she disappeared, Max trapped the ball the way Ahmed had taught him.

"Okay," he said in English. "What's the plan?"

Oscar translated for Farah, who replied to him in French too soft and fast for Ahmed to understand.

"She says she can call and cancel on the morning of the meeting," Oscar said. "Say she has a sickness."

"But Madame Legrand will just try to reschedule," Max said.

"And what if she tries to go to my mother?" Ahmed added. "She say this is possible."

Their plan was falling apart. Ahmed's gaze fell on one of the flowerbeds. It had been less than a month since he'd tidied up the garden, and already the weeds were taking over. He bent down and yanked out a dandelion, then another. It felt good to rip them out of the earth, to make room for the pale green stalks peeping through the dirt.

"You don't have to do that," Max said. "Madame Pauline knows you're here as a friend."

Ahmed shrugged. "Garden need it."

Farah kneeled down next to him and began pulling weeds too.

"Is there an adult you can trust?" she asked in slow, simple French.

Ahmed thought about this, then turned to Max so he could translate.

"Ibrahim, the man I came to here with, is possible stay with his family in Molenbeek."

A crack behind him made Ahmed jerk around. But it was just Oscar breaking a stick in half with his foot. He held a few others he had gathered into a pile. "What if he play uncle?" Oscar said in English. "Come to school in place of your mother?"

Max trotted over, looking excited. "Could you get him a fake ID, Oscar?"

But before Oscar could answer, Ahmed shook his head. "He may have lost his fight to stay, and even if not—I cannot ask this of him. He last sees me six months ago, and now I come, ask him to risk his own chance to stay by lying?"

He sank onto the damp grass. How long could they keep this up? New threats seemed to be emerging faster than the weeds in the flowerbed. But the thought of stopping school, leaving his friends . . . He had no interest anymore in running off by himself to Calais.

"Don't worry," Farah said in French.

"Yeah," Max said, "we'll think of something."

CHAPTER FORTY

Max tried to think of a plan. He tried at the School of Happiness, as he now thought of it, in between writing the *dictée* words that came so much easier now. He tried at Scouts (*Scoots* now, in his own mind), as he and Oscar practiced Morse code in the woods. He tried in bed, as he waited till it was late enough to visit Ahmed in the wine cellar. He tried at recess, now *récréation*, as he helped Oscar and the other boys lift Ahmed triumphantly onto their shoulders after a goal.

After school the following Friday, Max found an old soccer match on one of the Belgian sports channels and flopped onto his parents' bed to think some more. There was something calming about the announcer's patter, the smallness of the players on the large green field, the dull murmur of the crowd. But just when Max had begun to relax, Madame Pauline raced in and grabbed the remote. The soccer game vanished, replaced by a blurry image of police officers with helmets and assault rifles dragging a man in a white hoodie down the street. A news scroll in Dutch ran below it.

"What's going on?" Max asked.

"They've caught him!" Madame Pauline said, plopping down beside him on the bed.

"Who?"

"Abdeslam, the terrorist they've been looking for since Paris. They finally found him, here, in Molenbeek."

The fugitive terrorist had been caught! He'd been the whole reason for the lockdown, the whole reason for the police raids. Perhaps now that this bad guy was in custody, everyone would calm down. Perhaps they would even start feeling sympathy again for refugees like Ahmed.

"Took long enough!" Madame Pauline continued. "He was right under their noses for months, but of course the police and security forces do a terrible job of sharing information. That's what happens when you have nineteen police forces, one for every commune!"

"How'd they get him?" Max asked.

Madame Pauline snickered. "A pizza! The police were eyeing a suspicious apartment and then the woman there ordered too much pizza just for herself and her kids. The police realized that there was someone else staying there and raided the apartment."

"He was staying with this woman the whole time?"

Madame Pauline gave Max a hard look. "Of course not. He was hiding out all over the city. For four months! There's no way he could have done that by himself. I bet half of Molenbeek knew."

"It probably doesn't take that many people to keep someone hidden," Max said quietly.

"Have you been to Molenbeek, Max? It's like you're not even in Europe anymore."

Max almost mentioned that Farah lived there before he decided that Madame Pauline might take this as proving her point. She didn't know that Farah was the kindest person in his class, only that her mother wore a headscarf.

"I hope that woman and all the rest who helped him are sent to prison," she continued, "or better yet, back to where they came from!"

"But it isn't always wrong to hide someone from the police, right?" Max asked before he could stop himself.

"Of course not," Madame Pauline agreed. "Look at Jonnart. He not only hid that Jewish boy, he helped him escape."

Max looked at her, dumfounded. "Wait, Ralph escaped?! I thought the neighbor betrayed them, and that the Gestapo—"

"Yes, the Gestapo arrested Jonnart and Ralph's parents too in a separate raid the same night. But Jonnart knew it was them—who else would pound on his door at five in the morning?—so before he opened it, he sent his son Pierre—"

"The one who was Ralph's classmate?"

"That's right. He sent Pierre upstairs to wake up Ralph and tell him it was time for their emergency plan—"

"Hide in a secret attic?"

Madame Pauline paused dramatically. "Ralph climbed out the window and ran across the rooftops before climbing down to a neighbor's garden."

"But they still arrested Jonnart?"

"The Nazis weren't stupid. They searched the house and found an empty bed on the very top floor that was still warm. But by the time they realized this, Ralph had fled, so they could only arrest Albert. Pierre ran to the house of Jacques Breuer, the father of a friend from *Scoots*, told him what happened and asked him to help Ralph. Jacques was an archaeologist at the Cinquantenaire Museum, and he hid Ralph in the basement of the museum, as well as at his home, until the German occupation ended."

Max couldn't believe that he hadn't heard this exciting part of the story until now. It seemed to change everything.

"So Ralph survived the war!"

"Thanks to Jonnart and his family, as well as the Breuers. They were true heroes. But there's a big difference between hiding an innocent school boy and a terrorist."

Max felt a funny grin spread across his face. Madame Pauline was absolutely right. A boy like Ahmed deserved sympathy and help. Max knew, as surely as Albert Jonnart must have known, that he was doing the right thing. But he wouldn't have known this if he'd just called the police when he'd first found Ahmed or turned him away—if he hadn't had the courage to listen.

Later that afternoon, up in his bedroom, Max opened the window and stepped over the guardrail and onto the asphalt roof that stretched over the back of his parents' bedroom. He stayed close to the window, with one hand on the guardrail—he'd never liked heights—but he could see how the roofs of the town houses connected. It wasn't hard to imagine Ralph scrambling across them.

But with the last of the Paris terrorists finally in custody, Max was hopeful that Ahmed's story could end differently.

"ANY IDEAS?" Max asked Ahmed later that night as he sat down on the camping mat and handed Ahmed the tote bag. It had become their customary greeting ever since Madame Legrand had brought up the parent-teacher conference.

"No," Ahmed said. "You?"

Max cocked his head at the tote bag. "Open it. I brought good stuff: hummus, olives, bread—not too stale—and a piece of chocolate cake for dessert. You may have to share that, though."

"With who?" Ahmed asked innocently.

"You better share . . . I also have some good news."

Ahmed's eyebrows rose hopefully. "An idea?"

"We'll get to that," Max said. "But first, they caught the terrorist, the one they've been looking for since Paris!"

Ahmed gave such a full and genuine smile that Max wondered if he was already thinking along the same lines as he was. "This is very good."

Max grabbed his arm. "It's better than good! Now that they've caught this guy, everyone's going to be less worried. Less scared. Remember when I told you last fall that you couldn't hide forever? Maybe you no longer have to."

The smile dropped off Ahmed's face. "This your idea?"

Max knew he couldn't back down now. "Everyone at school

likes you! They know you now. And we can choose who to tell, which is a whole lot better than Inspector Fontaine or some other police officer catching on."

Ahmed pulled away and hugged his knees. Max worried that he'd pushed too far.

"It's up to you," he said carefully. "I'd never say anything if you didn't want me to. It's just that . . . You know I'm moving back to Washington at the end of the school year. That's just three months away. You'll have to tell sometime—"

Ahmed glared at him. "Of course, I know this! I am tired to lie. But you think so much will change because they catch this one man? What about next one? One man, two man in million is bad, so all refugees will again be bad. I want to tell, Max. But I do not want to leave yet—"

"Bonheur, I know," Max said. "But Madame Legrand likes you. She'll fight to keep you. I'll fight—"

"Not only school. You!"

A lump formed in Max's throat. "Maybe you can stay with us. My parents could take you in—?"

But Max knew his parents' reaction when they found out that Ahmed had actually lived with them for the past half year was not likely to end in adoption—unless it was Max's own adoption after his parents gave him up. From Ahmed's listless shrug, Max could tell he didn't really believe him either.

"Hey," Max said, meeting his eyes. "No matter what, I'm not going to abandon you."

"No one can say this, Max. No one is so powerful."

Max felt the lump in his throat thicken. This was the horrible truth; Ahmed had lived it. You couldn't always be there for the people you loved. You couldn't always save them, just as they couldn't always save you.

But you could try.

"I mean it, Ahmed. I'll make sure nothing bad happens."

Ahmed shook his head, like he didn't believe him, but his gentle smile told Max he was touched.

"I think about it."

CHAPTER FORTY-ONE

On the morning of Tuesday, March 22, Ahmed woke up after six. With the sunrise now around six thirty, he knew he'd have to get ready quickly. He threw on his clothes and rushed out to the furniture room to check the orchids. He was hopping on one foot, trying to shove on a sneaker, when he nearly toppled over. On the spike of the healthiest orchid were tiny, pale-green buds.

Only three days were left before the parent-teacher conference. Just as he'd promised, Ahmed had been thinking about what he wanted to do. It was hard to share Max's faith that adults would protect him, especially after he had broken so many laws. But he wouldn't be telling alone; Max would be with him. As he gazed at the buds, they seemed like a good omen, a message from the universe that everything would be okay.

By the time Ahmed scaled the garden wall and made his way to Square Vergote, the sky was turning a bright, cloudless blue. The peace it promised—of a sunny day, of warm moods lifted by spring, of friends and football—calmed him.

Only later did he realize that he had forgotten the most important lesson of war: when you least expect it, chaos always returns.

"JE VIENS CHERCHER MAX."

I've come for Max.

A familiar voice jarred Ahmed from Madame Legrand's lecture on the Thirty Years' War. He looked up to find Max's mother standing in the doorway. Wisps of hair stuck up around her face, and she sounded out of breath.

Ahmed glanced at the clock on the wall—it was barely nine thirty. Why was she picking up Max now? He hadn't mentioned a doctor's appointment.

Madame Legrand wrinkled her brow, clearly taken aback by the interruption. Ahmed looked at Max, but he just blinked and stared, as confused as everyone else.

"The *directrice* says it's okay," Max's mother said in French, waving Max up out of his chair.

Madame Legrand cocked her head at Max. "Go on."

Max quickly gathered up the books and papers on his desk, then, with an almost imperceptible shrug in Ahmed's direction, followed his mother out of class. As soon as the door closed behind them, Madame Legrand went back to discussing the Peace of Westphalia.

Ahmed told himself that Max's mother must have forgotten an appointment. But just as he began to focus back on Madame

Legrand's lecture, the door to the room opened and a man Ahmed had never seen before walked in. He too seemed breathless, like he was in a great hurry.

"I'm taking Charlotte," he said.

Outside in the hall, Ahmed saw a few other parents leaving with their kids. Something was going on. Something bad enough, frightening enough, that they were taking their children home. Ahmed could only think of one thing: a terror attack. His chest tightened; he couldn't breathe. Max's mother would get him home safely—they were only two blocks away. But what about Max's father and sister? The terrorists could be attacking government buildings, like the one where Max's father worked, or even worse, schools.

Madame Legrand had figured out that something serious was going on as well, because she walked the man who was clearly Charlotte's father out into the hall and closed the door behind them.

"What's going on?" Farah said.

As if in answer, a siren wailed in the distance. Jules and André ran to the window.

"No go near window!" Ahmed shouted.

Everyone stared at him. Ahmed felt his face turn red. He was just trying to keep them safe, but it might sound like he knew what was going on out there. What if they thought he was a terrorist or knew the terrorists?

A balled-up piece of paper landed on Ahmed's desk. He picked it up and smoothed it out.

"Stay calm," it read in English.

Ahmed caught Oscar's eye and nodded. But it was hard not to panic. He was an illegal refugee; he had forged paperwork. The whole city would be looking for young men like him. He just wanted to run back to Max's house and hide in the cellar. But running away now would seem suspicious. And he was safer here in school than he'd be on the streets with the terrorists and soldiers and police.

When Madame Legrand returned, she dismissed Charlotte, then went back to the history lecture. But this time, even she seemed distracted—forgetting her point and gazing out the window. It was a relief when Madame Bertrand, the *directrice*, walked in. She whispered for a minute with Madame Legrand, then turned to address the class. Ahmed understood some phrases: "explosion at the airport," "some parents have taken their children home," "the school is locked now." She seemed to be assuring them that they were safe, but the frantic bleating of the sirens outside made Ahmed wonder what she wasn't telling them.

The day continued as if it were no different than any other—Madame Legrand showed them how to solve for *x*, they learned a Zumba dance in gym and back in class they discussed the fables of La Fontaine and the moral lessons they taught. But it wasn't a normal day; no one clowned around or misbehaved, and Ahmed could see from the worried faces that everyone's thoughts were elsewhere. Ahmed knew exactly how they felt: did it really matter if they could solve for *x* when the city was under attack and their families were possibly out there? He wished he could tell them that it did, that even the illusion of normal life could help you put one foot in front of the other and walk the tightrope of disaster.

At lunch and over recess, rumors and stories began to spread. Oscar reported that he'd overheard the secretary telling one of the teachers that the airport had been blown up. Madame Mansouri had confided to Farah that the Maelbeek metro station had been attacked too. Ahmed felt ill as he remembered riding past this stop on the back of Max's bike on the way to the Magritte Museum. There was possibly also a bomb at the Schuman metro, near the European Commission headquarters, though no one knew for sure.

"This is bad," Farah repeated, again and again.

Ahmed knew she wasn't just talking about him and his life, but hers. Every Muslim in Brussels would be a suspect, at least in the minds of non-Muslim Europeans. Ahmed knew he could never tell the truth now. The authorities would lock him up or deport him back to Turkey.

As he played a halfhearted game of football during recess, Ahmed noticed that there were no commercial planes in the sky, only police helicopters, looping low over the neighborhood. The whoosh of the rotors reminded him of the helicopters back home, the ones that dropped bombs, and he had to stifle the urge to run inside.

"You're fine," Oscar whispered to him after one of the helicopters buzzed particularly low. "Just make it through the day; you'll be safe at Max's."

But Ahmed noticed that Oscar didn't talk about the next day and the day after that. In just a few hours, everything had changed. And Max wasn't there to reassure him.

By the afternoon, even Madame Legrand could no longer keep up the pretense that it was a normal day. For the last hour of school, she let them draw "*dessins heureux*," or happy pictures. Ahmed sketched without thinking. It was a way to keep his mind calm, clear.

"That's a beautiful garden," Madame Legrand said, standing over him.

"Merci, Madame."

He had drawn the garden behind Max's house. Madame Legrand asked him if she could hang it up in class. There was no polite way, Ahmed felt, to say no. But he would have liked to have kept it.

CHAPTER FORTY-TWO

All morning long, Max watched the same images loop in constant replay on CNN International and the BBC: screaming people running down the airport road as smoke billowed from the terminal behind them, bloody commuters stumbling out of the Maelbeek metro station. He watched them on the TV in his parents' bedroom as his parents and Claire fielded emails and calls from worried family and friends. Thirty-two people had died and hundreds more had been injured.

By afternoon, the images were seared into his brain, and the only thought that made him feel any better was that the people he loved were safe. His mother had not taken the metro that morning, deciding to walk instead. His father had picked up Claire and driven her home. And Ahmed was presumably still at the School of Happiness, which, like the rest of the schools in Brussels, had gone into lockdown soon after his mother had picked him up.

Around two, the doorbell rang, startling his mother.

"Who's that?"

His father jogged down the stairs. Could it possibly be Ahmed? Max darted after him.

"Don't open it if you don't know who it is!" his mother called after them.

For once, his father took her advice and looked out the kitchen window. "Don't worry! It's just that police officer."

Inspector Fontaine was standing on the stoop, a grave expression on his face. Max's heart thumped. Ahmed wasn't there, thankfully, but what if Fontaine wanted to see the wine cellar? Max wondered if he should run downstairs and clear out Ahmed's stuff, but there was no time. His father was already opening the door. As Fontaine stepped into the vestibule, Claire appeared on the stairs and bugged out her eyes at Max.

"I am sorry to disturb you, Monsieur *How-Weird*," Fontaine said. "But after the attacks of this morning, there is a state of urgency."

Max realized he meant "state of emergency," but Fontaine seemed rattled and Max wasn't about to correct his English. The cop's eyes darted from Max to Claire to Max's mother, who raced down the steps past Claire.

"It's horrible!" she said. "Do you think there'll be more?"

"I do not know, Madame," Fontaine said somberly. "The counterterror division has transmissions from the plotters and their accomplices. Many of them are coded, but I can assure you we are following every lead."

"I hope you catch them," his father said.

"I have made it my personal mission, *Monsieur*. But all of us must help. Which is why I have come by. I wish you to have my mobile number."

Fontaine scribbled on the back of a card and handed it to Max's father.

"If you see anything that is not ordinary, call me. Do not hesitate. These terrorists are not just in Molenbeek. Right now, they can be hiding anywhere. Arab men, young ones in particular, who are secretive, who act bizarre, who trespass—"

Max felt like he couldn't breathe. Fontaine was basically telling the whole neighborhood to look for someone like Ahmed. How long would it take for one of the neighbors to betray them, just as a neighbor had betrayed Albert Jonnart and Ralph?

"'See something, say something,' as we say in America," his father said.

"*Exactement*. And the children too." He glanced at Max, then Claire. "Listen to them. Sometimes they are more observant than the adults." Fontaine allowed himself a faint smile.

Max glanced at Claire, willing her to stay quiet. She turned away and headed back up the stairs. Fontaine gave him a reassuring pat on the shoulder.

"We will catch them, *Mex*, do not worry! *T'inquiètes pas*."

CHAPTER FORTY-THREE

When the bell finally rang for dismissal, Ahmed followed the rest of the class down to the courtyard. Only then did the strained calm of the day disintegrate; the parents and other caregivers who normally came into the courtyard for pickup were nowhere to be seen and the sliding door to the street was still locked. Everyone began to talk at once, and Madame Mansouri and the other aides were forced to shout over the hubbub. Since parents were not allowed to enter the school for security reasons, they explained, kids would be released to them one by one through the sliding door. Madame Bertrand, the *directrice*, was outside, explaining the new rule to parents.

Ahmed chewed on a dry cuticle.

"Did she say about kids who go home alone?" he asked Oscar in English.

Oscar shook his head. "Maybe you can just go?"

Ahmed slipped into the line already snaking through the passageway to the door. But when he finally reached the front, he realized that Madame Mansouri wasn't alone. Inspector Fontaine flanked the door on the other side. For the first time, Ahmed noticed a gun in his holster. But before Ahmed could back away, the police officer saw him.

"Ahmed!"

Ahmed's heart pounded in his ears.

"Bonjour, Monsieur," he said automatically. "How are you?"

What a stupid thing to say, thought Ahmed. But it was a wonder he could say anything. His legs felt like they might crumple beneath him.

"Not well. You know what has happened?"

His tone was sharp, as if Ahmed had had something to do with it.

Ahmed nodded. "It is very bad."

"Yes, it is," Fontaine said, as if Ahmed's response had been insufficient. He looked back and scanned the crowd of parents. "Where's your mother?"

Ahmed couldn't speak, so he just shook his head and held up his pass. But Fontaine didn't even bother to look at it.

"Surely your mother is coming."

He was right. What kind of mother would allow her child to go home alone on the day of a terror attack? Even if Ahmed said she was sick or couldn't get to school because the metro was down, it would seem strange that she hadn't sent someone else to fetch him.

"She not able," Ahmed choked out.

Ahmed could tell from the furrow that appeared in the

police officer's brow that this answer bothered him. Fontaine opened his mouth, but before he could say anything, a voice crackled over his radio. He pulled it off the clip on his belt and turned slightly away.

"Fontaine. I am listening."

Ahmed slipped past him, plunging into the crowd of parents.

The parents must have thought he was making his way to someone on the outer edge of the crowd because they easily let him through, then shuffled forward and closed ranks tightly behind him. It was as if, Ahmed thought, in their eagerness to collect their children and bring them safely home, they became his protectors too. Within seconds, he popped out on the other side of the crowd.

Just before he turned the corner, Ahmed glanced back. Fontaine was talking to the *directrice*. Ahmed hoped it was just about whatever he had heard over his radio. But then Fontaine pointed right at him.

Ahmed's every instinct blared an alarm: the police officer was on to him. Fontaine was asking Madame Bertrand questions that would lead to more questions. Soon enough, there'd be a knock at Max's door and trouble for everyone.

CHAPTER FORTY-FOUR

It had been a relief when Max finally spotted Ahmed scrambling over the garden wall at dusk. But there had been no way to talk to him. His parents were awake in bed, and the TV whined on until late in the night.

To keep himself awake, Max played one of his fantasy games, even though it was meant for multiple players. There was a comforting order to the rules, to the numerical values assigned to qualities like strength, craft and magic; to the bloodless fights between wizards and trolls, clearly determined by a roll of the die. The images of the attack faded and his thoughts turned to how he might calm Ahmed. It seemed best not to mention Fontaine's latest visit—at least right away.

A knock on the door interrupted Max's thoughts. He scrambled to his feet, imagining Ahmed, but when he opened the door he found Claire. She closed the door carefully behind her, then turned to face him.

"Is he home?"

There was no need to ask who she was talking about.

"Yeah. He's fine."

"That's great," she said, but Max could detect a note of sarcasm.

"What?" he asked.

Claire took a deep breath.

"You can't keep hiding him."

Max was surprised by how hurt he felt, as if she'd personally insulted him. "Yes, I can."

"Max, wake up. That police officer was here today looking for guys just like him. Guys who just blew up hundreds of people!"

Max stared straight at her. "Ahmed's not a terrorist."

"Look, I'm not saying he's a terrorist . . . ," she said carefully.

"So what are you saying?"

She looked away and her eyes passed over the character cards and board strewn across the floor. "This isn't some game, Max. Mom could have gotten on that metro today instead of walking to work. What if she were blown up?"

Max winced, but only because this dark thought had crossed his mind as well.

"Ahmed would never blow anyone up. I told you, he just wants to go to school. He has nothing to do with any of this."

Claire gave her long hair a frustrated shake. "It doesn't matter! Don't you get it? You're harboring an illegal refugee from Syria! And somehow you illegally enrolled him in school. The police came to our house today because there's a state of emergency! You're in over your head—"

"Don't you dare tell!" Max hissed.

"He needs to go. This is a mess."

Helping Ahmed was no longer "brilliant," Max noticed; now it was just a mess. But Claire wasn't so brilliant either. She seemed to have forgotten that he could make life difficult for her too.

"I'll tell on you . . . how during the Paris attacks—"

She gave a bitter laugh. "You think that scares me? Sneaking out to go to a party is *nothing* compared to what you've been doing."

She marched toward the door, but before she could yank it open, Max grabbed her hand.

"Please!" he pleaded. "I'll tell. Just don't make me do it now. It's the worst possible time—"

Claire bristled. "Did you ever think it was the worst possible time for me to move to Brussels? But Mom and Dad thought it was a good idea because of you! They kept talking about giving you a fresh start. But I didn't need a fresh start! They do everything for you!"

Max pushed down his anger. "Because they want me to be more like you!"

"Well, maybe you should be more like the rest of us and use your head! You're putting us all in danger."

"Ahmed is the one in danger, not us. Don't let Fontaine scare you—"

"Max, this isn't about being scared, it's about being smart!"

He was tempted to shout that being smart wasn't everything, that being kind counted for just as much, if not more. But he wasn't going to change her mind by yelling at her or making her feel like a jerk.

"Look," he said as calmly as he could, "I get it. I stress everyone out. I suck at everything. But I've kept Ahmed hidden. And I've kept him safe. I can't do a lot, but I can do this. I'm good at this."

He continued in an urgent whisper. "Please, Claire. I can't turn him out now. Please, just give me a little more time."

She didn't say anything, but she didn't run off either. Finally, she sighed deeply.

"Fine."

IT WAS NEARLY ONE in the morning when his parents' light finally switched off. Even though he could barely stand to wait another second to talk to Ahmed, Max forced himself to stay in his room another twenty minutes till he was sure they were asleep. Then he tiptoed down, filling his tote bag with leftovers in the kitchen as he thought more about what he would say to Ahmed. He definitely wouldn't tell him about Fontaine or Claire or that one of the terrorists was still on the loose. He would keep the conversation practical—the Belgian schools, surprisingly, planned to be open the next day, but since the metros, trams and buses weren't running, not everyone would be able to come. This gave Ahmed a choice: if he didn't feel comfortable going, he could just stay in the wine cellar without anyone getting suspicious.

Max knocked on the wine-cellar door.

"Ahmed," he said softly.

No one answered.

Max's breath came faster, his stomach tightened. But it was later than usual, he told himself, and Ahmed had probably just fallen asleep. He pushed open the door and stepped down into the cement anteroom.

"Ahmed!" he said again.

Silence.

Max rushed into the wine cellar, stopping short to avoid stepping on the camping mat. Only there was no camping mat. There were no blankets. There were no clothes. There were no books. There was no bag of food. There was no picture of the man who was a cage.

There was no Ahmed.

Max raced upstairs and threw on his jacket. His hand was on the doorknob when he heard a police siren wail outside. How would he find Ahmed at night, in the dark, with cops everywhere? He was more likely to be stopped himself and taken home.

He called Farah at the number for Ahmed's "mom." But the call just went to voicemail: *This is Reem Nasser. Please leave a message.*

He texted Oscar. But as long, silent minutes passed, Max realized that he, too, was probably asleep.

Ahmed couldn't have just left without a word, without even a goodbye. Max stumbled down to the front room of the basement and pulled back the shade. The orchids were still there, the grow lamp resting unplugged beside them. Their roots spilled over the sides of their pots, as if they sensed Ahmed had left and were feeling around desperately for him.

Max's eyes blurred with tears, but not before he noticed that the largest orchid was trying to say something. A scrap of paper was nestled among its roots. Max plucked it out and read:

Dear Max,

This one will bloom. Please take care of it.

Thank you for all.

Your friend,
Ahmed

CHAPTER FORTY-FIVE

Ahmed slumped against a lamppost. He couldn't take another step. His eyes blurred with exhaustion.

His first thought had been to find Ibrahim's relatives in Molenbeek—maybe they'd take him in for the night; perhaps Ibrahim would even still be there. But Molenbeek was on the other side of the city, and whichever way Ahmed tried to go, he'd found himself heading toward more police cars and sirens. The police, he realized, would be all over Molenbeek, searching for terrorists and asking to see people's documents.

So he'd reversed his route, making a wide loop to avoid the School of Happiness and Max's block before cutting back into Woluwe-Saint-Lambert. At least here, in the fancier neighborhood, there was less police activity. But he risked running into Fontaine; Ahmed had no idea how much of the commune he patrolled. He needed to get out of Brussels. But there were no buses or metros or trains running, and even if he managed to walk all the way out of the commune and into the countryside, he had no place to go. He had no money, and he couldn't imagine anyone willing to take him in after the attack unless they wanted to harm him, like Ermir.

This was when he'd collapsed against the lamppost, too hopeless to keep trudging on. He just wanted to go back to the cellar and to Max. He knew Max would be worried. He hadn't even said goodbye, except for his note. He'd told himself that there hadn't been time, but the truth was that it had seemed too painful.

On the other side of the traffic circle, a pair of stone towers rose over a small square like the minarets of a mosque. They drew him across the deserted streets, and he stumbled through them and into the iron arms of a large gate.

He found himself in a park, in front of the dry basin of a fountain. Paths stretched in several directions, lit by ghostly white lights. Ahmed chose one and started walking, past a large stone crucifix soldered to a rock. It made him feel as if he were trespassing, but he reminded himself that the gate was open.

How strange the path was—cobbled in the center, but paved with large flat stones on either edge. Wooden benches lined the path at intervals, tempting Ahmed, but he didn't sit down. To stop moving was to fall asleep, and he couldn't risk someone finding him lying out in the open. As his head drooped, he noticed rows of small holes in some of the big flat stones. The holes were all the same size and ran in neat horizontal lines. They seemed like a code. He wondered what the patterns meant—why some of the stones had the holes and others didn't. It was only as he passed under one of the ghostly white halogen lights that Ahmed noticed letters etched between the holes.

C-A-M-I-L-L-E, he read. Then on the next line, 1848–1877.

Ahmed jumped back. He was standing on a gravestone. The path was paved with gravestones. But he wasn't in a cemetery, was he? He looked around—at the wide grassy lawn, at a basketball court. No, he was definitely in a park. But it was a park where every day people walked over gravestones. Strollers and dogs and children on bikes wore them down till the names disappeared and all that was left were the holes of the chisel, and eventually just smooth, blank stone.

Ahmed sank into a crouch, blinded by tears. He knew it was silly to cry. Life was always taking place over death. But those fading names were his mother and father. They were Jasmine and Nouri. He suddenly realized that the bomb had fallen a year ago tomorrow, March 23. Except it was probably after midnight, which meant it was already tomorrow. And here he was, on the anniversary of their deaths, walking over them, grinding them deeper into dust.

He staggered to his feet, not bothering to wipe the tears that cascaded down his cheeks, but letting them fall on Camille's gravestone. School was gone. Max was gone. His family mattered to no one but himself. They were losers of history, names that would vanish and become anonymous numbers—one of ten thousand dead, a hundred thousand dead, a million. He had become a ghost himself, wandering the night, trying not to frighten anyone. He no longer had the strength to build a new life for himself, especially here in Europe, where he wasn't even wanted.

He looked up at the stars.

"You should have made the bomb fall at night, hitting us all!" he shouted in Arabic.

His voice echoed across the empty park. But he couldn't even stand there, shaking his fist at Allah. He couldn't even be that brave. His cowardly instinct to survive wouldn't let him. At the sound of his own voice—the angry, young Muslim everyone feared—he took off down the gravestone path. He ran till he saw a large wooden globe set high on a mound with several tubes poking off it. A fence surrounded this curious octopus-like structure, and it was only as Ahmed scaled it that he realized it was part of a playground and that the tubes were slides.

Ahmed stormed the rubberized mound and scrambled into the wooden globe through a small opening in its side. It wasn't much of a shelter—not with a draft of cool night air blowing through the opening—but at least no one could see him inside it. As long as he left by morning, when children and their parents would arrive, he was unlikely to be discovered.

He had found a way to stay hidden—at least till morning. But as he curled into a ball and rested his head on his school backpack, Ahmed felt no relief, only a hollow emptiness.

CHAPTER FORTY-SIX

The next morning, just before eight, the doorbell rang. Max ran to the kitchen window, hoping to find Ahmed. But instead Oscar stood outside, a battered racing bike balanced on its kickstand next to Max's.

Max grabbed his coat and backpack and ran to the door. His parents piled into the foyer after him.

"Hello, Madame, Monsieur *How-Weird*," Oscar said. Then he stepped past Max to kiss Max's parents on their cheeks.

Oscar probably had no idea how brilliant a move this was—his parents still weren't completely used to the customary Belgian greeting, and as they blushed and fumbled, Max took the opportunity to shoot out the door and down the steps. He unlocked his bike and nodded to Oscar, who had finished his kiss offensive and hopped back on his own bike.

"Where are you going?" his mother asked.

"We bike to school together," Oscar said matter-of-factly, as if they did this every day.

His mother took a step after them. "Wait, Max, I don't—"

"Oh, let them go. It's just around the block," his father said.

Max didn't wait for the argument he knew was coming. He just pushed off and started pedaling. "See you after school!"

"*Au revoir*," Oscar added.

They raced down the street, past Albert Jonnart's house, before turning onto Rue de Linthout. But at the end of the block, instead of turning right onto Rue Vergote and toward the School of Happiness, Oscar turned left. At the end of the block, he braked by a traffic circle and pulled out his phone. "I told Farah I'd call her as soon as we were together."

"Where is she?" Max asked.

"Home. Her metro is still closed."

"Hi," Oscar said into the phone. "It's me. Max is here."

He pressed Speaker and Farah's voice crackled over the line.

"I have an idea where Ahmed is," she said. "That man, Ibrahim, the one he came here with. If he was in trouble—"

"He'd try to find him!" Max said. "Didn't he have family in Molenbeek?"

"Yes," Farah said. "Ibrahim Malki . . . No, Malaki—that was it!"

Max squeezed the handles of his bike.

"You're in Molenbeek, Farah. Could you find him?"

"Because every Muslim knows every other Muslim? There are tens of thousands of people in Molenbeek!"

"I'll find him," Oscar cut in.

"How?" Max asked.

"I can use one of the computers at the commune to look up

anyone in the city. I'll just tell my mom I started feeling sick on the way to school—she'll let me hang out there."

Max grinned. "Criminal mind," he said in English. Then he switched back to French for Farah. "I'll bike to Molenbeek and find him."

"We'll go together," Farah said. "There are journalists everywhere trying to talk to people, and it's making everyone tense. It's not a good time to be wandering around by yourself. Meet me outside Forum at ten. It's this huge furniture store on Chaussée de Gand, the big shopping street, around the corner from the Place Communale. It used to be an old theater. You can't miss it."

AT A QUARTER TO TEN, Max rode into the Place Communale. After all the talk on the news and from Madame Pauline about Molenbeek being a terrorist training ground, Max was surprised to find a cobblestone square flanked by an elegant town hall with a copper dome and town houses with shops on the ground floors. The shops were a mix of Western (one with the illuminated green cross of a Belgian pharmacy) and Eastern (a shop that sold headscarves and other Muslim women's wear). A few were already open, and others were in the process of opening up. It almost seemed like a normal day save for the news vans parked in the square, satellites perched atop their roofs like huge white ears.

As Max turned the corner onto what Google Maps assured him was Chaussée de Gand, he saw more stores selling chandeliers, rolled-up carpets, lacy curtains, bolts of cloth. Most of the women on the street wore headscarves, and Max noticed that only men seemed to gather at the small cafés, where they drank glasses of steaming hot tea instead of wine or beer. But at the same time, Molenbeek didn't seem quite as foreign—or frightening—as he had imagined. The language Max heard most around him was French, and the curving street and buildings—with their tall windows and gabled roofs—were distinctively Belgian.

Minutes later, he spotted a white building with an enormous red marquee that once must have featured the night's acts but now simply read FORUM in big white letters. Before he had even reached it, Farah ducked out from behind the mattresses and dining sets that spilled out the front entrance and ran over to meet him.

"Oscar called me with the address," she said in French. "It's not far. Come on!"

Farah turned off Chaussée de Gand onto a residential street lined with apartment buildings and town houses. Then she stopped and pointed down a quiet block.

"That's where they caught Salah Abdeslam, the Paris attacker."

Max wasn't sure what he had expected, but it wasn't this, a slightly worn-down but still pretty block with ironwork balconies. He thought about what Madame Pauline had said. "Do you think a lot of the people knew he was here?"

"A few," Farah admitted. "It's hard when young men can't get good jobs and feel there's no place for them here in Belgium.

Some turn to crime and drugs, and there are radical mosques and imams who prey on them. But most people don't get involved in any of this. They just want to be left in peace."

"I'm not sure that's possible for anyone now."

Farah stopped in front of a tall brick apartment building.

"You may be right. But don't tell Ahmed—I'm sure he is frightened enough." She gestured at the building. "This is it."

Like the rest of the apartments they had passed, lacy white curtains covered all the windows. Max noticed a set of buzzers, but it was impossible to tell which apartment to ring since the names of the occupants had been scratched off.

"A lot of people did that after the lockdown," Farah said. "They didn't want the police to bother them."

"I hope Oscar gave you an apartment number," Max said.

"The address just said first floor," Farah said, pressing one of the lower buzzers. No one answered. She tried another.

A man's curt voice crackled over the intercom. "Who's there?" he asked in French.

"My name is Farah. I'm looked for an Iraqi family. Malaki—"

Then she said something in a language that Max guessed was Berber. The man answered her in this language and a few seconds later, the door buzzed open.

They scrambled up a steep, dimly lit stairwell to the first floor. Farah paused on the landing and pointed to a door to the right with an array of shoes laid out carefully beside it. "He said they live here."

Max rushed over and knocked on the door. He heard a bolt

slide and the door creaked open a few inches. A man with a creased, unshaven face peered out, his brown eyes blinking rapidly. It was clear to Max that he had no idea why he was there.

"I'm looking for Ahmed Nasser," Max said in French.

The man opened the door wider and gazed at Max, then Farah. "You know Ahmed?"

"We are friends of his," Farah said. "We mean him or you no trouble. We are simply worried about him and are looking for his friend Ibrahim Malaki."

The man's eyebrow twitched with excitement. "I am Ibrahim Malaki," he said in French. "Come in, children, come."

The warmth in his tone made Max hopeful that Ahmed was inside. He charged toward the door, but Farah grabbed his arm. "Take off your shoes," she said.

Max felt his face color slightly. He slipped off his sneakers and lined them up next to hers. Then they followed Ibrahim down a narrow hall into a room with several small carpets and futons. Max had hoped to find Ahmed sitting there, but the room was empty. Ibrahim called out in a language that Max assumed was Arabic, and a door off the room opened. A woman with shapely dark eyebrows bustled out, trailed by a wide-eyed little girl, and switched on an electric kettle in the corner.

"My wife, Zainab," Ibrahim said. "And my daughter, Bana."

Zainab greeted them with a nod and some Arabic words that Farah repeated back. Then she and Bana vanished behind another closed door, returning a few minutes later with a tray of teacups and flaky honey-and-nut-filled pastries.

"I am glad you come," Ibrahim said in French, settling onto one of the futons and indicating with a wave of his hand that they should do the same as Zainab handed them tea. "I too look for Ahmed."

Max's stomach dropped. "He's not here?"

Ibrahim shook his head. "I do not see him since he leaves me in August. But please tell me how you meet him."

Max sighed heavily—Farah's idea had seemed like such a good one!—but he knew he owed Ibrahim this much. He quickly explained how he'd found Ahmed hiding in his basement, how they'd enrolled him in school, how he'd impressed everyone with his hard work, how they'd become increasingly worried that Inspector Fontaine and Madame Legrand would catch on.

"I think the attacks were too much," Max admitted. "He was frightened. He just ran. But I was hoping he'd come to you or your family."

"I wish he does too," Ibrahim agreed.

Then he said something so extraordinary that Max thought he'd heard him wrong.

"I'm sorry. Can you say that again?" Max asked.

In a slow, clear voice, Ibrahim repeated, "His father is searching for him."

CHAPTER FORTY-SEVEN

The playground was so quiet when Ahmed woke that he figured it was still early in the morning. He sat up slowly, a little stiff, a little cold, but he had long before become accustomed to sleeping in uncomfortable places. It was only when he poked his head out of the wooden globe and looked up at the sun glinting high over the park that he realized it had to be nearly noon. But the playground was empty—there were no parents or grandparents sitting on the benches, no babies wailing from their strollers, no toddlers shouting up the slides or clambering up the mound. Ahmed instantly understood: people were afraid to be out. He had fled thousands of kilometers to escape the war only to find that it wasn't far enough.

Ahmed put on his backpack, then slid down one of the tube slides. He was too big for it, his hair nearly skimmed the top, but in case there was anyone on the other side of the fence, he didn't want to be seen. He had once loved slides—the rush of speed, the uncertainty of the final drop to the asphalt—but now he just felt heavy and had to push himself out at the bottom where the tube flattened out. He was relieved no one was there to see him: a possible terrorist popping out of a slide had to be a Belgian parent's worst nightmare. But it was strange to be alone at a playground on a sunny day, like the last living kid in the world.

What was Max doing now? He would be back at school if it were open. Of course, he'd be terribly worried, but Ahmed tried not to let his guilt bother him. If the police came, Max could honestly say he had no idea where Ahmed was.

Ahmed focused on his plan—he needed to make his way out of the city, perhaps to a larger, wooded park where he could hide until everything calmed down. And then? He tried not to think too far into the future; one step at a time.

His stomach rumbled and he was thankful for the banana and stale baguette he'd squirreled away in his bag. But he only allowed himself a few bites of each. Who knew how long he'd need these provisions to last? Then he scaled the playground wall and zigzagged around the ramps of a skate park until he rejoined the gravestone path. He could see more names in the daylight—*Auguste, Émile, À La Mémoire De Clémence*—but even the bright sun couldn't illuminate the names that were worn down and faded away.

The jingle of a leash made him look up. A small dog trotted over the gravestones, an old woman walking behind him. He knew he should just pass by without making eye contact, but in a flash of panic, he ducked behind a hedge.

Only after he heard the woman's footsteps pass and the

dog's tinkling leash fade did he allow himself to look around. He was in a small square set off the main path. On a pillar in the center was a life-sized statue of a woman with her arm draped around a child. The woman's hair was shorn, and she wore a shapeless dress. The child leaned against her. Ahmed translated the plaque beside them as best he could.

The Ravensbrück Monument . . . to women of the resistance and their children who died in German camps during World War II . . . The child represents the painful memory of loss . . . and the struggle to guard children, hope and the future.

Ahmed scowled at the words. What hope? What future? The women had died; their children too. Nothing was left of them but words hidden in the corner of a park.

And yet, the woman in the statue stared defiantly over Ahmed's head. It was as if she saw something in the distance that Ahmed had failed to imagine or understand. He swiveled around, tried to see it too.

CHAPTER FORTY-EIGHT

"Ahmed!"

Max stood in front of the dry fountain, hoarse from shouting.

On the way back from Molenbeek, he had searched Parc du Cinquantenaire, even peeking into the Great Mosque and the enormous carpeted prayer room. He and Oscar had agreed that it was best to split up the other parks near the house—Oscar, who could get there faster, would go to the larger Parc Woluwe, and Max would ride down Avenue Georges Henri to the smaller Georges Henri park at the bottom of the hill.

Ahmed couldn't have gotten far with all the metros and buses shut down. But what if he had hitched a ride? He wouldn't try that after Ermir, would he? Hopefully Ahmed hadn't been that desperate.

"Ahmed!" Max shouted again.

But the park was empty, save for an old woman walking her dog. She stared at him in an unfriendly way, but Max didn't care.

No one was going to stop him from finding Ahmed, not even Ahmed himself.

"I know you're good at hiding," Max said. "But I'm good at finding."

He left the fountain and jogged along the path of stone slabs.

"Ahmed!" he shouted.

He wasn't giving up.

CHAPTER FORTY-NINE

Ahmed froze. Was someone calling his name? It was probably just a trick of hunger and longing.

But no, there it was—again!

"Ahmed!"

Ahmed ran back out from the memorial to find Max sprinting toward him over the gravestone path. At the sight of Max racing toward him with a loud whoop, he burst into a smile. He couldn't help it. Deep down, he realized, he'd wanted to be found.

Max skidded to a stop in front of him. He was out of breath, panting.

"How did you—?" Ahmed asked.

"Searched different parks . . . But that's not important . . ." Max grabbed his arm. "Your father! He's alive."

Ahmed stared at him. Was this even possible? No, something was lost in translation. He had to be misunderstanding what Max was saying.

"Did you hear me, Ahmed?"

"About my father—?"

"He's alive!"

He shook his head. "This is . . . not possible."

But even as he said this, Ahmed felt a pang of hope.

"Your friend Ibrahim Malaki," Max panted. "He's still in Brussels. Last month, he charged his old phone . . . He found messages from your dad. The coast guard rescued him. He was in the hospital in Turkey for weeks, unconscious. By the time he was able to call, the smuggler must have had your phone. He couldn't reach you, so he left messages for Ibrahim."

Max would never lie; Ibrahim would never lie. It had to be true. Baba was alive!

Ahmed's legs crumpled and he sank onto the gravestone beneath him. Tears rolled down Ahmed's cheeks and splattered against the gravestone.

"He is still in Turkey?"

He looked up, but Max had kneeled beside him.

"No, he's in Europe. He was trying to find you. His last message said he was being arrested and taken to a detention center in Hungary."

The sentence landed like a blow. Of all the places in Europe that his father could have ended up, this was the worst. Hungary was the least welcoming country on the refugee route; Ahmed still remembered the hot, crowded Keleti train station in Budapest and the Hungarian police—how they would lie to refugees about where they were taking them, or even beat them. "Do you know where?"

"Ibrahim told me the name. He said there was also a refugee rights group in Hungary that was trying to help him—"

Ahmed jumped to his feet.

"I must go to this center. Now."

Max was up beside him, his hand on Ahmed's arm. "You can't just go to Hungary. The whole of Europe is on alert."

"But borders is still open?"

"I think so, but that doesn't mean that there won't be police at them now, checking documents."

"I have Belgian ID."

"A forged Belgian ID!"

Max was right. The Schengen Agreement kept borders open between European Union countries, but there would still be heightened security, especially in and out of Belgium. The trip would be incredibly dangerous. But so was the alternative.

"It is no longer safe for me here. Yesterday, after attack, Inspector Fontaine sees me leave school alone. He asks *directrice* questions."

"Is that why you took off?"

Ahmed nodded. "I must go right now."

Max crossed his arms over his chest. "You can't go—"

"Max—"

"Alone."

"You want to go with me?" Ahmed asked, but he already knew the answer. It made him want to hug Max and tell him to forget about it at the same time.

"We'll be less suspicious together. I have real papers and I can do the talking—"

What Max really meant was that having a white, European-looking schoolboy by his side would make Ahmed seem like less of a threat. Ahmed couldn't argue with this, but Max would make the journey riskier in other ways.

"Boy like me, people not worry if he travels alone, but boy like you—"

"In America, maybe, but parents here allow kids to be more independent, especially in groups. My Scout overnight next month doesn't even have adults going, just the leaders, who are, like, sixteen." Max's face brightened. "Hey! I know! We can dress in Scout uniforms, pretend we're going on a trip—no one will suspect anything; everyone loves the *Scoots*!"

"But your family—they will worry. They will call police."

Max took out his phone and began to type. A moment later, he held up the screen so Ahmed could see. "Look, Hungary is fourteen hours by train. We can catch a nine-twenty tomorrow morning to Frankfurt, that's the first leg. I'll pretend to go to school, and by the time anyone even starts to miss me, we'll be halfway to Hungary."

This was the same Max who had come up with a plan to sneak him into the School of Happiness—the same crazy, wonderful, naive, hopeful Max. But Ahmed shook his head. "No. I cannot ask this of you."

"You don't get it, do you?" Max said. He sounded almost angry. "I owe you."

"Owe *me*?"

"My whole life, I've felt so useless. Like I wasn't good at anything. Like all I did was screw up. You made me feel"—Max looked down, his face flushed—"like I could help."

Ahmed smiled. "Boy hero."

"No," Max said quietly. "Just a sidekick to one."

Ahmed couldn't speak, so he looked into the distance, the way the statue had, and concentrated on blinking back tears.

"Come on, Nabil Fawzi," Max said with a grin. "You'll stay with me tonight, in my room. The metro still isn't running. I'll tell my mom you need to sleep over."

"But Fontaine—?" Ahmed managed to choke out.

"He won't figure out where you are that fast, especially with everything else going on. Plus, he already came by once today. I doubt he'll be back."

CHAPTER FIFTY

It was after midnight when Max finally collapsed back onto the inflatable mattress on his bedroom floor. Ahmed was already fast asleep in Max's bed. He had tried to refuse, but Max had insisted: after months on a camping mat on the cold wine-cellar floor—not to mention outside on a playground slide—Ahmed deserved a good night's sleep.

So far their plan had worked perfectly. Max's parents had accepted Ahmed's story—although not for the best reason. Because of the metro shutdown, Madame Pauline was staying over too. His mother had set up a bed for her in the front room of the basement, leaving Max even more relieved that Ahmed wasn't in the wine cellar. While preparing the room, she must have rediscovered the orchids, because Max noticed they were back upstairs, lined up on the kitchen windowsill.

"New orchids?" Max asked.

"No, actually. They're the old ones. I stuck them in the

basement and forgot all about them, but they somehow recovered. Shows how damp it is down there."

When his mother wasn't looking, Max shot Ahmed a grin.

Madame Pauline spent most of the evening railing about terrorists and glaring in Ahmed's direction. But at least this embarrassed his parents into bending over backward to be nice to Ahmed. His mother even made a point of praising Ahmed's work on the garden. Claire ignored them both, avoiding Ahmed as much as possible. Max tried not to let it bother him. They would be out of her hair soon enough.

Max closed his eyes. He knew he needed to get some rest too, but he kept reviewing his checklist: He had locked his bike near the school so they could ride it to the train station. Their schoolbags lay next to them, packed with Scout uniforms, warm jackets and a couple days' worth of sandwiches and snacks. In addition to his birthday and Christmas money, Max had taken a few loose bills that had been lying around the house. They would buy the train tickets at the station—it would have been nice to do it online, where no one could ask questions, but that meant using a credit card and leaving an easily traceable record. He'd found his passport and zipped it carefully in his bag's interior pocket, next to his Belgian ID. He'd set up a new account and sent an email from it to the organization that was helping Ahmed's father in Hungary, telling them about Ahmed. He also had written down the group's emergency hotline number just in case. But after debating the matter with Ahmed, he had decided not to bring his phone. There was too much of a risk that it could be tracked, and he didn't want to deal with frantic calls and messages from his parents anyway. He could always buy a burner phone later. He would leave them a note in the morning.

Max had immediately let Oscar and Farah know that he'd found Ahmed and was taking him home. But he and Ahmed had made one other difficult decision: not to share their plan to find Ahmed's father. Oscar and Farah would figure it out easily enough, but this way, they could honestly say they weren't involved.

Max turned to look at Ahmed. He lay fast asleep, curled into a ball. A pang of fierce, protective love flooded through Max.

"*You'll see your father*," Max whispered. "*I won't let you down.*"

A LOUD BUZZ ripped Max from his dreams. He figured it was his parents' alarm. He kept his eyes shut tight, waiting for them to turn it off. He was still tired. But the ringing continued, urgently.

A hand shook his shoulder. Max turned over on his side. "Alarm," he muttered sleepily. But Ahmed shook him harder.

"Max, wake up! Doorbell!"

Max sat up fast, looked at his phone. It was 5:55. He could hear heavy footsteps, his father's, on the stairs.

"Stay here," he said to Ahmed. Then he ran downstairs, swerving around his mother, who was pulling on her robe on the landing, and catching up to his dad in the foyer. He wore a T-shirt and a pair of rumpled pants that he'd clearly just pulled on.

"Who is it?" Max asked.

His father shrugged. "I have no idea."

"Check before you open it!" his mother called after them.

Max ran to the kitchen window. Inspector Fontaine was pounding on the door, two police officers behind him.

"Don't open it!" Max shouted.

His father rushed into the kitchen and looked out the window.

"Max! What are you talking about?" his father said as he hurried back to the door. "It's the police."

Max raced after him, but he was already opening the door. Inspector Fontaine barged into the foyer, forcing Max and his dad backward as the other officers followed him inside.

"I'm sorry, *Monsieur How-Weird*, but I must see the wine cellar. Immediately."

"Excuse me?" his father said.

"We have become aware of an illegal, *Monsieur*."

Stay calm, Max told himself. But he felt like he couldn't breathe. Fontaine seemed so certain, like someone had told him . . .

His mother joined them. "What's going on—?"

Fontaine marched down the hall toward the basement door, the two policemen following behind him. Max's parents exchanged confused glances, then hurried after them.

The moment they were out of sight, Max raced upstairs. But as he rounded the second bend, he nearly collided with Claire.

She drew back, her face red.

"You!" he hissed.

"I told you to end it, but you wouldn't listen! Ahmed seems nice but . . . you don't really know him!"

"No!" he shouted. "I don't really know *you!*"

The basement door banged open, and Fontaine and the two officers ran into the hall.

"He's upstairs!" Madame Pauline shouted after them.

Max took the stairs two and three at a time. There was one more reason why he had insisted Ahmed sleep in his room. Albert Jonnart had taught him something else: the importance of always having a back-up plan.

"*Mex! Mex How-Weird!* You do not understand . . . This boy is dangerous!"

Max didn't stop to look back.

He tore into his room, slammed the door behind him.

"Ahmed, go!"

Then he grabbed the bags and raced to the window. Ahmed followed him without a word. Max opened the window.

If Ralph could do it, so could Ahmed.

And so could he.

"Go!" he whispered.

Ahmed scrambled over the safety gate and onto the roof. Max hurtled after him. But just as he cleared it, a strong tug yanked him back.

CHAPTER FIFTY-ONE

Ahmed was about to jump down onto the next roof when he heard Max cry out. He was certain that Fontaine must have grabbed him. Ahmed's every instinct told him to keep going. There was still a chance he could escape. Max's idea was a good one. The back roofs of the houses were connected; only the simplest of barriers stood in the way—low cement walls, skylights, slight differences of height that demanded stepping up a couple of feet or jumping down.

Instead, he turned around.

The strap of Max's bag had caught on the guardrail. Ahmed raced over to him, reached around and freed it just as Fontaine ran into the room.

"Stop!" Fontaine shouted in French. "We know who the gardener is!"

"What is he talking about?" Max asked Ahmed.

"I have no idea."

Ahmed ran to the side of the roof, pulling Max along with

him. They jumped together and landed on a skylight, nearly slipping on the slimy moss that coated the glass. Ahmed scrambled onto the roof of the neighboring house, then squatted to pull Max up after him. In the center of this roof were two large skylights. This time, Ahmed knew to avoid them and hug the wall of the house. A large brick chimney momentarily blocked his view of Fontaine, but he could still hear the police officer shouting.

"*Mex*, the counterterror police intercepted a message about 'Ahmed the Gardener,' the Syrian who 'fixed the flowerpots.' We think he makes bombs."

The dawn raid made sense now. Fontaine thought he was a terrorist, a bomb builder! This was far worse than just being an illegal; he would be jailed, interrogated, perhaps even beaten. But as frightening as this was, one thought frightened him even more: what if Max didn't believe he was innocent?

Ahmed turned to him. "This Ahmed not me!"

Max stared straight back at him. He seemed to be looking deep into him, into the Ahmed he knew from a hundred late nights. Max spoke quietly, but his voice didn't waver.

"I know."

There was no time to reply, no words anyway that could capture the joy Ahmed felt, even in the middle of a disaster. Ahmed just grabbed Max's hand and squeezed.

Fontaine appeared at the edge of Max's roof.

"*Mex*, don't be an idiot!"

"Jump!" Ahmed said.

Together, they jumped onto the next, lower roof. But the

height between roofs was greater than they'd anticipated, and they flailed through empty air before landing hard on their knees.

"You okay?" Ahmed asked, pulling Max back to his feet.

Max nodded, wincing. "Down. Where do we get down?"

"Next house is open on side, not connect," Ahmed said, grateful that he'd made his study of all the gardens and the easiest ways to slip out onto the street.

But to reach the last roof, they would have to scale a privacy wall that separated it from the one they were on. With Fontaine charging after them, would they have the time? The only other way across was to hold on to the end of the wall and reach a leg across the abyss to the ledge of the next roof. If they fell, it would be a direct drop to the ground, three stories below.

Ahmed could tell that Max had figured this out as well from the sheen of sweat on his pale face. Ahmed gave him a questioning look, but Max just nodded.

"Go."

Ahmed gripped the wall on both sides, then swung out a leg. He tried not to think about the empty air as he felt for the ledge. The front of his sneaker finally tapped against it, but only when he had his heel down did he shift his weight and swing his other across.

"Your turn!" Ahmed said.

Max's hand crept around the wall.

"Now leg!"

Max swung out his leg.

"*Mex!* Don't be an idiot! You'll kill yourself!" Fontaine shouted.

Max's leg trembled.

"I can't do this!"

Ahmed put his hand over Max's.

"I got you," Ahmed said. "You won't fall."

Max's foot touched down on the other side. Ahmed grabbed him and pulled him away from the edge. They could hear footsteps on the other side.

"*Mex!*"

"Quick!" Ahmed said, pulling him across the roof. "We need down."

"Go to the street!" Fontaine shouted back to the other officers.

Fontaine's hand reached around the wall. His brown leather shoe snaked around, looking for the ledge.

"How?" Max asked.

Ahmed was already clambering down over the edge. "Drain."

He hugged the drainpipe with his knees, then grabbed it in his hands. "Step on my shoulder!"

Max placed his feet on Ahmed's shoulders. Then Max let go of the aluminum siding of the roof and grabbed onto the drainpipe. Together they half shimmied, half slid down it. At the bottom, they jumped off onto a pebbly driveway.

They looked up to see Inspector Fontaine peering at them from the roof. "They're coming down near number forty-four!" he shouted into his radio.

Ahmed pulled Max into the backyard of the next house. They dashed around a trampoline, ignoring the barking of a dog. Lights turned on inside.

"They're heading toward fifty!" Fontaine shouted into his radio.

"Albert Jonnart!" Max panted.

Ahmed thought he understood. The officers were on Albert Jonnart, but if they could make it to Rue Vergote, where Max's bike was—

Ahmed swerved into a thicket of trees and bushes next to number fifty. He dragged Max through it till they reached a wall. In a single fluid motion, Ahmed hoisted Max over. Then he threw his backpack across and scrambled over after him. He fell to the other side and rolled onto the grass. Max had already scooped up his bag, and he yanked Ahmed to his feet. They could still hear Fontaine shouting into his radio, "One of you needs to get to Vergote. Rue Vergote, you idiots!"

Ahmed led the way through the yard, around the side of the house and out onto the street. Max ran to his bike, locked to a signpost. He pulled the key out of his backpack and fumbled with the lock. But he couldn't seem to get it open.

One of the police officers rounded the corner.

Max jiggled the key, then turned it.

"Hurry!" Ahmed said.

The lock popped open.

The police officer was running toward them, shouting.

Ahmed straddled the seat. He was relieved they'd ridden together before, knew exactly how to balance their bodies. Max threw his leg over the bar. Ahmed looked back—the police officer was only a few yards behind them, his arms outstretched, ready to grab him.

"Go, Max! Go!"

Max slammed his foot on the pedal. Ahmed nearly toppled backward as they shot forward, but he somehow managed to hold on to Max's shifting shoulders as the bike accelerated. Behind him, he heard the police officer mutter a defeated curse.

CHAPTER FIFTY-TWO

Halfway to the train station, Max locked his bike at a crowded public rack near the metro, hoping to throw off the police. It was after seven now, and bikes and cars jammed the streets; two days after the attacks, people were back at work and school, but parts of the metro were still closed, and Max had a feeling that many people were still too afraid to take public transportation. In the bathroom of a Starbucks, he and Ahmed changed into the Scout uniforms, then continued to Bruxelles-Midi station on foot. It was a slow trip; they had to keep changing their route to avoid the soldiers and police who patrolled outside the metro entrances, shopping centers and government buildings.

But there was no avoiding them once they reached the station. Camouflage army trucks encircled Bruxelles-Midi, and a long line of passengers waited in front of the central entrance, which was flanked by soldiers with assault rifles.

"What's going on?" Max asked a man in a business suit scrolling through his phone at the end of the line.

The man barely looked up.

"Security checks, delays. What a nightmare!"

The man's phone rang. "I'm trying to rent a car to drive down to Paris," he barked into it.

Max's chest tightened. What if they couldn't get out of Brussels? The train station was practically on lockdown. Max looked at Ahmed's watch. "Our train is supposed to leave in thirty minutes. We may not have time to buy tickets. And if they're checking IDs—"

Max didn't finish his thought, but he knew that Ahmed understood where he was going with it. Fontaine had likely alerted the entire security force to a Syrian boy terrorist and his American accomplice on the loose. But hopefully they wouldn't be looking for Scouts. And there was also a chance that the security forces at the station hadn't received the alert. Max remembered what Madame Pauline had said about the police—how with nineteen different forces, they were notoriously bad at sharing information.

Ahmed grabbed Max's sleeve and pointed to a small group of people waving tickets in the air. "Look. I think people selling their tickets. If we buy from them, we need not show ID."

"Good idea! Keep our place, and I'll check it out."

Max ran to where he could hear what the ticket sellers were saying:

"One Thalys ticket to Paris!"

"Three tickets to Aachen."

"Two ICE to Cologne."

The high-speed Intercity Express train to Cologne continued

on to Frankfurt. Max focused in on the seller. He was an old man, standing beside a gray-haired woman Max guessed was his wife.

"I'll buy them!"

The old man looked Max over. Max had the uncomfortable feeling that he was trying to figure out how old he was. He braced for a bunch of nosy questions. But the man merely handed him the tickets.

"Free to a *Scoot* and his mom," he said in French. "Or is it dad?"

"Dad," Max mumbled. "Thanks."

"Tell him you're welcome. And have a good trip."

As soon as the old man and his wife left, Max rejoined Ahmed in line and showed him the tickets.

"We might actually make it out of here after all."

Ahmed flashed a tense smile. "If we get through soldiers."

As he and Ahmed shuffled closer to the entrance, Max could see the soldiers pulling passengers out of the line and asking to see their ticket or ID or both. He hunched down and smiled, trying to look as innocent as possible. But when they reached the entrance, a hand instantly grabbed Max's shoulder and pulled him to the side. Max found himself standing in front of a tall soldier bulked up by a bulletproof vest. He yanked Ahmed out of the crowd too.

"Where are you boys going?" he demanded in French.

"*Scoot* trip," Max said. "Our group's already inside. We're late."

The soldier took in their faces. Max was certain he was putting it all together—how one of them looked Middle Eastern and the other was white, how Max spoke with an American accent, how they were traveling alone. He had to do something to distract the soldier before he demanded their IDs, something that would convince him they were just harmless Scouts.

Max began to sing.

"Scoot from elsewhere, Scoot from here,
You are my brother, my friend,
For today, for tomorrow—"

Ahmed mouthed along, pretending to know the song. But the soldier was too busy staring at Max in surprise to notice.

Then, with a self-conscious chuckle, he joined in.

"All united in a common project
Of justice, respect,
Home and fraternity."

The soldier gave them the three-fingered Scout salute.

"Hurry up, boys. Not good to be late, today especially."

Max forced himself to smile in *Scoot* solidarity. But his legs felt numb as they rushed away.

"Good idea, the Scouts," Ahmed murmured when they were out of earshot.

They were in, tickets in hand, with ten minutes to departure! But Max knew they couldn't relax till they were on the train and the train was on its way out of Belgium. He stopped in front of one of the electronic monitors inside the station. "Looks like we're boarding on platform 21."

This meant walking to the other end of the station, past more soldiers and police officers with Malinois, the Belgian police dogs that were more compact versions of German shepherds. The dogs' mouths hung open, revealing sharp teeth. Max could feel the officers' eyes pass over them. He made sure to talk to Ahmed in a friendly, animated way, even to link arms—to demonstrate that he was harmless. Ahmed seemed to understand; he grinned at Max and pretended not to notice the guns and dogs. But Max knew, from the way he tightened his grip on Max's arm, that he did.

By the time they reached the gate to platform 21, Max's Scout uniform was damp with sweat. But all they had to do now was board.

The sleek high-speed train was already filling up, mostly with business travelers to Cologne, men and women in suits stowing their briefcases and raincoats above. The sounds of people talking in French and German into cell phones filled the train car; several people talked about the attacks or remarked on the crowds and security. But to Max's relief, no one seemed to take any notice of two boys in Scout uniforms as they slumped in their seats and took out their books. Still, Max was only pretending to read *Boy Heroes*; his stomach clenched as he waited for the train to depart. Ahmed's eyes also kept flickering away from *The Calculus Affair* to the window, as if he expected one of the police officers or soldiers to come running down the platform and drag them off the train.

A mechanical chime rang out; with a jerk, the train began

to move and pulled out of the station. Max took a deep breath, resting his head against the window. The train rocked back and forth, picking up speed; electric transformers whirled by and the colorful town houses of Brussels flew past, jumbled unevenly against the horizon like in one of Magritte's crazy pictures. The feeling of needing to get away from Brussels receded, and Max was filled instead with affection for the strange, mixed-up city of languages and people that had become his home. He wished he could tell his parents that they had made the right decision to bring him here, that he would be okay, not just over the next several days, but in the future they always seemed so worried about.

He guiltily realized he had never left them a note. He instinctively reached into his pocket for his phone, then remembered he hadn't brought it. It was just as well. Surely they wouldn't believe Fontaine's crazy claim that Ahmed was a terrorist, but they would still be furious with Max for lying to them and running away. As for Claire, he certainly wasn't going to make her life any easier by checking in. He *hoped* she felt terrible. But knowing her, she was probably too busy pretending she'd known nothing about Ahmed and that Max was the family screwup.

"Max," Ahmed whispered.

Ahmed had swiveled around to stare down the aisle. Max followed his gaze. A burly, black-clad police officer with an assault rifle slung over his chest had entered the car and was checking documents. Max slid back down in his seat and looked at Ahmed. They were in serious trouble.

CHAPTER FIFTY-THREE

There was only one place to hide on a train. Ahmed stood up, grabbing his backpack, and waved Max after him. Then, as calmly as he could and without looking back, he walked down the aisle. He wasn't sure what he would do if the police officer called after them, and he tried not to think about the man's rifle. Hopefully, all he would see, if he noticed them at all, were the backs of two Scouts, heading to the café.

Ahmed pressed the electronic panel on the door that separated their car from the next. It slid open and he continued through a vestibule into the next car. At the far end was a sign for the toilets. Ahmed was relieved to find one unoccupied. He slid open the door, cocking his head at Max to follow.

They squeezed in together and locked the door. A light automatically switched on, casting a greenish glow over their faces. The only place to sit was the toilet, so they both stood. Ahmed could smell antiseptic soap and urine.

"If there is knock, you answer," he whispered to Max. Then he put his finger to his lips.

Max nodded. He seemed to understand the plan—that if the police officer knocked, he would pretend he was the only one there.

There was nothing to do but wait. Ahmed had no idea how long it would take for the police officer to make his way through their car, then the next. He leaned against the wall, closed his eyes and prayed. Ahmed remembered that Max didn't even believe in God, but that seemed like all the more reason to include his friend in his prayers.

There was a knock on the door, then a rattle as someone tried to yank it open. Ahmed wedged himself as far back as he could.

"It's occupied!" Max called out in French.

"Pardon," a woman's voice replied.

Ahmed exhaled, closed his eyes.

The minutes ticked by. Footsteps passed. Ahmed listened, wishing he could tell whether any of them belonged to the police officer. What if the woman told the conductor that someone was staying in the bathroom for a suspiciously long time? Survival didn't always come down to bravery or smarts; sometimes it was just luck in deciding between bad choices.

Ahmed caught Max's eye.

"Unlock door, go out. If you see police, come back like you feel ill."

Max undid the latch and pushed open the door. But he'd

hardly taken a step out when he turned around and held open the door.

Ahmed expected to see the police officer standing there, but instead an older man pushed past them into the bathroom. He scowled at Ahmed, but it seemed less out of suspicion than out of impatience. The police officer was nowhere in sight.

They returned to their seats and opened their books, trying to draw as little attention to themselves as possible. Ahmed hoped that the police officer would not be back—one pass through the train seemed plenty—but after the terror attacks and with a suspect still on the loose, he couldn't be sure. He distracted himself by thinking about his father. Every time Ahmed pictured him, his stomach fluttered with excitement. He imagined running into Baba's arms, telling him everything that had happened over the past nine months. He wasn't sure he could bear to wait even one more day.

The train hardly seemed to move, but finally, a half hour later, it pulled into a station.

"Look!" Max whispered.

Ahmed peered out the window just in time to see the Belgian police officer trot down the platform toward the station.

"Where's he going?" Max asked.

Ahmed spotted the horizontal black, red and gold stripes of the flag waving over the station and burst into a smile.

"Back to Belgium."

They had made it across the German border.

CHAPTER FIFTY-FOUR

In Cologne, they transferred to another train. Just over an hour later, it pulled into the glass atrium of Frankfurt Central Station. Ahmed turned to Max.

"You have been to Frankfurt?"

Max shook his head. "Never. You?"

"In August, on special train for refugees," Ahmed said. "The people are kind. When we come off train, they clap hands like we are heroes. They have balloons. They give us bags of food."

"It's weird how Germans used to be the bad guys," Max said. "And now they're the good ones."

Ahmed shrugged. "Maybe they learn."

There was no reception of welcoming locals, no snacks or balloons, but the moment he stepped off the train, Max decided that Frankfurt station offered something even better. The station was enormous. With more than a hundred tracks and five departure halls, it was easy enough to disappear into the shifting midday mass of travelers, beggars and railroad employees.

Although a few police officers stood around with assault rifles, everyone seemed less tense than in Brussels. There were no soldiers or random ID checks or dogs.

But they still had to buy tickets for the next leg, to Vienna. The ticket seller, a young guy with a hipster beard, gave them a curious look.

"American?" he asked in English.

"Yeah," Max said.

The ticket seller smiled as if this confirmed some suspicion. Max pictured a police bulletin in front of him—"Wanted: American boy, traveling with Syrian suspect—" He sucked in a breath. But before he could decide whether to grab Ahmed's hand and run for it, the man pushed two tickets across the counter to Max.

"I was in New York last year."

"Cool," Max managed to choke out as he snatched up the tickets.

"Have a good trip."

"You too," Max said.

Ahmed grinned as they walked away. "He doesn't go anywhere."

"Shut up. That felt like a close one."

"For Clark Kent. Not Nabil Fawzi."

Max rammed his shoulder. Ahmed rammed him back. Then they bought fries and Cokes at a McDonald's. There was nothing suspicious about hanging out there—the place was packed with kids. At 1:45, they boarded the train to Vienna. Max read for a while, then fell asleep.

He woke up queasy from the greasy fries and a nightmare he couldn't quite remember. It was twilight outside, fields and homes shape-shifting into silhouette, and as his eyes adjusted to the overhead lights, he had no idea where he was. Then he remembered his dream and twisted around to check for Ahmed. He was still sitting beside him, *The Calculus Affair* propped in his lap. He stared at Max with concern.

"You okay?"

"I dreamed they took you away."

Max didn't say who "they" were, and Ahmed didn't ask.

"I am here," he said.

Max took a deep breath and propped himself up. "Where are we?"

"Austria. Soon to Vienna."

Max rubbed his eyes. "I slept a long time. What have you been doing?"

"Read, think."

"About your dad?"

Ahmed nodded.

"You'll see him soon."

Ahmed's dark eyes crinkled. He looked even happier than he had the morning Max had walked him into school.

"Also, I wonder something. When Fontaine comes, how you know to run over roofs? You have this plan?"

Max smiled. "No. Not me."

Ahmed's brow wrinkled. "Who then?"

"Monsieur Jonnart."

"Jonnart, like our street?"

Max realized that he'd never told Ahmed about Albert Jonnart. The story had seemed too depressing, especially when he'd thought that the Nazis caught Ralph. But now he wanted Ahmed to know how history had saved them.

"The street was named for him after the war," Max explained. "In 1942, he—"

As he launched into the story, the world outside vanished into the soft, spring night. It was almost as if they were being transported back in time, as if three-quarters of a century was no more than the blink of an eye.

CHAPTER FIFTY-FIVE

Luck, Ahmed felt, was with them. With minutes to spare, they'd caught the last train of the night from Vienna to Budapest and had even found seats together in the second car. In just two and a half hours, they would arrive in the Hungarian capital. But now, as he sat next to Max, he knew that this luck had a name—Albert Jonnart—and that it wasn't just luck, but kindness. He thought about the boy, Ralph, who had lost both his parents, who'd had to start life over after the war. Ahmed knew he must have been wracked by guilt and despair, just as Ahmed himself had been. Ahmed hoped Ralph had found peace.

There was nothing to look at anymore—the world outside the illuminated train car was dark and seamless. Borders and boundaries were invisible now, and across them Ahmed imagined the flow of millions of feelings: of hope and longing and love. He thought of his mother, of Jasmine and Nouri. Perhaps death was just another border, a line his body couldn't cross but that his heart kept slipping over.

The train slowed down, distracting him from his thoughts. Max noticed as well and looked up from his book.

"The border?"

Ahmed looked at his watch. It had been forty-five minutes since the train had pulled out of the station in Vienna. He remembered that the Hungarian border was not very far.

"I think."

The train pulled up to a deserted platform and idled there.

"What are we waiting for?" Max whispered.

"I do not know."

Ahmed shifted in his seat, his hands clammy. Last August, as he'd held Bana on his lap, stuffed onto a train full of refugees heading in the opposite direction, he'd sworn he would never step foot into Hungary ever again. He remembered how the police had pushed men carrying children, detained families for hours without water and later thrown bags of food at their faces. The message had been clear: that they were pests, animals, not people. But then he thought about how his father had leapt into the sea to save him.

"Look," Max whispered, pointing out the window at a group of uniformed conductors walking down the platform. "I think they're switching the crew."

A few minutes later, there was an announcement in Hungarian and German. Ahmed understood neither language, only the German word *willkommen*, which meant welcome. He knew he wasn't welcome in Hungary no matter what the conductor said, but at least he and Baba were finally in the same country. The train jerked forward.

"I guess that was just a normal stop," Max whispered.

"Yes," Ahmed agreed. But nothing seemed normal now that they were in Hungary. Every noise, every shadow, every station seemed to pose a threat.

Max checked Ahmed's watch.

"I don't know how late the local trains run. We may have to stay in Budapest tonight, then take the first train to Kiskunhalas in the morning. The detention center is less than three kilometers from the train station, so we can just walk there."

Ahmed shuddered at the memory of being marooned in Keleti, the Budapest train station. There hadn't been enough trains for all the refugees, so they'd camped out on the platforms with hundreds of others. He remembered hearing that mothers were bathing their children in the bathroom sinks and that smugglers offered taxi rides to the border in exchange for people's life savings. He remembered seeing the desperate crowd—even old people and pregnant women—rushing the trains when they arrived. But at least Ahmed had explored the station in his search for water and food and knew it well. "I spend two days in this train station the last summer. I know places to hide up to morning."

Max smiled. "I'm not worried. If there's anyone who's good at hiding, it's you."

Ahmed found himself on the verge of laughter, the silly kind that strikes during a nervous time. "This *is* my great talent."

"Don't sell yourself short," Max said. "You're also good at running."

"Ha," Ahmed said.

But before he could think up a better comeback, the door to their car opened. A conductor in a blue uniform and cap with a black purse slung over his shoulder strode in and started checking tickets.

"They already did this," Max whispered.

"In Austria," Ahmed whispered back. "They must do again in Hungary."

As the conductor neared them, Ahmed shrank down in his seat and stared out the window. He didn't even look when Max handed the man their tickets, hoping the conductor would just peer at the tickets and ignore him, as the Austrian conductor had done. But he could hear the conductor address Max in Hungarian.

"English?" he heard Max ask.

"Where are you coming from?" the conductor said.

"Vienna."

"Alone? Without parents?"

Ahmed didn't like the question, but it was nighttime now, and traveling alone seemed more suspicious.

"We're going on a Scout exchange," Max said.

"You and—"

"My friend."

Ahmed turned and smiled as pleasantly as he could. The conductor stared at him.

"You have ID?"

Without a word, Ahmed handed the conductor his Belgian ID. He barely glanced at it.

"Passport?"

"He doesn't need a passport," Max said. "He's traveling within the European Union."

"Are you his lawyer?" the conductor snapped.

"No, but—"

"I have passport," Ahmed cut in, holding up the forgery.

The conductor glanced at the eagle and shield emblazoned on the front, then waved it away. "Is someone meeting you in Budapest?"

"Yes," Max said. "Our scout leader."

The conductor nodded and handed back their tickets, then continued down the aisle.

"He not like us," Ahmed whispered as soon as he was out of earshot.

"But he didn't stop us either," Max said. "He just wanted to give us a hard time."

Ahmed elbowed him to be quiet. The conductor was walking back past them to the front of the car. Ahmed noticed him glancing in their direction before the door shut behind him.

"I hope you are right."

The train slowed down, stopped at a station. The doors sprang open, and Ahmed had a sudden urge to grab Max's hand and run out. But this was the last train of the night, and he had no idea where they were.

The doors closed and the train pulled away. Seconds ticked into minutes. The lights in the train flickered, then the ring of a mobile phone pierced the silence, startling Ahmed. An announcement crackled over the intercom; some passengers started packing up their computers and fetching jackets and bags from the overhead rack. They were approaching the next station.

The train slowed and people moved into the aisles, anticipating the stop. Ahmed watched them open the door and move into the vestibule.

All of a sudden, the line jammed and people backed up. The conductor pushed past them through the door and pointed in Max and Ahmed's direction. Behind him, Ahmed saw the crimson beret of a Hungarian police officer.

Ahmed jumped to his feet and pushed Max into the aisle.

"Back, go back!"

Max gave a quick glance behind him, then turned around and ran. Ahmed grabbed their bags and raced after him.

"Stop!" voices shouted.

But Ahmed kept running. At the end of the car, he reached around Max and slammed his palm against the electric panel that opened the door. The door flew open and they scrambled into a packed vestibule. Ahmed's first thought was that they would be trapped here, but Max was small enough to slip through the gaps between people, and Ahmed elbowed his way after him. They sprinted into the next car, weaving around the passengers blocking the aisles. Ahmed glanced behind him and saw that it wasn't so easy for the officer and conductor, who were larger and needed more room to pass.

"How do we get off?" Max asked as they shoved their way across the next vestibule.

"Station soon. Just keep going!"

The train was continuing to slow down. But what if they reached the last car before the train reached the station?

Ahmed glanced out the window. There was the beginning of a platform, yellow station lights, a long, rectangular building that he guessed was a station. The train was creeping now. They could stay ahead of the police; they just needed a few more cars. But an overweight man completely blocked the next aisle.

"Seats!" Ahmed said.

They vaulted over the empty seats on either side of the man, then continued to run. Ahmed could hear the police officer shouting, presumably for the man to move. The train inched forward. Any moment it would stop and the doors would open. Outside, it was dark; they could find someplace to hide.

But just as he was thinking this, Max stopped short and Ahmed nearly crashed into him.

Ahmed didn't have to ask what the matter was. He just looked up. The door at the end of the car was marked with a large red circle with a white line cutting through the middle. It was an international symbol, one Ahmed knew well, one that seemed to symbolize his entire life: No Entry.

CHAPTER FIFTY-SIX

Max froze. They were cornered, trapped. But it was only in that panicked instant, when he'd stopped moving, when he was standing absolutely still, that he realized the train wasn't moving anymore either.

He spun around and pushed Ahmed back toward the vestibule. A blast of cold air gave him hope. He could tell that Ahmed felt it too. Ahmed grabbed Max's hand, and they burst into the vestibule toward the open door.

But just then, the policeman ran in from the other car, shouting at the group of passengers waiting to disembark who stood between them. Frightened, the passengers moved in an uncoordinated way—some to the side, some backward, some toward the door. In the chaos, Max and Ahmed shoved past them and leapt out the door and onto the platform.

Holding tight to Ahmed's hand, Max landed on his feet. His ankles throbbed with the shock of the concrete, but he immediately began running. They raced down a staircase, through an underpass and into a station. Ahmed was running so fast that Max felt his arm being pulled in the socket. He worried it would either rip off or he would trip and his legs would fly out from under him. But the policeman's shouts behind them made him determined to keep up. Max hardly took note of the station or the staring faces as he tried to ignore the burning in his legs.

The station wasn't large—a minute later, Ahmed rammed open a door and they were back outside. He paused just long enough for Max to take in a darkened square surrounded by gabled stone buildings before he pulled Max across the street toward it.

They kept close to the silhouettes of trees as they ran, trying to stay away from the beam of the flashlight that was following them. Max was afraid they would be trapped again, but Ahmed pointed to an opening between two buildings. He pulled Max through it onto the sidewalk of the next block. Max hoped they might rest a moment, but Ahmed didn't even stop to check if the cop was still behind him. Dragging Max along, he raced past an enormous illuminated building with a clock tower and spires—a town hall perhaps, or a courthouse, but not a place to hide.

"Park," Ahmed gasped.

Looking up, Max realized where Ahmed was heading: a dark cluster of trees that seemed to stretch for several blocks. With his last remaining energy, he sprinted toward the park. Seconds later, they plunged into its shadows. Ahmed kept running, but Max tripped on the uneven ground. He landed on wet grass and lay there.

Ahmed stood over him. But he didn't urge him up, and from the way his chest was heaving, Max could tell he didn't have it in him to run much farther either. He crouched down and pointed to a clump of bushes.

"Behind."

Then he pulled Max to his feet and the two of them stumbled to the bushes and crawled beneath them.

The only sound was their own labored breathing, so loud that Max was sure that anyone passing the bush would hear it. Every muscle in his body ached and he realized, as the wet grass soaked into his shirt, that he had forgotten his coat on the train. Ahmed had noticed as well, because he took off his jacket and spread it over both of them.

A few minutes passed. Then, on the other side of the bush, they heard voices, footsteps. The smell of cigarette smoke tickled Max's throat. He tried to work up spit in his dry mouth to soothe the cough he felt building. But when he finally had enough to swallow, he heard a loud gulp in his eardrums and worried it echoed out into the park.

Gradually, the park became quiet. The clock tower bell tolled.

"What now?" Max whispered. "We stay here till morning, then get back on the train?"

Ahmed had closed his eyes—as if not seeing himself could make him more invisible—but now he opened them. Max was struck by how sad and defeated he looked. Hadn't they just escaped the police?

"No more train."

"You sure they'll be looking for us?"

Ahmed nodded.

"Maybe there's a bus—?"

Ahmed frowned. "Bus, train, taxi—policc look for us now on all."

"So what are we going to do?"

"Walk back to Austria border. Try to cross on foot."

"What about your father?"

"Max, they look for us now."

Max scrambled up to his elbows.

"There's got to be a way to get there. Someone who could drive us—"

"No smuggler!"

Max couldn't blame Ahmed for rejecting the idea after what had happened in Brussels. He fell silent, thinking. It was ridiculous to get this far and give up. He thought of Albert Jonnart and Ralph. What would they have done? He had no idea. As far as Max knew, they'd never been in Hungary. But Ralph had been in a country where the authorities were hostile to him. And he'd survived, not because he'd paid anyone to help him, but because, even in the darkest times and places, there were always good people, people who would help others out of the kindness of their hearts.

Max grabbed Ahmed's arm.

"I know what to do! But we need an Internet connection."

CHAPTER FIFTY-SEVEN

Just after the hand of the Seamaster struck one, a car pulled up next to the park and flashed its headlights three times.

"That's him," Max said.

Ahmed jumped down from the bow of the wooden pirate ship they had stumbled upon in a playground. It had been a perfect lookout, allowing them to see out to the street but also to duck behind the hull when they heard voices or passersby. He felt exposed as he crossed the sand, and he couldn't help but imagine Ermir as he followed Max to the little white two-door. But he told himself that this driver would be different.

Max reached the car first and opened the passenger-side door. Ahmed froze, startled by the person inside. The driver was not the man he had imagined, but a pretty young woman in a red coat, her shoulder-length dark hair streaked with blond.

"Come in quick," she said in English. "Ahmed in back."

Max folded the seat forward and moved to the side. Ahmed

climbed in. The car was warm inside and a wool blanket was folded on the seat next to him.

"You can sit in front," the driver said to Max. "You are less suspicious."

Max folded the seat back up, climbed in and closed the door. Ahmed wrapped the blanket around him. He wondered if he should lie down beneath it so anyone looking into the car would see only two heads—Max's and the driver's.

The woman swiveled around so she was facing them both. "I'm Reka. Daniel says you're going to Kiskunhalas?"

"Yes," Ahmed said. "To find my father."

It had been Max's idea to contact the refugee rights group that was helping Ahmed's father. After a short search, they'd found a hotel close to the park with a business center. Ahmed had waited outside—keeping watch for the police—while Max had played the part of the American tourist, greeting the night clerk in English and mentioning his parents upstairs as he sauntered in to use a computer. By messaging the emergency hotline of the refugee rights group, Max had been able to reach the coordinator, Daniel, who'd promised to send help. Max had already sent him a message back in Brussels, so their request didn't come as a complete surprise.

Reka shifted the car into drive and pulled back onto the street. "Kiskunhalas is about two and a half hours away. When we get there, you can stay in a friend's flat."

"Thank you," Ahmed said.

Reka shrugged as if driving two underage fugitives through Hungary in the middle of the night was hardly a big deal. "No one will bother us so late. You can rest, sleep. There are sandwiches and Cokes in the bag at your feet."

Ahmed's memories of Ermir faded as he took a cheese sandwich and a Coke out of the bag, then passed it to Max. He was hungry now, and he guessed Max felt the same—relief reminded him of the empty stomach he had ignored. Reka played some English music on the car stereo, but when they were finished eating, she suddenly turned it off.

"I hope you don't mind my asking what's your plan."

Ahmed was caught off guard, even though he knew he shouldn't have been. She had every right to ask.

"We were going to go to the center in the morning and ask if Ahmed could visit his father," Max said.

In the rearview mirror, Ahmed noticed Reka smiling the way adults do when they think kids don't know how the world really works. Ahmed might once have smiled that way too. But Reka didn't know how many of Max's crazy schemes had actually worked.

"You know that Hungary closed its borders to refugees last fall and is arresting anyone who crosses into the country illegally. What if they try to take Ahmed into custody?" she asked.

"I have Belgian ID," Ahmed said.

He didn't mention it was a fake, and neither did Max.

"That's worth something," Reka admitted. "But how old are you boys?"

Reka laughed at their silence.

"Okay, you don't have to tell me. But you're young enough that you can't just walk into the reception center at Kiskunhalas by yourselves without raising questions. You need an adult with you, if only to make sure they respect Ahmed's documents."

Ahmed knew she was right. Getting to Kiskunhalas had been hard enough; because of that, they hadn't quite thought through what they would do when they got there.

"Can you help us?" he asked.

"I'm glad you asked, because the only way I will let you go there is with me. In the morning, we'll go together. The guards know me. I'll make sure they don't lock you up too."

Ahmed grinned. Luck was with them after all. "You are very kind!"

"Thank you," Max added.

"But you need to promise me one thing—"

"What?" Ahmed asked.

"Max needs to call his parents and let them know where he is. Tonight."

"They know where I am," Max lied.

In the rearview mirror, Ahmed could see Reka raise a skeptical eyebrow. "They let you come here all by yourself?"

When Max spoke next, his voice was quiet but firm.

"I'll call them after Ahmed sees his father. I'm sure they're asleep now anyway."

Reka thought about this for a moment.

"Okay. But this is a promise."

A peaceful silence filled the car. Ahmed curled up on the seat and drew the blanket up over him. In just a few hours he would see his father again. He couldn't wait to touch him, smell him, feel the bristle of his beard against his cheek. The rumble of the car lulled him; his eyes closed. In his mind, he saw his father, asleep on a dormitory cot. Ahmed imagined he could whisper into his dreams.

I'm almost there, Baba; I'm so close.

Reka's voice roused him from the sleep he hadn't realized he'd fallen into. She was talking to Max in the front seat. The car was still moving, the only light on the dark road. Ahmed kept his eyes closed, listened.

"There are plenty of us who disagree with the government," she was saying. "Who are ashamed of the way they treat refugees, who want to help them."

Ahmed smiled softly to himself. Max had been right not to give up. There were always people who cared.

CHAPTER FIFTY-EIGHT

Just after nine a.m., Max stepped out of the car into the parking lot of the Kiskunhalas detention center. As he looked around, he was glad Reka was with them. A five-foot-tall metal barrier topped with barbed wire stretched around the perimeter of the center. It walled off the parking lot from an oblong, gray building. Metal bars covered the windows.

"Are you sure it's for refugees?" Max said. "It looks like a prison."

"Yes and yes," Reka said. "It's a prison for people who haven't committed a crime."

Max glanced at Ahmed, but he barely seemed to have heard them. He was staring at the building, his eyes shining, and Max realized he wasn't even really seeing it. He was seeing his father inside, as if love was a superpower that let him see through walls.

They left the parking lot and walked around to the street-side entrance. Hungarian and European Union flags hung side by side over the door. But Max also noticed a security camera monitored the entrance.

Reka pressed a bell; a few seconds later, the door buzzed open and Max and Ahmed followed her into a sparsely decorated waiting area that reminded Max of a doctor's office. A 2015 calendar still hung on the wall, and a stack of Hungarian sports magazines was piled on a side table. Sitting behind a desk was a skinny woman in a blue uniform with a matching cap. She spoke to Reka in Hungarian. Reka responded—her voice polite and calm. As the woman disappeared through a door in the back of the waiting area, Max wondered if she even spoke English.

"You might want to sit down," Reka said. "This could take a while."

Max plopped down on one of the hard plastic seats, Ahmed next to him. Max could tell he was anxious by the way he jiggled his leg.

"Daniel sent me your father's case file last night," Reka said. "A few weeks ago, he crossed the Hungarian border from Serbia after a smuggler led him astray. So the border police arrested him."

"What is to happen to him?" Ahmed asked.

"Hopefully we can make a case now for him to join you in Belgium. It's good you are registered there."

Max and Ahmed exchanged a worried glance. At some point they would have to tell Reka the truth, but not before Ahmed had seen his father.

The door in the back opened, and Ahmed bolted from his seat. Max stood up as well, hoping to see Ahmed's father. Instead, two guards, guns swinging in their holsters, charged toward

Ahmed. Reka grabbed Ahmed by the arm and pulled him behind her.

Max frantically turned to Reka. "What's happening?"

Reka ignored him and spoke to the guards in Hungarian. One of them gave a curt reply while the other darted around her and grabbed Ahmed's arm. Max knew whatever was happening couldn't be good, because Reka began to shout. Max pulled at the guard's arm, trying to free Ahmed. Behind him, he heard the door open and someone else enter the room, but he didn't turn around for fear of losing his grip on the guard's arm. Ahmed stopped struggling and stared with disbelief. For a split second, Max thought Ahmed's father must have entered the room, but then he heard a familiar voice, speaking English.

"*Mex*, stop. Ahmed must go."

Max spun around. Inspector Fontaine stood in the doorway, as out of place as in a nightmare. Max just stared at him, unable to speak.

Only Reka seemed unfazed. "I'm sorry," she said in English to Fontaine. "I don't know who you are, but I just explained to them, they can't take Ahmed into custody. He has a Belgian residency card."

Inspector Fontaine smiled at her. "It is a forgery. Believe me, I am Brussels police."

Reka was looking at Ahmed now. "But you registered in Belgium? When you arrived?"

Ahmed glanced hopelessly at Max, then down at the floor.

Reka's voice sounded more desperate. "You must have opened a case file?"

"No," Inspector Fontaine answered for him. "He did not. He stayed in Belgium illegally with forged papers."

"He's not a terrorist!" Max cut in. "No matter what you think. You're wrong! He wouldn't hurt any—"

"I know!" Fontaine barked.

Max stared at him in surprised silence.

"I made an error," Fontaine said gruffly. "Though perhaps if Ahmed hadn't fled like he was guilty, I would have figured this out sooner."

"So he can go back to Belgium with his father?" Max asked hopefully.

"Absolutely not! His father must stay here in Hungary, and this is where he too will register with the authorities."

"But that's not fair!" Max shouted.

"What is not fair, *Mex*, is how you have worried and frightened your family, not to mention broken the law. It is time I take you back to Brussels."

Inspector Fontaine put his hand on Max's shoulder, but Max shrugged it off and ran to Ahmed.

"I'm not leaving you!"

He threw his arms around him. But Ahmed couldn't hug Max back—the guards were holding his arms.

"Max," he said softly. "How they say in the soldier book? We are overnumbered."

"Outnumbered," Max managed to choke out.

The next thing Max knew, he was bawling. He didn't even care that he was thirteen years old and everyone was watching.

"Please." Ahmed blinked and blinked. "Don't cry."

But this just made Max sob harder, messy tears streaming down his face.

Reka's voice trembled as she spoke to the guards in Hungarian. A second later, they sheepishly released Ahmed's arms, and Ahmed hugged Max back, tight.

"Max, it is okay," Ahmed whispered. "I will be good here."

"I failed you," Max whispered back.

"No, you bring me here."

"To a prison!"

"To my father."

Ahmed started to pull back, but Max couldn't let go. "I can't—" he said between big gulps of air.

Ahmed looked him straight in the eye, as if he knew more about Max than Max did himself.

"It's just for a moment. You take care of orchids, okay?"

Then Ahmed let Max go. At the same time, Inspector Fontaine pulled Max away.

"Come, *Mex*. We have a plane to catch in Budapest. We must go."

This time, Max didn't fight. There was no point. He couldn't bring Ahmed back to Brussels, back to the School of Happiness. There was nothing he could do other than croak a final goodbye.

CHAPTER FIFTY-NINE

There was no time for Ahmed to think about what had just happened. All he knew was that he had to be brave, if only for Max. The moment the door closed behind Inspector Fontaine and Max, the guards grabbed his arms again. Reka pleaded with them in Hungarian, but they half walked, half dragged him to the door that led deeper into the detention center.

"Ahmed, I can't come with you, but we'll try to help!" Reka shouted after him.

Then he was through the doorway and her voice was muffled as the door slammed shut behind them.

The guards deposited him in a chair.

"Is my father here?" Ahmed asked. "Can I see my father?"

"No English," the larger of the two guards said.

"*Français?*" Ahmed asked hopefully, but the men just shook their heads.

They took off his backpack and searched through it, laying everything out on the floor—his clothes, *The Calculus Affair*, even his half-finished cheese sandwich. Then they patted him down for knives and guns and even made him take off the Seamaster so they could inspect it. One of them took a photo of him and uploaded it to a computer. Another fingerprinted him. Finally a third man, thin and gray-haired, joined them. He sat behind a desk and asked Ahmed questions in English.

"Full name?"

"Ahmed Abdullah Nasser. Can I see my father?"

"We must do your paperwork first."

"But he is here?"

"Age?"

"Fourteen."

The man raised an eyebrow. "The dentist will check your teeth."

They didn't trust him, and the feeling was mutual.

"Nationality?"

"Syrian."

"Your passport is a forgery."

"I am Syrian."

The questions went on like this for a long time. What was his hometown? His home street? How had he become separated from his father? Why had he gone to Belgium? What had he done there? Ahmed answered them as calmly and truthfully as he could, but after a while his head hurt and his throat felt dry. They hadn't even offered him a drink of water.

And then, suddenly, it was over.

CHAPTER SIXTY

Max stared out the window at the Ryanair plane pulling up to their gate.

"That's us," Inspector Fontaine said in French.

Max didn't respond. He hadn't said a word to Fontaine since they'd left Kiskunhalas, not on the two-hour car ride to Budapest, nor as they'd waited in various lines at the airport. Fontaine had tried—he'd offered him a sandwich, a Coke, a candy bar; he'd asked him about Scouts, school. But even his kindness felt like treachery, like he was enticing Max to forget about Ahmed and accept the better treatment freely given to him as a white American boy. Every attempt Fontaine made to help or comfort him just made Max angrier and angrier. It was Ahmed who needed apologies and second chances, not him.

A few minutes later, they boarded the plane, and Max took the window seat Fontaine pointed him toward. Fontaine sat beside him.

"Your parents will be waiting to meet us in Charleroi," he said in French.

Max had seen on the monitors playing CNN International in the terminal that the Brussels Airport was still closed after the attacks. They would fly into Charleroi, which was an hour's drive to the south. Max guessed that Fontaine had flown to Hungary out of Charleroi as well.

"How did you find us so fast?" Max asked him in English. "Claire didn't know where we were going."

A smile flickered on Fontaine's face, though Max couldn't tell if he was proud of his effort or was just happy Max was finally talking to him.

"After you ran off, I asked the *directrice* to show me Ahmed's identification card. When I saw it, I knew there was only one boy who could make an actual card of identification at the commune. So I found Oscar."

"He told you?"

Fontaine laughed. "He claimed not to have made the card, to know nothing about this affair. Of course, he was lying."

Max was glad to hear that Oscar had protected them. He hoped from the way Fontaine seemed more amused than angry that Oscar hadn't gotten into too much trouble.

"It took some time," Fontaine admitted, "but then Madame Pauline mentioned the girl, Farah—"

Max stiffened. Farah had been in the room when Ibrahim had told him that Ahmed's father was at Kiskunhalas. Max hadn't told her their plan, but she could have easily guessed.

"But she too said she knew nothing. Her father said he was very strict with her, that she does not involve herself in mischief."

Max gently let out his breath, relieved that Farah also had defended Ahmed. But he was sorry he had put her in a situation where she too had to lie, especially to her family.

Fontaine gave a small shrug, as if he didn't quite believe Farah or her father but didn't much care. "That afternoon, I looked at the history of recent searches on the computer Oscar used in the commune. I found a search for an address for an Ibrahim Malaki in Molenbeek—"

Their plane picked up speed. The engines roared and the cabin vibrated; it was too loud for Fontaine to continue. But Max already knew the rest. Fontaine had spoken to Ibrahim and learned that Ahmed's father was at Kiskunhalas.

The nose of the plane lifted off the ground. Normally, Max loved this moment, when the plane seemed to defy gravity and escape the weight of the earth. But now all he could think about was Ahmed: He'd never had the freedom to fly above borders and barriers. He didn't even have the freedom to leave the detention center.

A hand seemed to pull the plane directly up into the sky. Fields shrank into green squares, highways into gray lines. Ahmed was a dot on a dot on a dot somewhere below. Max wanted to scream but instead he turned to Fontaine.

"How could you think Ahmed was a terrorist?"

He wanted Fontaine to apologize, but the police officer just gave a shrug.

"You must admit, he did act like one. Hiding, breaking the law—"

"Taking care of your grandfather's garden." Max stared at him hard. "He loved it. Like you do."

"*Mex*," Fontaine said gently, "he could not love it like I do. It is my garden. I played in it as a boy."

"You've told me," Max snapped.

"I have such happy memories of life there—football with my cousins, my confirmation party, the summer fête when all the neighbors would come and Grandfather would set up a tent by the roses. My childhood was peaceful, serene. But my parents' was not—"

"Because of the war," Max cut in.

Fontaine nodded. "You have never lived through a war, Max. It is a terrible thing."

Max didn't even bother to conceal his irritation. "Ahmed told me."

But Fontaine didn't seem to hear him. "Europe was in ruins in 1945, but by the time I was a boy, just a few decades after, it had rebuilt itself. There was unity, cooperation in Western Europe—even between countries that were once enemies."

"What does this have to do with Ahmed?" Max interrupted.

"Migrants are threatening this unity. Do you realize that more than a million of them came to Europe last year? Our union is young, *Mex*, *fragile*; if it breaks down, Europe could fall again into chaos."

"But chaos and war is exactly what Ahmed was escaping! If you know how horrible this is from your own history, you shouldn't turn your back on people like him. You should have compassion, like Albert Jonnart!"

"Jonnart?"

"The man they named my street for. He saved a Jewish boy during the war. Your grandfather must have—"

Fontaine glanced away.

Max stared at Fontaine, amazed it hadn't occurred to him earlier. "Was it your grandfather who betrayed him?"

Fontaine turned back, a fierce scowl on his face. "My grandfather did nothing! He was not a hero like Jonnart, but he was not a collaborator either."

Even if Max believed him, there still wasn't anything honorable about doing nothing. "But you agree Jonnart was a hero because he helped a refugee—"

"Ahmed's situation is different—"

"Ahmed just wanted to go to school," Max said. "What's so dangerous about that?"

Fontaine waved his finger. "I don't think you understand. Ahmed broke the law by staying in Belgium, and you did too by registering him in school. The law is important, *Mex*. Society cannot function without it."

"What if the law is wrong?"

"What if the heart is wrong? What if you let all these people into your country, your home, and they turn out to be bad people who want to harm you and change your way of life? What if they are not worth your sacrifice?"

Max wished he could tell Inspector Fontaine that until Ahmed had come into his life, he hadn't felt worth much himself.

But instead he just said, "You can't know what anyone's worth unless you give them a chance."

"Ah, to be young," Fontaine said. He shook his head. "Cheer up, *Mex*. Ahmed is with his father, where he belongs."

Max could grant Fontaine that. But there was something else he was just as sure of: Ahmed belonged in school, not in a prison.

CHAPTER SIXTY-ONE

The guards will take you back," Ahmed's interrogator said, motioning for him to stand.

Ahmed's breath quickened. He was barely even aware of the guards shoving him through another door until the cool air hit him and he realized he was back outside. They led him into another building and down a long corridor until they reached an open door. Then they pointed Ahmed inside.

The room was bare, with nothing on the walls and no furniture save for two bunk beds. The windows were narrow and barred, but in the dim light, Ahmed could see a hunched figure on the bottom bunk, reading.

"Baba?"

The book fell out of the man's hands, and he scrambled to his feet. Ahmed stared at him. He was thinner, grayer, shorter (but he couldn't be shorter, Ahmed realized, it was he himself who had grown!). There was a scar on his father's neck that hadn't been there before. But his eyes were the same, his barrel chest, his smile.

"Ahmed!"

It wasn't a dream or some hopeless fantasy. His father was here now, rushing toward him in this time and place. Those strong arms were around him, squeezing his shoulders, his arms, as if checking to see if he too were truly there. Then his father's lips pressed against his cheek, his forehead, his lips.

"My son," he said again and again in Arabic.

His father was laughing and crying, and Ahmed felt the same way, all mixed up between joy and sorrow.

"Baba," he said between sobs. "I thought I'd lost you forever."

His father cupped Ahmed's chin in his hands and smiled.

"Hush, my soul, it was only for a moment."

Ahmed closed his eyes, relaxed his head against his father's shoulder. As if Baba had uttered a spell, Ahmed felt time flow backward—his memories rewinding past Europe and the terrible night at sea, Turkey and the bomb, to the dirt and bloom and buds of his grandfather's nursery, to his mother quietly singing *Rima tnam* to a sleeping Nouri, to Jasmine laughing as she played *hajla*, to his father greeting him after school with a kiss.

"Don't cry, Ahmed."

He was a small boy and an ancient traveler. He was four and fourteen. He had scraped his knee. He had pricked his finger on a rose. He had heard a noise in the night. Nothing more. He was safe now.

Ahmed unfastened the Seamaster, tried to hand it back to his father, but Baba refastened it around his wrist.

"Keep it. It is yours."

The lines of the ancient Sufi poet echoed in Ahmed's mind: *Why did you teach me to love / Then leave me when my heart became attached to you?*

Now he knew the answer:

So I could know how much I love you.

CHAPTER SIXTY-TWO

With a loud ping, the seat belt sign switched off. Passengers sprang out of their seats, pulled down bags from the overhead luggage bins. But Max just stared out the window at the bruise-colored clouds. This hadn't been the plan. He wasn't supposed to be back in Belgium without Ahmed.

Fontaine's phone buzzed as he switched it off airplane mode. He turned to Max.

"Your parents are at Arrivals."

Max's stomach flip-flopped. He didn't feel ready to face them. This was way worse than the crazy eighth grader's broken arm. He had lied, stolen, forged documents, run away, broken countless rules and laws. He tried to imagine what they would do. Ground him until he turned eighteen? Send him to one of those wilderness programs for bad kids where he'd have to survive on dew and berries? *At least*, he thought bitterly, *I've learned a few tips in the* Scoots.

The passengers clogging the aisle surged forward. Fontaine stood up. "Come along, *Mex*. They wait for you."

There was nothing to do but get it over with. Max hoisted his backpack onto his shoulder and slumped after Fontaine.

The terminal was packed with travelers whose flights had been diverted from Brussels. They waited with tense expressions in front of the Departures boards or in the long lines for ticket agents. Police and soldiers with rifles milled through the crowd. Everyone was clearly nervous that there would be another terrorist attack, but all Max could think about was his parents. He expected them to shout and scold, lecture and sob in despair over what a disaster he was. He took a deep breath, then followed Fontaine through a security door and into Arrivals.

He spotted them immediately, their necks craned toward the security door. But as soon as they saw him, they did the one thing he hadn't expected: they rushed over and hugged him.

Max did something he hadn't expected to either: he hugged them back.

His mother started crying, but what surprised Max even more were the rhythmic spasms of his father's shoulders. He had never seen his father cry.

"It's okay," Max said, blinking back tears of his own. "I'm home."

His father clutched him tighter. Max pictured Ahmed's father doing the same, and for the first time since he'd left Ahmed, Max felt he hadn't entirely failed him.

His father's shoulders stopped heaving, and when Max

finally looked around, he realized that Fontaine had left. Then a more important absence hit him.

"Where's Claire?"

His mom dabbed her eyes. "At the house."

Coward, Max thought. She couldn't even face him. But he was glad that she hadn't come too.

His mother touched his chin, tipped his face toward hers. Her eyes were bloodshot, with deep shadows beneath them. Max realized that she probably hadn't slept since he'd left.

"Max, do you know how much we love you?"

He wanted to say, *I do now*. But instead he just lowered his head.

"I'm sorry. But I had to help Ahmed—"

His father held up his hand. "You're in some pretty serious trouble, Max. You betrayed our trust and a lot of other people's too—"

"I know," Max muttered. There was no point in denying this.

"But we're proud of you."

Max scrunched up his eyes, certain he hadn't heard his father right.

"You *are*?"

"You did something most people can't. You put yourself at risk for another person."

Max could feel his cheeks burning with his father's praise.

"So, you're not angry?"

His father gave a loud snort. "I didn't say that. You're

grounded for the rest of the year. And if you ever do anything like this ever again, your mother and I will—"

"Kill me?" Max offered.

"Give every device you own to Claire," his mother said.

Max gave a melodramatic moan. "It'd be kinder to kill me."

His father grinned. "I know. But the world needs a kid like you."

CHAPTER SIXTY-THREE

His first few days in Kiskunhalas, Ahmed hardly even noticed where he was. All that mattered was that his father was with him. If there were guards and walls and wire, they made no impression. There was so much to catch up on, so many stories to tell. At night, Ahmed left his own bunk to sleep with Baba in his. His father moved over without complaint, wrapped his arms around him.

"Twice, I've waited nine months for you," he'd whisper in Arabic. "The first time for you to be born, and the second for you to find me. Each time you've given me great pride and joy."

Then his rough hand wiped away Ahmed's tears.

"Hush, my soul."

"I wish they could come back too," Ahmed said.

He didn't need to say who "they" were. His father knew. That was the unspoken language of family. Baba just held him tighter.

On the third day, after a dentist verified Ahmed's age, a

supervisor moved them into the family barracks. Slowly, the world around Ahmed came into focus. The other families detained with them were from a multitude of countries—Afghanistan, Syria, Iraq, Eritrea, Kosovo, Nigeria, Pakistan, Somalia. The few Ahmed could communicate with didn't seem to understand why they were being held. They prayed in an indoor gym and shared two hot meals a day in the cafeteria—breakfast and lunch consisting mostly of rice, potatoes or bread and a tiny bit of fruit or vegetables. The guards distributed a cold dinner, usually tinned fish and crackers, toward evening. At night, they locked everyone in their rooms, cursing if someone was too slow returning from the filthy outdoor toilets.

But the guards weren't even the biggest problem. As Ahmed exhausted his supply of stories, he realized that the real danger of Kiskunhalas was boredom. There was only a single small TV for two hundred people, and fights broke out when someone tried to change the channel. The two Ping-Pong tables were always in use, and the only books Ahmed could find were in Hungarian (the guards had never returned the contents of his backpack). A truck from a Catholic youth charity provided eight hours a day of Internet access, but the lines to use the computers were so long Ahmed barely managed to write a few sentences to Max before his turn was up. There was no phone.

Every day, they were sent outside into an enclosed gravel courtyard for an hour. There was a playground for the younger kids and a bench press and a few other exercise machines. But there wasn't even a football to kick around, and only a small canopy to protect them when it rained. Often, Ahmed and his father just spent this time washing their clothes in a plastic bucket since there didn't appear to be any laundry machines. They dried them on the bars on the windows of their room.

"Don't worry," his father said. "They'll let us out soon. You must have faith."

Ahmed began to understand the toll of captivity and uncertainty: the women who complained daily of headaches; the men who chain-smoked for hours; the little kids who clung to their mothers, peevish and whimpering, the older ones glassy-eyed from too much TV. He slept more fitfully, even with his father beside him, and woke up gasping for breath. But he still tried to remain optimistic, especially in his messages to Max:

I have not much time at computer so I tell you all is well.
My father and I have great happiness together. There is much time to rest and talk. I teach him some words of French.
Your friend, Ahmed/Nabil Fawzi

CHAPTER SIXTY-FOUR

On the morning of Monday, April 11, Max waved goodbye to his parents and plunged into the stream of kids sweeping through the passageway to the School of Happiness. Only two and a half weeks had passed since he'd last stood in the courtyard, but it felt like much longer. Over the Easter break, the trees had unfurled a canopy of new leaves, and the birds had turned up their song. There was even sunshine and a sky that seemed impossibly blue, perhaps Max thought, because he was not used to seeing it without its veil of clouds. The day was so close to being perfect. If only . . .

"Max!"

A football flew toward him. He ducked just in time.

Oscar raced up to him with a grin.

Max rammed Oscar's shoulder. "I missed you too," he said in French.

"I miss Ahmed. He would have trapped that."

"Thanks," Max said, pretending to be offended.

"At least he found his dad. You know, I always had this crazy fantasy—" He looked down, gave a sharp exhale.

"About your dad?"

Oscar spoke so softly that Max could hardly hear him. "That he was still out there somewhere."

"That's not crazy," Max said. "It just means you miss him."

Oscar didn't say anything. He just nodded.

"How did it go with Madame Bertrand?"

Max and his parents had met with the *directrice* the day after he had returned to Brussels. "Fine. She said she could expel me, that I broke practically every school rule, but that I hadn't really broken the spirit of the rules so she was letting me stay. My parents didn't understand anything she was saying except that she was letting me stay."

"You're lucky. My mom understood everything. I've got to stay off all devices until—"

Max smiled. "Next week?"

Oscar's eyes narrowed mischievously. "Something like that."

"At least Farah didn't get in trouble."

"You mean at school . . ."

Max stared at him. "But Fontaine said her dad didn't believe him!"

Oscar gave a snort. "The guy's not an idiot."

"We texted. She didn't tell me—"

Oscar shrugged, then cocked his head. "Your girlfriend's coming. Take it up with her."

Max spun around to find Farah racing toward them.

"She's not my girlfriend," he muttered, but he could feel his heart thumping.

Her big eyes were staring anxiously at him from behind her glasses. "How's Ahmed?"

She didn't seem angry. But Max still knew what he wanted to say.

"I'm sorry. For getting you into trouble with your dad."

Farah's forehead wrinkled. "*You* didn't get me into trouble."

"Claire did," Oscar added.

"I'm still not talking to her," Max said. "But it's my fault too. I was the one who convinced you—"

Farah waved her hand in the air as if brushing away a fly. "I got *myself* into trouble, and you know what? I don't care. There are some people worth getting into trouble for."

Max felt like throwing his arms around her, but he knew he'd never hear the end of it from Oscar, so he just smiled. "Thanks, Farah."

"How's Ahmed?"

"He's okay, I guess."

But Max knew Ahmed well enough to know that the messages he sent him were meant to reassure, not to reveal the truth of his life at Kiskunhalas. Max had responded with his own optimistic reports:

My dad and I worked on the garden together during the break. He and my mom have promised to put in some calls for you. I've been taking care of the orchids (don't worry, I'm not letting my mom near them). There are more buds, and they look like they'll bloom soon—maybe by the time you're back?

"Any news from Reka?" Farah asked.

"She says they can detain families with children only for thirty days," Max said.

"And then?"

"I don't know," Max admitted. "But at least they won't be in prison."

The bell rang and kids started grabbing their backpacks and heading inside, but Oscar didn't move.

"So, Criminal Mind, what's the plan?" he asked.

Max realized they were both looking at him, waiting for him to tell them what to do. His friends back home had never looked at him like that. He was tempted to come up with some crazy idea just so they wouldn't be disappointed. But that didn't seem right either. Good ideas, like orchids, took time, patience. He needed to give the adults trying to help Ahmed a chance as well.

"We wait."

Oscar frowned, but didn't protest. Max understood how he felt. The old Max wouldn't have been able to wait either.

"It's not the same thing as giving up." Max stared hard at them. "We're not giving up."

But it was hard not to feel that Ahmed was gone forever, especially later that morning, when Max noticed a drawing tacked to the wall of Madame Legrand's classroom. It was a picture of the garden behind Max's house, and Ahmed's signature was in the corner. There were flowers in bloom everywhere—roses, forsythia, irises, azaleas and others Max didn't know by name, that he guessed weren't even native to Belgium but instead, like the orchids Ahmed had saved, came from more distant corners of the earth. It seemed to Max as if Ahmed had drawn the garden not the way it had been when he'd lived in the wine cellar, but the way he'd imagined it could become with care and affection.

Madame Legrand had tacked the drawing beside the map of the world, and the juxtaposition between the entire, vast earth—with all its fear and violence—and the peaceful, miniature world of the garden made Max miss Ahmed more than anything else.

A shadow fell over him. He looked up to find Madame Legrand. He expected her to tell him to keep his eyes on his work, but instead, she squeezed his shoulder as if she understood.

CHAPTER SIXTY-FIVE

On the twenty-ninth day, one of the supervisors summoned Ahmed and his father to the front office, where they found Reka waiting for them with a thick folder.

His father spoke in English for them both.

"Miss Reka, we are so happy to see you!"

But Ahmed noticed her brow was creased with anger.

"I have been trying to get in to see you for weeks! I am so very sorry it has taken this long—"

Ahmed cut in. "Max write me they must have to free us soon—"

Reka sighed. "He's right about that. But then they will deport you back to Greece. There is no legal way to get you to Belgium or even Germany. Those countries are not taking in any more refugees for the moment, except through Turkey."

Ahmed pictured taking a crowded ferry back to Izmir—after everything they'd gone through, he couldn't bear for them to just turn back around. He slumped in his chair.

"So we have to return to Turkey to have a chance to come back to Europe?" his father asked.

"The conditions at the camps in Greece are very bad right now because all migration north has been stopped. But if you are willing to stay in Greece for a while, my contacts there will see what they can do."

"Thank you," his father said.

He patted Ahmed's hand as if this was good news. But Ahmed wasn't fooled. Bad choices were all they ever had.

He looked up at Reka. "Have you explain this to Max?"

Reka nodded. "He's still trying to find a way to get you back to Belgium."

In spite of everything, Ahmed felt himself smile. "Of course."

Ahmed imagined Max was probably thinking about Albert Jonnart, trying to figure out if there was some other lesson in his story that they could apply to their own. But Jonnart's story hadn't exactly had a happy ending either. He had died in captivity, far from Belgium; seventy years later, his story was mostly forgotten. Had it been worth it? He had saved a single boy, one life. And who even knew what had happened to Ralph after the war, how long he had lived or whether his life had been a happy one?

Ahmed thanked Reka, then followed his father and the supervisor back to their room.

"Don't worry," his father said in Arabic. "At least we are together."

Ahmed forced a smile. How powerful, in the end, was a

single story? Powerful enough to reunite a father and son, but not powerful enough, it seemed, to change their destiny. One story couldn't change the world, just like one person couldn't. But two—

Ahmed's breath caught. He broke away from his father, ran toward the mobile Internet unit.

"What is it?" his father called after him.

"I need to write Max."

CHAPTER SIXTY-SIX

Max sat in the kitchen polishing off an after-school snack of sausage and baguette when the message from Ahmed popped up on his phone.

"Max, ready for *dictée*?" called Madame Pauline from the dining room.

Max stared past her at the white orchid flowers in bloom on the living room windowsill. They reminded him of Ahmed and the resilience Ahmed had taught Max.

"I can do it myself."

Madame Pauline didn't argue. They had developed an understanding since Max had returned: Madame Pauline didn't talk about Ahmed—or Muslims in general—in front of him anymore, and although she kept a hawkish eye on Max (probably on his parents' orders), she didn't boss him around quite so much. She seemed to realize he cared about school now and could focus on his own.

Max retreated to his room, lay down on his bed and opened Ahmed's message. It wasn't very long, but right away it was different than the others. As soon as he'd finished reading it, Max ran over to his desk, opened his laptop and did a few searches on Google. Then he opened a new Word document and began to type.

He was hardly aware of time passing as he wrote and deleted, weighing each word. Only when he heard the knock on his door did he look at his phone and realize it was after five thirty.

"What?!"

Claire pushed open the door.

Max turned away and closed the laptop so she couldn't snoop.

"What do you want?" he asked without looking at her.

"Look, we can't go on like this forever—"

"I can. You betrayed me."

"Can you just turn around, Max? Look at me for a second?"

Max looked at her, then turned back around. "That was a second," he mumbled. He knew he was being childish, but he didn't care.

"I'm sorry, Max, okay? I was just trying to protect you, to keep our family safe."

"From what?"

"I don't know."

Her voice sounded tight, like she was going to cry. Max glanced back. Her eyes were bloodshot, like she hadn't been sleeping well.

"I was just . . . scared. All these crazy things were happening that I couldn't control and the thought of losing Mom and Dad . . . or you—"

Max rolled his eyes the way she had always done at him. "As if you care about me."

"When you ran off—" She shook her head. "Everyone was so freaked out—"

"I had to help Ahmed."

She didn't seem to hear him.

"I kept thinking of what could happen to you. You're my little brother."

Max felt a lump form in his throat. But he wasn't going to let her off so easily. People justified doing some pretty awful things in the name of protecting their own families. The neighbor who had betrayed Albert Jonnart had probably thought he was keeping his family safe by helping the Nazis.

"You didn't have to be scared of Ahmed."

"I messed up, okay?"

She turned to go. Max watched her pull open the door and start to walk out. It occurred to him that she had never apologized to him for anything before. But he had to admit, she was trying.

"Wait," he said.

She whipped around so fast he could feel her relief.

"I need your help."

"With what?" she asked eagerly.

"I need you to look at this letter. Tell me if it's any good." He waved her over and shoved her lightly into his chair. "Read."

The letter had to be good, the best story—or stories—he'd ever told. But his sister's face was blank, motionless except for her blinking blue eyes as they darted across the page. Max tried not to loom over her. He paced back and forth until, after what felt like forever, she turned around.

"It's pretty bad, huh?" he said. "That's why I asked you. You're much better at this—"

"Max—"

"You can change anything. I mean, maybe I should have started with Ahmed, not Albert Jonnart and Ralph, but they were our inspiration and our stories go together, they're powerful together—"

"Max!"

Here it came, the criticism. But he'd take it because if he'd learned anything over the past nine months, it was that no one could be a hero alone. He never would have been able to help Ahmed find his father without Farah and Oscar and Reka. In some mixed-up way, he was even grateful to Madame Pauline for telling him the story of Albert Jonnart, and to Inspector Fontaine for making Ahmed run away so they could discover his father was still alive. But the real hero was Ahmed: he himself had come up with the idea of writing a letter to Jewish aid organizations and asking for help. Now Max needed Claire to help him do his part.

"What?"

Claire read the first sentence out loud: "'I'm writing you about two people, Ahmed Nasser and Albert Jonnart, whose stories changed my life.'"

He had included what Madame Pauline had told him about Jonnart's life, then added the details he'd found in his French Google searches of newspapers and archives: How Jonnart had continued to help fellow resistors even in prison—in one of his last letters to his wife, Simone, he'd written, "*Je ferai mon devoir jusqu'au bout,*" "I will do my work till the end." How after the war, the Jonnart family had continued to live on the block alongside the family who'd betrayed them. Max didn't include the family's name, but he noticed that it wasn't Fontaine. How Ralph, whose parents were murdered at Auschwitz, had moved to Canada, then returned to Brussels; how he'd married but never had children. How every year until Madame Jonnart's death in 1985, he'd sent her flowers on the anniversary of Albert's death. How after Ralph's death in 1998, at the age of seventy-four, the Jonnart family had received a card: "To all those who softened my existence with their feelings, I address an ultimate thank-you and goodbye."

Then Max had written Ahmed's story—the story of a boy who lived in a wine cellar, who saved orchids, who just wanted to go to school.

"'I tried to soften Ahmed's existence, but it was really he who softened mine. I've said thank you. But neither of us are ready to say goodbye.'"

Max's cheeks burned. "It's too much, isn't it?"

Claire pushed back the chair and stood up to face him.

"No, Max. It's perfect."

CHAPTER SIXTY-SEVEN

Thirty days became forty. Forty became fifty. Families left. April turned to May. And still no one came to release Ahmed and his father from Kiskunhalas.

"Reka says this is a delay with our paperwork," his father reported after speaking with her briefly. "But maybe it is better here than in Greece. You must have faith in Allah's plan."

Ahmed would have to try; he had lost faith in his own. Would a Jewish organization really want to help a Muslim boy? They probably just resented the comparison between his plight and Ralph's. People were always weighing their suffering against others', not using it to form bonds. He wrote to Max: *It does not work.*

Be patient, Max wrote back. But the fact that Max wrote nothing more just made Ahmed feel more hopeless.

The single tree in the courtyard had unfurled its leaves, dappling the ground beneath it with shade. An hour a day outside was no longer enough; Ahmed felt jealous of the birds that flew over the fence, of the laundry that hung outside the barred windows, flapping in the breeze. He learned a few phrases of Hungarian, and one afternoon, one of the guards who appreciated his efforts brought him a football. Ahmed kicked it as hard as he could against the fence, trying to break the barrier open. But the fence held, and eventually the guard took the ball away and gave it to some younger kids. After that, Ahmed mostly just sat beneath the tree, imagining his life back at the School of Happiness—hopping the garden wall, Madame Legrand praising his *dictée*, football with Oscar and Max.

One morning in late May, as he leaned against the tree trunk deep in one of these reveries, he heard his father's voice.

"Ahmed, up, up! I have news!"

Ahmed jumped to his feet. His father was running toward him across the courtyard, waving a piece of paper.

"What is it?"

"Our petition was approved! We're going!"

"To Greece?"

"No, my soul." His father threw his arms around him and gave him a kiss. "To America!"

"But . . . how?"

With a trembling hand, his father showed him the piece of paper. It was a letter from the Hebrew Immigrant Aid Society in Silver Spring, Maryland.

"Reka told me earlier that they'd heard about you and were trying to help us. But America is only accepting ten thousand Syrians. There is even a candidate for president who wants to ban all Muslim immigrants. So I didn't want to say anything till we were sure."

Ahmed leaned against the tree trunk. His father had tears in his eyes, but Ahmed wanted to cry for a different reason. He wasn't going back to Belgium. The School of Happiness was gone forever. He would never be a student there again.

Then he remembered: in just another few months, Max would be moving back to America.

"Where?"

His father pointed to the last paragraph of the letter.

"Charlottesville, Virginia. It's a town three hours south of Washington, D.C.—"

"Where Max lives!"

Ahmed took a deep breath, pushed down the tide of sadness. Enormous challenges awaited him—a new country, a new culture, a new school. Ahmed knew it wouldn't be easy. But his father and Max would be near.

"Baba, I feel it again."

"What's that, my soul?"

Ahmed touched his father's shoulder the way his father had once touched his on that moonless night at sea when he thought they'd never find a shore, never mind a home.

"Hope."

A CONVERSATION WITH KATHERINE MARSH

1. Nowhere Boy *brings together the stories of two boys, Ahmed and Max, who both find themselves far from home. What was your inspiration?*

   In July 2015, I moved from Washington, D.C., to Brussels, Belgium, so my husband, a newspaper reporter, could cover European security. We moved into a beautiful old house with a walled garden on—you guessed it!—Avenue Albert Jonnart. A sign at the end of the block gave a short history of Jonnart's life: how he had hidden a Jewish teenager in his house during the German occupation of the Second World War and how this act of resistance cost him his life. I thought of Jonnart's story when I discovered a wine cellar off the basement of our new home. It seemed like the perfect place to hide someone.

2. *How did your experience as an American abroad inform your perspective as you wrote* Nowhere Boy*?*

   I set the story on our street and in our house, as well as at a fictionalized version of my children's school. When they started school, my children only spoke a few words of French and were the only English speakers in their class; like Max, my son had to do battle with a fountain pen and the weekly *dictée*. I, meanwhile, had to puzzle out confusing school notices and instructions from the commune using rusty high school French. Navigating daily life as a foreigner was exhausting and stressful, even for a family with considerable advantages, like mine. It gave me a deep sense of compassion not only for my three immigrant grandparents, but for the million refugees arriving in Europe that year with so much less.

3. *How did you experience the refugee crisis in Belgium and how did this shape the book?*

In Brussels, the most visible symbol of the refugee crisis was Parc Maximilien. Like many others, I felt deeply ashamed that men, women and children were sleeping in tents in the middle of the city. By far the most vulnerable refugees were unaccompanied minors: children under eighteen—mostly boys—like Ahmed. Many of these children had been traumatized by war or violence and had lost years of their education. Of the 2,650 who applied for asylum in Belgium in 2015, 15 percent were *under* fourteen years old.

But there was an inspirational story as well: Parc Maximilien was run totally by volunteers—including several of my neighbors and friends, who gave selflessly and without prejudice. The spirit of Albert Jonnart was clearly still alive, but as the idea for this book started to gel, I realized it was also in jeopardy. Not everyone in Europe, or the United States for that matter, was happy about the influx of mostly Muslim refugees. This wariness only increased with the Islamic State terror attacks in Paris, Brussels, Nice and other cities.

4. *Why did you decide to work these current events into* Nowhere Boy*?*

I felt it was important to describe the fear people were feeling. During the Brussels attack, I ran to my children's school, like Max's mother, and picked them up. In the weeks that followed, I thought a lot about my fear that something could happen to me or the people I loved, and how easy it was to let that fear distort perceptions and facts. I decided to put this struggle in the book and to try to do it honestly—not just through the examples of characters like Madame Pauline, who refuse to grapple with their fear, but through the examples of characters like Max, who do.

5. *Obviously, you had a lot of personal experience to draw upon for Max's perspective. But how did you come up with Ahmed's story?*

In imagining Ahmed's life, I was helped enormously by several families and individuals from Syria, mostly from Aleppo, who generously shared their memories—both from Aleppo and as refugees—and answered my endless questions. I'm also fortunate to live in an age of great journalism, and I used details from news accounts, blogs and nongovernmental agency reports. I interviewed reporters, aid workers, refugee advocates, members of Brussels's Muslim community and an unaccompanied minor. Every individual's experience is unique, but I tried to capture something of the larger emotional truth.

6. *As Max learns more about Albert Jonnart and Ralph Mayer, he recognizes some stark parallels between the treatment of the Jews during World War II and today's Syrian refugees. What do you hope readers will take away from this book?*

One of the experiences I cherish most about working on this book was meeting Bénédicte Jonnart, the granddaughter of Albert Jonnart. Several years ago, Bénédicte heard about the Righteous Among the Nations, a special designation from the State of Israel honoring non-Jews who risked their lives to save Jews during the Holocaust. Immediately, she thought about her grandfather. For him to qualify, Bénédicte had to provide evidence, and so she became her family's unofficial historian—collecting letters between Albert and his wife, Simone Deploige; conducting interviews with surviving family members; and even locating a classified postwar lawsuit against the neighbor who betrayed Jonnart, which included Ralph's firsthand testimony. As a result of her efforts, in 2013, both Albert and Simone were designated Righteous Among the Nations and their names appear on a wall in the Garden of the Righteous in Jerusalem.

It's impossible to include all the amazing details of the story Bénédicte shared with me. But every detail included in this book—including Ralph's rooftop escape—is true. Colette Dubuisson-Breuer, the daughter of Jacques Breuer, the archaeologist who hid Ralph after Albert Jonnart was arrested, also shared his story with me, as well as her own memories of Ralph, who remained in touch with both the Jonnart and Breuer families.

A few postscripts deserve additional mention here: Pierre, Bénédicte's father and Ralph's classmate, left home after his father's arrest to join the resistance; he passed away on March 1, 2018, at the age of ninety-three. Bénédicte was careful not to mention the name of the neighbor who betrayed her family, and even though I know it from legal documents, in keeping with her example, I've chosen not to share it. Albert Jonnart's story isn't about betrayal or anger. Rather, it's about what I hope readers will take away: the incredible importance of decency and kindness, especially to those who aren't family or tribe, but "others."

Katherine Marsh

April 2018

Brussels, Belgium

ACKNOWLEDGMENTS

I could not have written this book without an international cast of heroes:

I had the good fortune to be reunited with my first editor, Jennifer Besser, and to remain with her through two fabulous publishers. Her keen insights into character and plot helped me deepen and polish Max and Ahmed's story. Alex Glass, my longtime agent, believed in this book from the beginning; for over a decade now, he's been my champion. I am grateful to Jason Richman at United Talent Agency for helping me think about this story cinematically. My gratitude also goes out to Rotem Moscovich, Abby Ranger and Christian Trimmer for sharing their wisdom and enthusiasm for this book in its early stages. A huge thank-you to the team at Putnam, including Kate Meltzer, Nicole Wayland, Cindy Howle, Jen Loja and Jocelyn Schmidt. An equally heartfelt thanks to the team at Macmillan—including Allison Verost, Kathryn Little, Molly Ellis, Luisa Beguiristaín, Lucy Del Priore, Jennifer Sale, Morgan Dubin, Johanna Kirby, Katie Halata and Nancy Elgin—for taking this book to the finish line with great enthusiasm and support.

I am deeply grateful to the insightful readers who helped me shape this story: Valentina Pop, Rami Midani, Caroline Hickey, Lyda Phillips, Karen Leggett Abouraya (with an assist from Tharwat Abouraya) and the Wise family (Jill, Russell, Raleigh, Nell and Jack). A special thanks to Valentina, who also shared her firsthand knowledge of the refugee route, toured me around Molenbeek, connected me to refugees and helped me devise realistic plot twists. Her powerful reporting on the migrant crisis for *The Wall Street Journal* is a must-read. I am also especially grateful to Rami Midani for his read for accuracy and sensitivity from a Syrian perspective.

Bénédicte Jonnart shared her family's memories, as well as historical documents, photos and memorabilia, with a warmth and openness that brought her grandfather Albert Jonnart and the wartime history of Brussels to life. Nicole (Colette) Dubuisson-Breuer related the story of her father, Jacques Breuer, as well as her own firsthand memories of the war. Special thanks to her late husband, Louis Dubuisson; her son, Baudouin Dubuisson; and her grandson, Jean-Christophe Dubuisson, for arranging and enriching the interview with their presence.

Rehab Alhdad, Muhamedkher Alhjibrahim, Sabah Sheikh Fadhel, Moundher Dawoud and Yazan Rajab generously shared their memories and stories of life in Aleppo and their experiences coming to Europe as Syrian refugees. Sabah Fadhel also cooked an out-of-this-world Syrian dinner for me. Abdulahi

Abdulkadir Omar shared his own brave story of arriving in Belgium in 2015 as an unaccompanied minor. Elke Zander, Barbara Winn-Hagelstam and Amy Anderson embody the spirit of helpers throughout history; I am grateful for their help connecting me within the refugee community.

Sofia Mahjoub at Child Focus, the European Center for Missing and Sexually Exploited Children, helped educate me on the challenges of undocumented minors in Europe. Semma Groenendijk at Minor-Ndako shared her firsthand experience working with undocumented minors in Belgium. András Léderer at the Helsinki Committee for Human Rights shared reporting that brought Kiskunhalas and the Hungarian detention centers into stark relief.

Jamal Khayar introduced me to the warm, rich culture of Moroccan Belgians. Anahita Nickdast corrected the French in the book; Jennifer Walsh Weyers, Jessica Barist Cohen and Mouhamed Farouk helped translate oral interviews in French and Arabic. Hendrik Verstraete at Petrens & Co., a fifth-generation orchid nursery, and Dr. Anne Ronse at the Botanic Garden Meise helped me write more accurately about orchids.

Thanks to Celeste Rhoads and the staff of the American Library in Paris for the chance to debut a chapter of this book, and to Jennifer Dalrymple and Luis Roth for introducing me to this vibrant literary community. I am grateful to Amy Huntington and the Performing Arts Forum (PAF) in France for a productive retreat. I am also grateful to Amy and my fellow PAF writers for helping me brainstorm the title of this book.

Over the past several years, Teresa Cuvelier, Aida Radović, Katy Hull and Katy Walters Brink have encouraged me and kept me sane over croissants, coffee and Belgian beer. Amie Hsia and Ben Harder have cheered me on across time zones and on wild holidays through Europe. I am grateful to my parents, Elaine Milosh and Ken Marsh, for teaching me to value storytelling and creativity. I am also indebted to my late grandparents, Natalia Ostapiuk Milosh, John Milosh and Leo Marsh, whose spirit of hope brought them to America as immigrants.

My deepest thanks to my family—Julian E. Barnes, who took the plunge to move to Belgium and supported this book and me every step of the way, and my children, Sasha and Natalia, who braved a new country, a new language and a new school. I am particularly grateful to Sasha for his willingness to read this book in countless drafts and to share his experiences and correct my cultural misunderstandings. A very special thanks to their school, the real Ecole du Bonheur, which welcomed our family with open arms and whose staff and community epitomize the kindness and decency of the Belgian people.

Finally, thank you to the two people who inspired this story: Ralph Mayer, for his courage to persevere in the face of unbearable tragedy, and Albert Jonnart, for his courage to live a moral life.